SNOW-BLIND

SNOW-BLIND

ALBERT M. TREYNOR

CHAPTER I
"ARE YOU THERE?"

"This," said the bland voice on the air, "is Station WBZ, Springfield, Massachusetts, broadcasting greetings from the home folks to the far-advanced outposts of the Royal Canadian Mounted Police. I have a letter for Sergeant Buck Tearl at Port-o'-Prayer in North Saskatchewan. Good evening, Sergeant. Are you there?"

And then the message went into space on the waves of the ether. Like a ripple on a pond, widening to the shores, the voice ranged all directions to reach an audience half a world away. It was heard, no doubt, by many lonesome chaps with ear-phones clamped to their heads: trappers in snow-buried shacks, scattered over a hundred thousand miles of forest and mountain and blizzard-scourged tundra; factors and bush-rovers at the remotest fur-factories; whalers in stout ships, nipped in the polar drift; frost-bitten policemen in barrack and camp, stationed here and there in the great midnight around the curve of the arctic circle, the uttermost videttes of the northern law.

"It is a queer message," pursued the radio announcer in his pleasantly modulated speech. "Maybe the man for whom it is meant hears me and will understand. Here it is:

"Sergeant Buck Tearl, R.C.M.P., Port-o'-Prayer." There was a momentary pause and the voice cleared itself of a faint husk—a strangely personal and familiar sound that for a moment seemed to bring the speaker out of distance and invisibility into the very presence of the listener.

The man at the microphone went on with the letter.

"The dead do not always die," he read. "If you can find Kablunak's band of A-hi-ag-muit Esquimaux, who winter, they say, on Queen Maud Sea, make them tell you the truth."

"I don't know whether I pronounce the Esquimaux names correctly," ended the announcer, "but anyhow, that's the letter, and it's signed—Diane."

Of course the broadcaster could not know whether Sergeant Tearl had a radio receiver or was tuned-in that night on the wavelength of WBZ. Nor could he have guessed that there was another man named Tearl, who happened to be listening-in at this very moment, and in whose quiet New York apartment that cryptic message arrived like an exploding grenade to rearrange violently the whole of his future life.

Kitchener Tearl found WBZ by accident when in an idle moment he had given the radio dial a careless spin. This much was fate or coincidence, or whatever mischievous force it is that is constantly unsettling people's nicely settled affairs. But all that happened afterwards followed as naturally and inevitably as blood follows the knife or youth after its own reckless bent or birds take the course of the southerning sun.

The greater part of the broadcasted messages in themselves were not of much interest to an eavesdropper.

"Mother sends love." "Father's rheumatism is better." "Bella wonders if you remember her." "Did you get the socks we sent last July?" "Baby Nellie, born August second, is waiting for her first glimpse of Uncle Jack." Small, homely, intimate matters such as these were discussed in the hearing of the rest of the world and flung off into the night to end up under the crackle of the northern lights.

The messages would not have made Kitchener Tearl forget an engagement he had made for that evening; it was the visioning of the men who were receiving them. His imagination soared off to far, strange places which he had never seen, nor ever expected to see, but which were names that had been thrillingly real to him since his earliest days of boyhood.

The whirr of the elevator outside the foyer of his apartment, the rumble of traffic coming up from the pavements of Park Avenue, were lost in the sorcery of his straying thoughts in other, greater sounds: The grumble of ice-floes, the slash of sleet on cabin walls, the rabid cry of the wolf pack, the wind in the pines.

His lean, hard-kept body was sprawled motionless in his chair as he listened and stared into immeasurable distances with one keen eyebrow quizzically upcocked, seeing not the bright window-squares in the apartment building across the way, but big timber and ice barrens and mountains stacked behind mountains and the auroral glimmer on the Arctic sky.

The fascination of the northland for Kitchener Tearl was a part of the tradition of his blood and kind. One of his grandfathers long ago had been a factor of the Hudson's Bay Company, and he died with his moccasins on in the frozen forests of Keewatin.

William Tearl, Kitchener's father, had followed the trails that had been broken ahead of him by Factor Jacob Tearl. He was an inspector in the old Royal Northwest Mounted Police.

The story of Inspector Bill Tearl was left a grim, unwritten chapter in the territorial records. Somewhere in the Ottawa files, after his name and service reports, was set down in fading red ink the word—"missing." One night, more than twelve years ago, Bill Tearl had walked out from a sub-post somewhere in the then-uncharted Vermilion River country, and was never seen nor heard of again.

Tearl's Yankee-born wife happened to be visiting in New York at the time of the inspector's disappearance. With her were her three children, Gerald, who was sixteen years old, Kitchener, twelve, and Jane, an elfish, jewel-eyed girl of nine.

An inheritance of money from her own side of the family had enabled Mrs. Tearl to provide for the three fatherless youngsters, to send them one after another to college, and to plan for a life of future comfort. And then, the year Jerry graduated from the university, where he won renown as one of the most ferocious half-backs who ever tore cleat-marks in the Yale bowl, his charming mother was taken ill and suddenly died, and Jerry became the head of the Tearls.

The two grown-up brothers and the growing sister went on living together, a bit quarrelsomely, but with a fierce and undying loyalty. Jerry gave promise of becoming as great a man in the business world as he had been on the college gridirons. But tragedy once more stepped in to decimate the family ranks.

The ex-line-plunger was notoriously quick-tempered. Nobody had ever found out what it was all about, but he got into a fearful argument with a man on a Broadway street corner, and had three-quarters killed that man with his bare hands. A warrant of atrocious assault was issued by the nearest magistrate, but Jerry left town a couple of jumps ahead of the police. Kitchener and Jane never heard another word from him. Like his father before him, he had abruptly quitted his place in the world to be engulfed in the mystery of the passing years.

This had happened a long while ago. Kitchener was now twenty-four, the elder of the remaining Tearls. In all this time he might have lost the image of his prodigious brother in casual forgetfulness. But in his case the hero-worship that had grown in the heart of boyhood still lingered with all the sweetness of the earliest memories. The hearing of the name Tearl choked him with a surging of emotion such as he would have felt if his brother's sinewy hand had been laid suddenly upon his shoulder.

When Kitchener's sister came home at one o'clock that morning from some sort of a party she had been attending somewhere or other, she found the floor of the living room carpeted with her father's old police maps, while her brother crawled over them on his hands and knees, a strange look in his dark, eager eyes.

"What the deuce, Kit?" she demanded from the doorway.

"I think I know where Jerry is," he said.

Jane dropped the wrap from her fine arms and shoulders and came into the room. "What?" she ejaculated.

Kitchener stood up and showed her the message he had taken down on paper.

"Diane!" read Jane, womanlike, noticing first of all the woman in the case. "Who's Diane?"

"She sent the message over the radio. I've never heard of her before."

Jane wrinkled her short nose as she perused her brother's hasty scrawl. "Who's Buck Tearl?"

"Sounds like Jerry to me," declared Kitchener.

"Why?" Jane had grown calm and skeptical. "Why would it be Jerry, when it's Buck?"

"There are not many Tearls in the world," Kitchener reminded her. "It isn't like Smith or Einstein or O'Toole or Jones. As far as the nickname goes, a man like Jerry would be apt to pick one up wherever he went. And it just naturally ought to be 'Buck.'

"Funny I never thought of it before," he mused. "Knowing Jerry as I did, I can't understand now why I never guessed it. He went back where he belonged, of course—the north and the Mounties." Kitchener faced his sister in tense excitement, "It's Jerry, you can bet on it. He joined up, and naturally by now he'd be a sergeant at least."

Jane laughed, and then stopped and sighed. "We're an odd outfit," she said, "each of us wasting our affections on the one up ahead. Dad thought grandfather was a stupendous man, and Jerry worshiped Dad, and you adore Jerry, and here am I, the last, with nothing to do but to be simply foolish about you."

He squeezed her graceful shoulders, and then turned away. "Don't be an ass," he said.

"Can I help it?" she grinned.

"Listen here!" he said soberly. "Did you get the possible meaning of that message?"

"About so-and-so's Esquimaux?"

"No," he returned, "the other part," and repeated the line: "'The dead do not always die.' Does that by any chance make you think of Dad?"

4

She looked startled for an instant, and then closed her firm mouth and shook her head. "No. Why should it? You'd be crazy to get any such ideas. Dad went—mother used to say—*écarté*—lost, frozen in the drifts, and was never found. Or perhaps he was ambushed by some outlaw he was after. Whatever happened, it was the end."

"Are you so sure it was the end?"

"As sure as I can ever be in this life."

"I'm not." Kitchener gathered up the tattered police maps, refolded them gingerly, and restored them to the keeping of the old mahogany highboy. "You don't know everything," he remarked over his shoulder. "For instance, you never heard of the Tearl annuity."

"The which?" she asked.

"The year Dad was lost," Kitchener informed her, "an express money order for five thousand dollars was delivered at our address here in town. The envelope that contained it was mailed in San Francisco, postmarked January first. There was no writing—no mark to identify the sender."

The girl stared with a quick contraction of her jade-tinged eyes. "You mean—?" she began, and then left the rest unasked.

"I don't know," answered her brother. "I only know that another five thousand came the next January and the next, and so on, every year, as regularly as the months rolled around. One draft was sent from Portland, another from Sitka, one from St. Johns, Newfoundland, two from Quebec, one from Kamchatka, Siberia."

"You've tried to trace the sender?"

"Mother first, then Jerry. Lately I've been trying. No use! If our unknown friend were a skulking criminal he could have taken no greater pains to keep his tracks covered."

"You think it could have been—" The girl's speech checked for an instant on a failing breath, and then she ended in a whispered word, "Dad?"

"Who knows? If he were alive and could send money he could have written to us. You were old enough to remember what he was like. It wouldn't have been like him to duck his family. No matter what had happened to him, he surely would have sent us word. And yet—"

Kitchener took a turn the length of the room, and then came back to stand head-high above his sister. When he was in deadly earnest over something his left eyebrow had an unaccountable habit of cocking itself at the jauntiest angle, as though he had thought up something funny to say.

Jerry used to tell him he looked at such moments like a wily, black-headed crow getting ready to guffaw over his sins.

Jane knew that expression of old, and she knew that whatever notion was sticking in his head, all the world could not shake it out. "Hello, Cocky-bird!" she exclaimed. "What's up now?"

"I'm going to find Jerry," he said.

No Tearl was ever much astonished by anything another Tearl ever decided to do. She faced him anxiously, but without the least show of surprise. "When?" was all she said.

"As soon as I can pull out."

"But you're by no means certain that Sergeant Buck Tearl is Jerry."

"Yes, I am. And if by any chance he didn't receive to-night's message, I want to see that he gets it. And I want to see Jerry."

"You know what it means, of course. The rail head doesn't go near Port-o'-Prayer. The rivers will be frozen up there. No canoes. You haven't been in the forests since you were twelve. You'll have to walk, my boy!" Her smile did not quite hide the dismay that had suddenly drenched her eyes. "You'll never make it."

"That money," he pursued, without looking at his sister. "We never spent any of it because we didn't know whether it was ours to spend. Mother put it in the bank. She called it the mystery fund. She deposited five thousand every January—then Jerry—then I. I only learned about it a short while before Jerry left. Didn't think it was anything to bother you with. But I'm telling you now. There's sixty thousand dollars all told, plus the interest. I'll turn the book over to you. Whatever you do about it is your own business."

"It's all settled, then? You're going?"

"I don't see any way out of it," said Kitchener.

Jane's hands reached up to smooth her brother's raven-black hair. Then she stood a-tiptoe to kiss his cheek. "If you think not," she said, "there's no way out of it."

CHAPTER II
AFTER MANY YEARS

When Kitchener Tearl left New York the city was basking in a spell of sultry, Indian Summer weather that had lingered into late October. As his Pullman traveled up the length of the Hudson Valley he saw robins in the orchards and flocks of belated blackbirds hovering about the meadows and fields. The hills and mountains still loomed green against the line of a soft and sunny sky.

Farther north he found notable changes in the climate and the scenery. On the other side of the border the air tingled with a frosty crispness, and the fringes of the forest were blazoned with the colors of the dying season. The people of Ottawa were wearing overcoats and keeping their hands in their pockets. On the way across Ontario the harvested acres reached sere and bleak to the chilly horizon. At Winnipeg the edges of the forked rivers were rimed in the morning with a first film of ice. Traveling from Saskatchewan into Alberta he saw long chains of wild geese, swans, and ducks in clouds, fleeing ahead of winter. Near Edmonton he caught sight of a man walking alongside a pond with a string of muskrat traps slung from his shoulder. The train going north on the branch line ran through snow flurries that increased in frequency and severity all the way to Fort McMurray.

Here he threw away his timetable and opened up his maps. From this point on his life would be regulated, not by the hours of a clock, but by the changing seasons.

He dug out of his baggage a pair of scarlet "four-point" Hudson's Bay blankets—heirlooms that had been in his family for more than half a century—and he went to bed warmly in the unheated inn and dreamed gratefully of Grandfather Jake Tearl who for twenty years had defied the cold of Keewatin in these same red, imperishable blankets.

The trip down the river afforded him three weeks of complete idleness. The boat ran aground on all the charted shallows, and the crew of Indian stevedores would lighten ship by lightening the cargo: afloat once more, they would re-load and go hopefully northward for a few more miles, until they stuck on another bar. Kitchener had traveled up this same river on this same scraped-bottom steamer with his mother and his brother and his little sister Jane, when they undertook their fateful journey to the city, twelve years ago. He spent the short, gray days on deck, facing sleet and swirling snow, trying to pick out old landmarks as he watched the endless marching of the great spruce forest along the white streaked hills.

They cracked ice the last hundred miles, before they reached the long, black lake that is the geographical key to all the wild watercourses to the north and the west and the east. The captain of the boat hoped to go on down Mackenzie River, but his solitary passenger never learned how far he got. Kitchener had his baggage dumped on the shore near a

7

Chippewyan encampment, and although sheet ice enclosed a part of the lake, he hired two Indians with a canoe, and crossed in a headwind and a heavy sea to his destination at the farthest lonesome harbor. So his sister Jane's dismal prediction came to nothing. He reached Port-o'-Prayer and had not walked a step of the way.

Kitchener left his belongings on the beach and strolled up the hill towards the group of white-painted buildings that huddled at the edge of the vast forest. There was a sort of inn near the landing, a story and a half log building, with battened doors and windows and an unsmoking chimney. Nobody lived there at this season. Farther on were the company's store houses and the residency of the store-keeper. The buildings were shuttered and silent, not even a dog was visible in the snowy compound.

In the spring and early summer, when the trappers had come in from the forests, Port-o'-Prayer looked like a populous village. Now the store-keeper was the sole remaining inhabitant. He had sent out his furs long since and had hibernated for the winter.

Kitchener routed the man out of his quarters and found him to be an untalkative, sad-featured Scotsman. He was so lacking in curiosity that he did not even show wonderment at the sight of a tenderfoot who had journeyed into the back-country while winter was beginning to close up all the routes of retreat.

He answered the newcomer's questions with an air of pained but patient politeness. Yes—a Sergeant Buck Tearl had stopped here at the post. But he went away again, after a couple of days. This was nearly a month ago.

Where had he gone? North somewhere, into the Vermilion River country. There was a police look-out station there at *Saut Sauvage*, on the ground that vaguely divided the Esquimaux from the forest tribes of the Cree and Yellow Knives. The sergeant was making an Arctic patrol, presumably on the trail of evil-doers.

What was he like, this Sergeant Tearl? He was a big man, who spoke softly, and yet had a hard and dangerous-looking mouth. While he was at Port-o'-Prayer he had kept on his lynxskin capote and the store-keeper had seen only his mouth and nose and his disconcerting eyes.

Even this meager description set Kitchener's pulses tingling. Having come this far he had no thought except to go on, as far as *Saut Sauvage*, if need be. This man surely was his brother Jerry.

Had Sergeant Tearl picked up a radio message sent to him on the twenty-fifth of last month? The store-keeper didn't know. He himself had no interest in hearing things out of the air. The company had given him a receiver last year, but it was too much trouble to buy new batteries for it. If he wanted to hear voices and songs he could go sit in the Chippewyan camp up the river.

Kitchener decided to go on at once. He would need a sledge and a train of huskies. It was snowing steadily and drearily now, and the trails would lie under shrouds to-morrow. What about dogs? The store-keeper had a couple he could sell. One of them would do all right for a king-pin. The Indians probably could spare two or three others. But they would come high—a hundred dollars a dog at least. Men were feeding their draught animals again, and weren't kicking and clubbing them away from the camps as they did in the summer. This was dog-time.

Fortunately Kitchener had no need to stint himself in money. He acquired the store-keeper's two spare huskies, a serviceable sledge, a pair of snowshoes and a load of Hudson's Bay company staple groceries. At daybreak next morning he hitched in the two dogs, set his face to the snow-laden wind, and was off on the river route.

Years ago young Kit Tearl had followed his brother or his father through another spruce forest on such white, blustery days as this, sturdily planting a pair of toy-sized snowshoes in the tracks of the bigger raquettes ahead. He hadn't thought of that boy in a long while. But when he shoved his toes into the *babiche* thongs and started out through the powdery drifts he was surprised to discover that snowshoeing was a logical and familiar method of locomotion.

It was the same with the "gee" pole and the dog traces and the dogs. As he coursed through the thickets at the edge of the freezing river, he found himself trudging along effortlessly, managing his sledge and the tandem of trotting dogs with a subconscious facility, as though a long-forgotten part of himself had breathed the tang of the wilderness and suddenly awakened to take charge of his affairs.

The lessons of childhood may be buried deep by passing time and quite forgotten. But things well learned are never really lost. He strode forward with an easy swing of the hips, his toes pointed straight ahead, as a woodsman walks. Eyes accustomed to look placidly and rather humorously upon the world, somehow had grown sober and restlessly alert. It did not seem like a recollection of ancient teaching, but an instinct, rather, that prompted him to keep a lookout twenty paces ahead for trail signs and to pass invariably on the windward side of the denser thickets.

He would have said yesterday that he did not know a word of any Indian language. But when he pulled into the Chippewyan encampment he was amazed to discover his tongue twisting into strange clicking and grunting sounds of speech. He understood the talk of the sooty-skinned men who emerged from the huts and teepees, and it was evident that they understood him.

Yes, the tribe had a few very good, excellent sledge dogs for sale. After long dickering Kit purchased a couple of undersized, slinking starvelings, which he had to accept because his sharp-dealing hosts would not part with any others. But when he tried to obtain a guide for his northward trip, business relations promptly ceased.

The tribesmen could think up a hundred reasons why nobody wanted a job. The whitefishing at this moment was too good to be neglected. One man had promised his squaw not to leave Port-o'-Prayer, another's moccasins hurt his feet if he walked too far, a third felt his rheumatism coming on, a fourth would have to go down to church on Christmas. Besides, the proposed journey would reach the country of the Dog-Ribs and Yellow-Knife Indians. Nobody was afraid of these bad men, the Chippewyans wanted it to be known: they simply weren't going, that was all.

While Kitchener was engaged in his most persuasive efforts the flap of one of the teepees was jerked back and a voice spoke to him in English. He turned to face a white man who had come out to join the group by the sledge.

The newcomer fixed Kitchener with a long, measuring stare. He was a gaunt, big-boned man, slouchy and loose-knit of body, with lengthy, dangling arms hinged powerfully to the knotted muscles of his stooping shoulders. The temperature was approaching zero, but he stood unshivering in a sleeveless athletic undershirt and without any hat. There was a swipe of lather across the bulge of his hard, bluish jaw. Evidently he had been interrupted in the act of shaving. His lean, dark face was marked here and there with glaring white lines that might have been scars of knife cuts, and his close-cropped scalp likewise showed the seams of old wounds. Although Kitchener himself stood an even six feet without his pacs and snowshoes, this stranger overtopped him by a full two inches.

"North myself," said the man. "Shoving off two hours before to-morrow's daylight. You can come with me."

He spoke with a sharp-clipt brevity and without any trace of accent. Kitchener should have been glad to find a man of his own language and race for a companion. But somehow he was taken aback by the abruptness of the proposal. The stranger's deep-set eyes looked cold and calculating in the winter twilight.

Kitchener had a feeling that he would have preferred an Indian. "Where are you going?" he temporized.

"Not as far as *Saut Sauvage*. But I can put you on the track when you turn off."

"What's your name?" asked Tearl.

"Jim," said the other. "What's yours?"

"Kit," answered Kitchener, and checked a smile. He could be reserved too if there was any reason for it.

"All right. You have your muts fed and ready to leave by six."

Kitchener nodded. There was nothing further to be said. The man had overheard him appealing to the Chippewyans for a guide. He could think up no excuse for refusing the services that perhaps were offered with honest intent.

He swept the man with a speculating glance, wondering who he might be. If he were an ordinary bushman he would have been out on his trapping grounds before now, circling his lines. His high boot-pacs and his Mackinaw trousers were new and obviously of city manufacture. Nevertheless he must be a forest man or he would not be pushing off with such quiet confidence into a country that was barely known to the outer world.

Although he had removed his upper garments to shave, he had kept on a cartridge belt and a holster, from which frankly jutted the ivory handle of a heavy revolver. Outside of the police, men of the wilderness carried rifles habitually, but seldom burdened themselves with pistols.

It was a very fine weapon this stranger carried. Kitchener's eyelashes blinked as there came to him from out of the obscurity of memory or imagination one of those dim and tantalizing flashes that try to bring back a sound or a sight or an experience, once familiar, and afterwards faded to dreamy inconsequence. The butt of the revolver was made of two pieces of old, yellow ivory, handsomely carved and scribed. Kitchener had a queer, startled feeling that he had seen it somewhere before.

He found the stranger's formidable eyes upon him, and he looked up and said anything to cover his momentary lapse of mind. "I'll be glad to make a deal with you."

"Deal?" echoed the other coldly. "What do you think I am—a professional guide? I've asked you to go with me. Come or not, it's all the same."

"Thank you," said Kitchener. "I'll come."

The Chippewyans gave the two white men a sleeping space in one of their skin teepees, and after taking potluck at the camp kettle, Kit rolled up in his grandfather's red blankets and went to bed. He tried to sleep, but his thoughts kept going back to the ivory-handled revolver. It belonged somewhere in the past, either this or a gun exactly like it. Time after time the recollection almost came to him, and then escaped behind the curtains of the mind.

Four or five Indians were soddenly asleep on the farther side of the airy teepee. Jim, the stranger, was stretched out in the open space between, a relaxed and quiet shape, breathing slowly and regularly. The faint radiance of the northern night reached through the smoke hole of the lodge poles to outline his sleeping form. He had unstrapped his cartridge belt, and the ivory-handled revolver lay within reach of his right hand.

Kitchener tried to make himself comfortable, first on one side and then on the other. But he remained awake, hearing the cracking of branches and the whisper of snow on the caribou skins. After a long while he flung off his blankets and sat up. He might as well settle this thing that was destroying his night's rest.

The stranger was obviously asleep. Kit moved forward on his knees, and the man did not budge. He reached the cartridge belt, extracted the revolver from its holster and crept across the teepee to the flapping doorway. None of the sleepers spoke or stirred.

From his shirt pocket Kitchener produced a match. He waited for a moment, and then struck a light, cupping his hands carefully to break the reflection behind him. Peering tensely, he turned the weapon in front of the match. The blued steel of the barrel bore the manufacturer's trademark, with the patent-rights dates, and on the frame was a small, silver shield, carrying a line of fine engraving. He bent closer and read the inscription:

"W. T., insp., R. N.-W. M. P., '16."

Kitchener went back on his hands and knees and replaced the gun in the holster. Then he drew his blankets about his shoulders and sat huddled and shivering—staring into vacancy—

He saw far back through space and time. He remembered a twelve-year-old boy seated on the steps of the barracks of the police. It was a sweet, green afternoon with the spring sun flecking the parade ground between rustling branches, while robins and red-polls and pipits flashed singing among the trees. There was a tall, soldierly figure in a scarlet coat, standing before a group of uniformed men. He recalled that one of these men—a grizzled sergeant of police—had made a sort of awkward, halting speech. In a presentation case of mahogany and velvet lay an ivory-butted revolver.

These men had assembled to say good-by to their commanding officer, who had been assigned to a far-distant post. They wished him to accept this beautiful six-shooter as a memento of their affection and esteem. The sergeant had said: "May it never fire first; may it never fire too late." And the twelve-year-old boy had listened and swelled with the glory of the moment.

The tall officer was Kit's father, and on that occasion they had seen each other for almost the last time. Inspector Bill Tearl had buckled on his big, new gun and voyaged away to the north.

To-night, after the long lapse of years, Kitchener had looked again at his father's revolver, and another man was wearing it.

CHAPTER III
DISMAL TRAIL

At the coldest and dreariest hour of the morning, in darkness and silence so intense that an early riser must feel the snow stinging his face to know that it was still snowing, Kit Tearl was out of his blankets, poking the night fire and thawing out the coffee pot.

The Indians would lie sluggishly until daybreak, but the other white man aroused himself a few minutes behind his traveling companion. Before he donned his fur parka and mittens he stood half naked outside the teepee, revolving his body in the weather, and stretching his sinewy arms, as though he took relish in the snow beating upon his skin.

The two men barely exchanged greetings, and they ate breakfast without a syllable of speech. The stranger fed and harnessed his dogs and waited in dour silence while Tearl was putting his sorry team into the traces.

When the Chippewyan curs and the huskies from Port-o'-Prayer found themselves in harness together for the first time the inevitable dog-fight took place, and ended in as many seconds as there were dogs. The leader, a red-furred Chinook cross called Buzz-saw, walked back through his team-mates and left them on their backs, howling.

The tall man stood aloof until the trouble was settled. "Men could learn something from the dogs," he remarked. "When two or more start some place together they ought to fight it out before they take the trail. Then there'd be no future arguments."

"As long as you know the trail, and I don't," said Kit, smoothly, "we don't have to prove which is the king-pin. You lead, I'll follow."

Until the dull, leaden daylight seeped through the forest Kit drove his team and followed in the crunching furrow left by the vaguely seen figure that stalked ahead.

He had said nothing about the ivory-handled revolver and was careful to give no hint of last night's discovery. Since their first meeting the stranger had inspired him with distrust and an unaccountable feeling of apprehension. To mention the fact that the gun he carried belonged to a mysteriously "lost" police officer might precipitate a show-down such as Kit was not yet prepared to meet. Common sense advised him to wait and keep his eyes open, to find out who this man was and whence he came. If he had any part in the tragedy of Inspector Tearl's disappearance, it would be insanity to question him or put him on his guard. He could vanish permanently into the storm if he chose, or simply turn with a single shot and let the ivory-handled revolver preserve its own ancient secret.

Kit was carried along by a grim excitement as he dogged the footsteps of his laconic companion. It was an odd whimsey of fate that had brought them both on the same day into this out-of-the-way part of the wilderness. For twelve years a great force of relentless, sharp-eyed man-hunters, with every resource of experience and organization at their command, had searched ceaselessly for news of a lost comrade. The scarlet-clad brigade does not lightly abandon its own. Countless patrols had turned up, time after time, with "nothing to report." But where a thousand seasoned bushmen had sought fruitlessly, young Kit Tearl, on his first night in the big timber, had stumbled upon a clew that perhaps might lead to the knowledge of what had happened to the missing inspector of police. His errand had suddenly changed to such grave import that he was almost afraid to look into the future. A huge responsibility had fallen upon his shoulders. Of secondary concern now was the finding of Sergeant Buck

Tearl. His new mission was to hold the trail and, by hook or crook, to ferret out the history of the man with the ivory-butted gun.

The short day broke sullenly to the steady accompaniment of falling snow. Kit and his traveling mate were cruising through a dense spruce forest. There were no landmarks visible—nothing but trees and trees and trees, with the endless expanse of snow underfoot and snow-chinked ceilings of greenery above.

Men and dogs were like shadows stealing through muffled, unechoing corridors of whiteness. The only sounds to be heard were the silken whisper of sledge runners, the padding of industrious feet, the creak of raquettes sliding through the feathery drifts.

The motions of snowshoeing came naturally enough to Kit, but by the end of his first couple of hours on the march he began to feel acute little pains in his ankles and calves and thighs. Since his graduation from college his most arduous journeys had been undertaken by subway between his apartment and the law office in which he had hoped in time to become a junior partner. He was in for a few days of torment before his muscles hardened up; meanwhile he shut a stubborn jaw and held the pace.

A while before noon they halted for a breathing space and to give the dogs a drink. They picked up a cold snack and Kit's companion squatted by his sledge, unsociable and saturnine, crunching with strong, white teeth the bannock and hard chunk of pemmican which he had produced from his pack.

The taciturnity of the man was beginning to wear upon Tearl's nerves. If he would only say something, even to grouch at his fellow traveler! But his harsh mouth stayed shut and his eyes remained as cold and unfeeling as the wilderness that reached into mysterious silence for a thousand miles about him.

They had left the river far behind and were traveling a diagonal course across the spruce ridges. To ignore the natural guidance of the valleys and waterways is the easiest way of getting lost in the big timber. Each wooded crown or hollow looked exactly like the hills and hollows ahead or those left behind. Had Kit been alone he would have been hopelessly muddled long ago. But the stranger apparently scorned the need of route marks. He plowed on tirelessly and without hesitation, having neither sun nor compass to correct his turnings, driving his dogs through the unbroken leagues of the forest, breaking trail and never at loss in his points of direction.

Kitchener at first thought that the man's silence was due merely to a surly and unfriendly disposition. But as they traversed the miles of solitude, it occurred to him that perhaps there were grimmer reasons for keeping so quiet. He noticed that his trail-mate continually shifted his glance, right and left, and whenever he came to an open glade in the woods, where a moving object would stand out boldly against the snowy backgrounds, he invariably skulked close to the edges of the fringing thickets. At every high ridge he paused to scan the surrounding landscape and to watch briefly over his own back-trail.

Once when the dogs started up a snowshoe rabbit and gave chorus excitedly, their driver sent them back to their business with a savagely curling whiplash, and within ten seconds had reduced them to whimpering obedience. On another occasion the man checked his team in mid-stride on the slant of a sheer hillside. He crouched to stare fixedly across the valley, and, with a quick, reflexive jerk, his hand reached for the rifle that rode under the lashings of his sledge. Whatever he thought he saw or heard, it failed to reveal itself. By the time Kit had scrambled across the slide, he had straightened again and was ready to send his team onward.

"What was it?" Kit asked.

The man gave him a stony look from under his wet, bristling eyebrows.

"Habit!" he explained in a voice that he was cautious to keep lowered. "It gets to be second nature to keep a lookout around you."

"You were grabbing for your rifle," Tearl observed.

"Thought I saw a moose," the other returned sourly, and commanded his team to *marche*!

Kitchener followed without further comment. But he knew that the man was lying. The sledges were overloaded now, and it would be impossible for either of them to take on any extra haunches of meat. Besides, no moose would ever have allowed them to approach that close on his windward side, as this woodsman knew perfectly well. It was evident that he was on his guard against somebody or something that he feared was on his trail or ambushed in the dim coverts ahead.

The winter darkness overtook them in mid-afternoon, and they promptly made camp. In a deep little glen, screened densely by the alders, where a spring of water welled forth in a half frozen trickle from underneath an old, fallen hemlock, they erected shelter sheets and spread their blankets. Jim built a tiny fire of knots kicked off the rotting tree, and took pains to keep the flame low and well hidden in the deepest pocket of their retreat. It was not an honest fire of logs that a care-free bushman would have ignited to warm himself on a winter's night. Obviously the man did not wish to risk the attention of spying eyes.

Kitchener was too tired to perturb himself over the significance of all these precautions. He fed his dogs, helped to drain the pot of coffee, wrapped his aching frame in the red blankets, and in ten seconds had fallen into profound sleep.

What it was that aroused him he could not have said. The wind had died during the night and the forest was invested in utter quiet. Jim had trampled out the fire before he turned in. The faint aurora of a northern white night lent a magical unreality to the muffled shapes of the surrounding forest. Great downy snowflakes sifted interminably through the weary-drooping branches. Kitchener had no idea whether it was midnight or the edge of daybreak.

A drift of snow had formed over his feet and a current of outside air had found a way in between the flaps of his blankets. He was curled up in a tight ball, cramped and shivering. With clicking teeth he sat up, intending to remake his bed.

His companion had bunked down on the opposite side of the spring. Kitchener looked sleepily in that direction, and then his eyes blinked wider and he looked harder. In the obscurity he could just make out the oblong shape of the folded robes. But they lay flat on the ground. There was nothing under them. Wonderingly, Kit crept forward to make sure that he was not deceiving himself. He pulled back the furs, and saw in the snow the deep impression of a man's body. Jim had rolled up under his covers for a while—presumably until he was sure that the other man was safely asleep. Then he had got up again, and disappeared from camp.

At first Kitchener supposed that the man had decided to rid himself of his traveling mate and had sneaked away into the night. But a hurried glance around corrected that notion. Jim's packed sledge still remained where he had unhitched the evening before on the other side of the brook, and on the neighboring slope, where the dogs had buried themselves in the snow, a group of little hummocks, like grave mounds, tallied in number with the count of the two teams. The man had slipped off somewhere on some benighted business of his own, but it would seem that he expected to come back.

Kit fastened his boots and picked up his rifle. The other man had taken his own gun from the sledge, and his broad-toed snowshoes also were missing. It was merely a question of casting across the brook to pick up the web-scuffled marks in the snow. Jim had climbed out of the hollow and, for some unguessed reason, had struck back over the windings of his own down-country trail.

There was no hesitation on Kit's part. Here was a chance for discoveries. It must be a momentous errand to pull a man out of his warm robes in the middle of such a night. He noticed that his fellow traveler wore broad snowshoes with a peculiar square web packing. An inspection of the departing prints showed only a light powdering of new-fallen flakes. Presumably the man had quitted camp only a short while ago. Kit scrambled up the embankment, intending to follow.

From a distance of a half-dozen paces he could dimly make out the furrowed line that curved down through the spruces. By staying off at one side of the trail he could pursue the back-track without being betrayed later by his own footsteps.

Kit reached the top of the first terrace and there halted with a startled abruptness. He had an impression that something had stirred behind him. A bulky shadow loomed in the alder thicket. Before he had half turned a brawny arm reached suddenly forward to crook itself about his head, and an astounding voice accosted him.

"Hello, Cocky-bird!"

For an instant Kit felt as though his heart had gone dead in his chest, and then all his blood coursed through him again in a wild, warm resurgence. He knew without looking around. The low, mocking laugh, the bearlike embrace squeezing his head and pinching his ears: there was only one person in the world who ever hugged him like this, or chuckled at him with such ironic amusement. It was Gerald Tearl. It could be nobody on earth except his brother Jerry.

CHAPTER IV
A GHOSTLY VOYAGEUR

The arm in its rough, icy sleeve clutched Kit tightly, and in that breath-taking moment he neither moved nor recovered the voice to speak. It was as though time had swept backwards to rediscover the heart of an eager, small boy, whose bigger, rougher brother sometimes stalked up behind him with laughter to clench his head like this. The pain of his ruffled ears had always seemed to him a very trifling price to pay for the ecstasy of being noticed by the redoubtable Jerry. Even to-night Kitchener was conscious only of a sudden, blinding happiness in feeling himself caught in that harshly affectionate grip, in knowing that his brother had found him.

"I saw your funny old face this morning," said the man behind him. "You stopped on a hillside and goggled your eyes my direction. And then I knew it was you, Cocky-bird."

Kit broke the muscular hold and squirmed around. He saw a tall, deep-chested figure in duffles and furs, and wearing the royal insignia of the northern police.

"Jerry!" he gasped.

The other man grinned at him, displaying teeth as white as the snow that clung to his hood.

Jerry had matured since Kit last saw him, and seemingly had grown in stature and taken on several more inches of girth. The eyes that twinkled in the half-light were older with knowledge and experience. Even in smiling the mouth held something of the ruthless inflexibility of a wolf-trap. He looked harder and more competent than ever before, and also, Kit fancied, with a touch of misgiving, much more self-willed and reckless and devil-may-care.

"Are you Sergeant Buck Tearl?" Kit asked.

"None other. Almost demoted now and then, but still Sergeant Tearl. What are you doing here, Oakheart?"

"I intercepted a radio message for you from WBZ. It was about some Esquimaux and the dead not dying. I've got it written down for you. I was sure this Buck party would be you."

Jerry laughed quietly. "The same old Cocky-bird! Would hike three thousand miles through a freeze-up of hell—if you take the notion—just to tell me you got WBZ on your radio. That would be little Kit—always. Too bad, after all your trouble, but I got the message too. I carry a small, portable set on my sledge, and I picked it out of the air the same night you did, about a month ago."

"Then you must know—" Kit regarded him sharply. "What does it mean? Who's Diane?"

Jerry shook his head. "I'll tell you about that later when we have a little more time—all that I know, at least. It's a strange story, and may bring on things still stranger before we're through. Just now we have more immediate things to think about. How do you happen to be consorting with this egg I saw you with to-day?"

"Jim What's-his-name? I ran into him at Port-o'-Prayer, and he offered to guide me part way to *Saut Sauvage*, where they said you had gone."

"That's all you know about him?"

"No," said Kit, "that isn't all I know about him." He stole a glance around the thickets and dropped his speech to a whisper. "He's got Dad's old ivory-butted gun."

"All right."

Sergeant Tearl accepted the fact with a nod that might have seemed almost indifferent. "He's the mug I thought he was. I've been hovering on him for several days, and of course he knows that I came in through Port-o'-Prayer, just as you knew. He thought he saw me yesterday noon, when I was watching from the opposite hill. He did, but it's a good thing for all of us that he changed his mind and decided he didn't. It's too soon to kill him."

Kit stared at his brother, chilled not so much by the remark as the matter-of-fact tone of its utterance. "Who is he?" he demanded.

"I don't know what name he's going by now. His real name is Simeon Bent, but the guards down at the prison in Ottawa called him 'Hell' Bent. You can draw your own conclusions. He just finished an eleven-year stretch, and they let him out a few weeks ago."

Kitchener studied the dim vistas of the snowy landscape. "He told me his name was Jim. But perhaps I misunderstood. He may have said 'Sim.' Where's he gone now?"

"Just took a saunter down through the forest to find me. People are so ready to accept the belief that it is easiest to murder a policeman when he is in bed asleep. You're supposed to sleep soundest in the small hours of the morning."

"You don't mean—" Kit gasped.

"Why not?" observed Jerry placidly. "He knows I'm around here somewhere. He has a pretty little job afoot, but he can't go ahead until the field is clear. He's got to get me out of the way. I was sure he'd strike back to-night to intersect my sledge tracks. He won't find the trail until he's five miles up country. I detoured widely and came in here from the east instead of the south.

"Caught a little sleep about a hundred yards from here." The sergeant pushed back his sleeve to observe the luminous dial of the watch strapped around his big-boned wrist. "One-thirty now. It'll be three before Sim makes the circuit. That gives us time for a family reunion. How's little Jane?"

"She's a grown woman, Jerry. Pretty and sweet and stubborn as a mule."

"Little Jane!" ruminated the sergeant, with the faintest break in his voice. "She's the best of our tribe. Give her a kiss from the outcast, if you ever see her again. I'm not at all sure that you will." Jerry measured his brother's straight-standing figure with a critical eye. "I've got to use you, Mr. Stoutenberg, now that I've got you. Sorry!"

Jerry reached forward a mittened hand and his iron fingers clamped down for a moment on the other's shoulder. "Did you make the varsity squad, Cocky-bird?" he asked, as he prodded his brother's wiry muscles.

"No," said Kit regretfully. "Not enough weight for my height. The best I could do was the cross-country team and captain of the pistol team."

"You always were an ugly shot with a gun," remarked Jerry. "And there may be times when that'll get an alumnus farther than a Phi Beta Kappa key."

"Jerry," demanded the younger brother abruptly, "why did you run out on us the way you did? I know you got yourself into a mess, and all of that, but there was no reason why you couldn't have written. It was rotten never to send any word to Jane and me."

"Maybe," agreed the other. "But I'd thought it all out and I never was going to. It was fairer not." He laughed heavily and ended with a sigh. "That man I smashed—I've almost forgotten who he was and what it was about. There was a girl mixed up in it somewhere—as unimportant as that. I went off my chump, and might easily have killed the poor devil."

"He recovered, though," Kit said. "You could go back and square it up and be yourself again. There's no need of burying yourself alive for life."

"I am myself," Jerry returned somberly, "and there's a beastly streak in me. What happened once can happen again. I'm not going to risk another chance of disgracing you and Jane, or keeping you in a nervous stew over my running amok again. I'm better off forgotten."

"That's fool talk," the younger brother protested.

"If I turn violent any time now," grinned Jerry, "I'm acting in the name of the law. This is the right job for me."

Kitchener regarded him curiously. "Do you like it?"

"It's my job," the sergeant reiterated briefly, and changed the subject. "Hitch your dogs," he ordered. "You're coming with me."

It was characteristic that Kit should accept unquestioningly his older brother's decisions. He roused the sleeping huskies from their nests under the snow, pitched them a fish apiece, and then hustled them into the sledge traces.

Jerry looked on without offering to help. "You'll find as you go along that you remember things you thought you never knew," he remarked as the younger brother smartly swung his leader into line. "You and I cut our milk teeth on the butt of a dog whip, and took our first bath in a snow drift. I'm glad you're here, Crow-eye."

"What about Sim?" asked Kit as he packed up his bed.

"Let him find you gone. He'll see I've been here and that we've gone off together. Let him think what he pleases. I'm going to pass him along later to the captain of the varsity pistol team." Jerry finished with an ironic laugh. "Ready?"

As he approached the neighboring hillside a half dozen animated bundles sprang yapping from the drift to claw and leap at Jerry for a moment, and then to round in a wolf-like pack upon the strange huskies. The sergeant booted his own beasts back into their traces, and within ten seconds had quelled the riot. Then he gave the command and the team launched forward into the night.

Kit had thought that his companion of the first day's march was a snow-traveler, but he was to learn what it really means to cruise. His dogs were forced to stretch their gaunt bodies to the utmost to hold the pace of the police malemutes and the lusty sergeant who broke trail for them.

Years pass and seasons change and men grow older. Times there had been when a short-legged, anxious-faced little chap used to tag after his elder brother, taking two steps for one, stumbling and breathless, yet keeping up somehow. To-night it seemed to Kit as though a ghostly young familiar were running with him, sharing his distress as the miles lengthened and his wind gave out and his aching legs grew heavier, but pushing onward, nevertheless, hanging on in spite of everything, not once losing sight of the big hurrying shape ahead of him.

An hour or so on the shadowy side of daybreak Jerry at last decided mercifully that they had come far enough. He halted his team in the darkness of a wooded ravine at the head of a tiny, ice-bound brook. Then with a crooked grin he turned to look back as his brother kicked out of his snowshoes and sank down upon the ground.

"Same old Kit!" he said. "Cheerio! You'll toughen up."

He disappeared in the thicket with an ax, and for a few minutes the morning stillness was broken by a cheerful ringing of steel. Presently he returned with an armful of white birch billets and started a brisk fire.

"You and I must have an understanding before we split directions," he remarked. "I've got my job to do, and you'll have yours. We'll breakfast first. Meanwhile, let's see what Diane has on her mind."

"Diane?" echoed Kit, staring blankly.

"See if she's asleep, will you?" Jerry nodded casually towards the sledge. "Maybe she'd like something to eat."

"To eat—? Diane?" Kit regarded his brother slantwise, as though he were in momentary doubt of the other's sobriety, or sanity. The policeman was absorbed in measuring coffee from a muslin bag into a tin pot, and he did not look up.

Kitchener stood up and paused uncertainly. "What are you talking about?" he demanded.

"Here's the key," said Jerry. He fished in his pocket and handed his brother a tiny, metal object that glinted in the firelight.

Young Tearl held the key between his fingers, looking at it vacuously. "What am I to do with this?"

"Let her come to breakfast, if she wants any," said Jerry, and turned his back again.

Kit stood irresolute for a moment, and then, with a bewildered glance at the policeman, he moved over towards the sledge. He halted to gaze in sagging-jawed wonderment.

Jerry's sledge was bedded deep with duffle and blankets and soft, warm furs. In the cozy nest thus formed he made out the contours of a slight figure, and saw the oval of a feminine face and a pair of dark, living eyes glowering up at him.

As he stood awkward and unreasoningly embarrassed, a pettish, slightly husky voice spoke sharply from the smothering furs. "Unfasten these!"

The robes were lifted and thrown back, and two hands stretched themselves towards Kit. He was aghast to discover that the woman's wrists were held together by the steel links of handcuffs.

CHAPTER V
THE GIRL IN HANDCUFFS

The key was in Kitchener's fingers, but at the moment he seemed to have no idea what its purpose might be. He bent above the sledge, gawking absurdly, utterly at loss to know what to say or to do. In the half light of dawning he saw the curve of a full, firm cheek and was aware that the woman's mouth was drawn tensely in a fierce and bitter line. It rather increased his distress to discover that she was quite young and extremely indignant.

She tried to sit up, rattling the nickel-plated chain that swiveled one wrist close to the other. He perceived then that the handcuffs were secured by a short length of cord to one of the braces of the sledge.

"Will you," she said in a panting fury, "kindly take these things off of me?"

"Certainly," said Kit, who was beginning to win back his self-possession. He dropped his mittens and took her hands in one of his. Her fingers, he noticed, were warm and soft and gracefully slender. After a fumbling attempt or two he fitted the key in its apertures and shot open first one and then the other of the locking wards. The woman cast off the ugly circlets, dumped the robes overside, and flung herself from the sledge. Without a word to her deliverer, or a glance towards him, she stalked off through the snow to confront Jerry.

She was a small young woman, with a body as slim and supple and emotionally reactive as a reed in a gusty wind. She wore calf-high boots with moccasin feet, a pair of forest-green breeches, and a green camel's hair parka with the hood thrown back. From the opened throat of her upper garment her slender neck emerged to hold high a prideful and shapely head. Her nose was slightly upturned and a shade too short; her mouth was generously wide and warmly crimson, and, at this moment, insolent. In the daytime her elongated, dark-fringed eyes were probably a clear hazel color; in the light of the birch fire they gave back ruddy, sherry-tinged glints. Her reddish hair, short and electrically unruly, flaunted its disorder in the reflection of the leaping flames.

"If it takes me the rest of my life," she said to the policeman, "I'll pay you for this!"

"Why, bless your heart," said Jerry affably, "it wasn't so much to do. Baby Bunting in the warm rabbit skins. I didn't mind taking you bye-bye." He had pronged a brochette of bacon strips, and was watching the grease drops fall and explode in the fire. "I hope you had a nice nap."

"You—" The girl stopped and choked in her wrath. "You—devil!" she wound up impotently.

Jerry turned his head slowly, and for the first time paid her the tribute of looking at her. Then he shifted his glance to Kit. "This is the one, Buck," he said. "This is Diane."

Kit in bemusement regarded first the girl and then the man. In his brother's lightness of speech he recognized a serious and purposeful undercurrent. Jerry had called him "Buck." Why? He couldn't guess. Only he realized that there was some queer and subtle game afoot. He would have to watch closely and pick up his cues.

Jerry's eyes held him, and he caught the warning in their smiling depths. "This," the policeman informed the girl, "is Sergeant Buck Tearl of the royal stuffs. He told me that he wanted to find you and ask you about that radio message. And here you are!"

Kit advanced a pace or two, but was careful not to reveal himself too closely in the firelight. For some incomprehensible reason Jerry was asking him to shift identities—to pretend that he was a policeman. All his life he had been playing up to his big brother's whims, and it seemed but the normal and natural thing now to follow the lead that was offered him, whatever the hidden motives might be. There would be no difficulty in playing the part. He stood back in the shadow, and even if the girl looked at him too observantly she could learn nothing from his appearance. As far as she knew he could be wearing a police uniform under his outer garments.

"I want to know," he said, "what you meant by sending me that stuff in the air. 'The dead do not always die,'" he quoted. "And by the way, who's Kablunak?"

The girl shifted her hostile stare his direction. "I don't know what you're talking about," she said.

"Why did you ask WBZ to relay your message?"

"I sent no message to anybody," she snapped.

He interrogated her with a measured frown. "Your name's Diane?"

"Yes, it's Diane."

"What's the rest of it?"

"Is this supposed to be a court-martial?" she asked. "Or are you just a fresh young man?"

"She told me her last name was Durand," put in Jerry. "Diane Durand." He moved over a few inches on a log that he had recently brushed clean. "Won't you sit down?"

"No," she said.

"What are you doing here alone in the woods?" Kit asked.

The girl had turned with a malevolent impulse to Jerry. "I want to tell you something," she declared. "You claim to be a policeman too. Well, there's an inspector somewhere in charge of this district. When I tell him that one of his brave officers overpowered a helpless and harmless girl and handcuffed her and dragged her around through the woods on a sledge, you know what'll happen to you. They'll break you, my man, and throw you so far out of a decent service that the lowliest Dog Rib will be ashamed to walk in the same wilderness with you."

Jerry stripped several crisp bacon slices from his toasting switch and arranged them neatly on a tin plate. He added a couple of pieces of buttered bannock, and offered the dish to the girl. "Won't you eat some breakfast?" he asked.

"No," she said.

"My dear," he informed her pleasantly, "your unsupported word won't get you anywhere with the inspector. Inspector Bowman's in charge just now. And you could never in your life convince him that one of his trusted, gentlemanly boys would do a vile trick such as overpowering a frail and innocent girl, and slipping the nippers on her pretty wrists, and dragging her around the woods on a sledge. He just couldn't believe it, and that would be all of that."

"How did you chance to wander into this part of the territory—all by yourself?" persisted Kitchener, making his voice as gentle and polite as he could possibly manage.

"Her dogs," said Jerry, "ran away from her and left her on her own.... Her own what?" He questioned himself interlocutorily, as though he were a one-man minstrel show, at the same time inspecting the small feet in the half-knee-high boots. "Dogs," he replied.

The girl's mouth curled contemptuously. "The comedy," she said, "hasn't a laugh in it."

Kitchener's grave eyes wrinkled at the corners and, quite unwarrantedly, he himself laughed.

The girl looked startled, and then glanced full at him and for the first time appeared to recognize him as a fellow being. For just an instant a responsive glimmer heightened her expressive features, as though she were on the point of grinning back at him; and then the flickering brightness was gone and the look of sullen resentment had returned.

"If I hadn't picked her up," remarked Jerry, "she no doubt would have starved to death and frozen to death and lost her way home."

"I wasn't lost," she declared furiously. "If you'd kept your hands off I'd have found the man I was looking for."

"Who was he?" Kitchener inquired.

"My uncle," she told him.

The coffee pot had reached a boil. Jerry tossed a handful of snow under the lid, and then poured out a steaming cupful, into which he dribbled a sticky, white fluid from a punctured can. "May I give you a cup of coffee?" he inquired of the girl.

"No," she said.

Kitchener was watching her face with reflective curiosity. Suddenly he tried a blind shot. "Is your uncle's name Jim?" he asked.

For a second she hesitated, and then threw up her head.

"Yes," she said.

"Tall, stoop-shouldered party with scars on his face and head?" questioned Kit. "A burly-looking bird who shaves in blizzards and eats up the weather?"

This time she was really interested. "Yes," she said, and her straight eyebrows drew anxiously together. "Have you seen him?"

"Jim who?" temporized Kit.

"James Durand."

"It isn't Sim, is it, instead of Jim?"

"What?"

"Simeon Bent?"

The girl stiffened perceptibly and the space between her eyelids narrowed ever so slightly. She seemed to swallow something in her throat. "What do you mean?"

"Is Jim Durand also Simeon Bent?"

"He is not," she declared.

"Do you know Simeon Bent?"

She hesitated for half a breath, and then shook her head. "No," she said.

"Where do you live?" Jerry cut in.

"New York, Philadelphia, Edmonton, Portland, Montreal, North Saskatchewan." She rattled it off as glibly as a railroad brakeman.

"Ottawa too?" suggested Jerry. "Why discriminate against Ottawa?"

"Yes," she answered surprisingly. "I did live in Ottawa for a while. I went to school there."

"Recently?"

"Quite recently."

Jerry smiled. "Do you still want to meet your uncle?" he inquired. "If you do it's easy. We just came from his camp. All you have to do is back-track the sledge runners to the place you came from. It isn't five miles."

The girl regarded him suspiciously, and then glanced at Kit as though for confirmation.

"Right!" he assured her.

"Won't you have some coffee before you go?" invited Jerry.

"No," she said.

She walked to the sledge, picked up a pair of snowshoes, and pushed her toes into the thongs. For a moment she lingered, holding a pair of boyishly competent hands towards the fire. Then she shoved her hands into the fur mittens that dangled around her neck on a cord. Without a word or a backward glance she walked away.

They saw her for a moment moving sturdily across the snowy hillside, and then the slight figure faded in the morning gloom and was lost to sight.

CHAPTER VI
THE GREAT OWL MURDER

With a plate of beans and bannock and bacon in his lap, and a tin mug of coffee gripped in his fist, Kitchener sat down by the camp fire and faced his brother with an unwonted lack of approbation.

"I had believed," he remarked, "that chivalry towards women was supposed to be one of the higher virtues of the honorable northern police."

"All of that," agreed Jerry easily. "And 'never fire first.' You've heard that one too. But strictly *sub rosa*—to uphold the law a police force needs a few in its ranks who walk a little roughly and who sometimes neglect to remember that women are ladies, and who are just a hair firster on the gat than the other guy." He shrugged his shoulders. "They didn't make me a sergeant for spreading my cloak in the mud for the village queens, or for waiting for crooks to take a crack at me, while I counted 'one-two—it's my turn next.'"

"What about this girl?" mused Kitchener. "She seems to me—sort of—a square-shooter."

"She's Hell Bent's niece," said Jerry.

"Tell me about her," invited Kit after an almost imperceptible pause.

Jerry glanced at his brother's left eyebrow, which was crooked upwards at its sharpest angle. "Hello, Cocky-bird! By the barometer I see there's danger of muggy weather. I'd be careful."

"Don't you worry about me."

"I ran into her yesterday evening—and she acted lost and strayed. She was looking for some man who was coming in from Port-o'-Prayer, and it struck me that it might be this Bent onion. Then she told me her name was Diane. I asked her if she was the WBZ Diane, and she said no. But it seemed an odd coincidence that I should pick that name off the air, and the very next woman I meet calls herself Diane. It gave me reason to pump her a little." Jerry shook his head. "A deep well, and Heaven knows what's at the bottom."

"Why did you give her the wristlets?" asked Kit.

"Before I decided she was interesting I'd told her of crossing the trail of a tall, stoop-shouldered snow-plodder back a ways in the forest. She was all for going and finding him at once. That didn't suit me. I didn't want the tip-off to reach Bent that I was flanking him—not until I could have an understanding with you. Also I didn't want her to see you before I did. I expected you two to be making faces at each other, and I was particularly anxious for you to know first what sort of a face yours was to be."

Kitchener prodded the ground with the heel of his snowshoe, and said nothing.

"So when she started to go off to find her uncle," Jerry pursued, "I told her this morning would be soon enough. She didn't agree in the least: so what else could I do except to present her with the shining bracelets and tuck her away comfortably for the night. She had nothing to complain of. She had a snug sleep and a pleasant sleigh ride all over Saskatchewan."

"Do you think she did radio that message?"

"I don't know. She, perhaps—or somebody using her name—thinking I'd heard of her, and might heed it."

"What would be the object?"

"To get me out of the country."

Kit looked up searchingly. "What's it all about, Jerry?"

"Dad!"

Jerry spoke the word solemnly, and just for that moment his look of grim bantering was erased from his face.

Kitchener waited with a sudden physical tensing that seemed to strain every muscle of his body.

There followed an interval of profound silence while Jerry stared off northward through the falling snow. "Kit," he blurted out in a constricted breath, "there is a dark and horrible crime that has gone unsolved and unavenged for twelve long years!"

Still Kitchener sat without speech.

"Since I came back into this country," Jerry went on in a slow, brooding tone, as though he had forgotten that any one else was present, "I've spent every day and night and thought with just one object. I've gone through all the department records, I've talked with every policeman who has traveled the old-time trails, I've questioned every trapper and bush-ranger and every one of the sooty-brothers, Indian and Esquimaux, that I've met in the wilderness. I have spent years trying to find out what happened to Inspector Bill Tearl."

"You've found out—"

"Not much actually, and yet—maybe a lot."

Jerry put down his empty coffee cup, dug in his shirt pocket, and then twisted and licked a cigarette into shape. "Did you ever know there was gold in this country?"

Kitchener shook his head, and his eyes begged his brother to get on with the story.

"I didn't either. But there must be. Of course the color may be found almost everywhere. But what I mean is a lode or pocket or placer drift in which the raw, yellow wealth has clustered like the raisins in a pudding. Enough of it to shovel out with a scoop and load up a dog sledge."

"And where is this fabulous hoard?" asked Kit.

Jerry shrugged indifferently. "Who knows? You've got ten thousand miles of territory to guess in. That part of it doesn't mean anything in our lives. Maybe some Indian found the deposit in the first place, or perhaps it was rifled by one of those wandering, crack-brained prospectors whom you're apt to meet almost everywhere. The loaded sledge is plenty for us to worry about. For all we know it may have been hauled half-way across a continent and passed from murderer to murderer before it reached its ultimate tragedy.

"The police," Jerry went on, "maintain a little advance post near the edge of big timber, some few days northeast of here at a place called *Saut Sauvage*. At the time I am talking about a sergeant and two men were wintering at this post. Dad, as you recall, was then the inspector in charge of this district. Twelve years ago this December, Dad went out on an inspection patrol and paid a little visit to the *Saut Sauvage* boys. It was at that time, as you know, that he disappeared."

"Where does the sledge-load of gold come in?" inquired Kit.

"I have this part of the story from Inspector Bowman, who, twelve years ago, was the sergeant in command at *Saut Sauvage*," said Jerry. "Much of it never went into the official records, and almost all of it was hushed up by the higher officers. Even Bill Tearl's family wasn't told all of the facts. You'll see why when you hear what happened.

30

"On the particular day I have in mind," Jerry resumed, "when Inspector Tearl was a guest at *Saut Sauvage*, a man and a woman came in from the north somewhere, driving a train of huskies and a sledge. Bowman doesn't remember what they said their names were, or even whether names were mentioned. He recalls only that the man was a lanky, rather good-looking chap around thirty or so. The woman, he introduced as his sister. She appeared to be near her brother's age—an athletic-looking woman with an astonishing lot of golden hair—they didn't bob it in those days. I gather from the inspector that she was a knock-out."

The policeman pitched a couple of fresh birch logs on the fire, and then moved a foot or two farther away to escape the heat. "The stranger and his sister, it seems," he went on, "had been up on the barrens hunting musk-ox. They had started out with guides and packers—three men, whites or breeds. What happened I don't know. But there was some sort of trouble, and either their men left them, or they cleared out and left their men. It doesn't matter about that. The two were alone when they arrived at the police post. They had been caught by winter and were hurrying to reach the outside before the big snow trapped them.

"One who lives in this country," Jerry ruminated, "is apt to lose his sense of wonderment. If you told me that you had found diamond pipes in the hills yonder to rival Kimberley, I would say, 'why not?' There's everything else—coal and iron and copper and platinum and gold fields, untouched as yet, and for the greater part undiscovered—waiting to be dumped into a world that's already too fat with wealth. Oil, illuminating gas, water-power to run all the earth's industries in high. I've seen a natural gas vent up on the rim of the Circle, which some passing Indian ignited, possibly a hundred years ago, which is burning to-day, and perhaps will be spouting its fifty foot jet of flame a century or two or three from now."

Jerry sighed and shook his head. "It's a pity to think that some day this will all be filled up with sweaty ditch diggers and shrieking machinery. Thank God, you and I will be dead."

He looked into the darkness and stretched his arms in a wide gesture. "It still belongs to you and me, and it hasn't changed much since the first white man found it. A wilderness bigger than the whole United States. Peopled by a few of the simple, sooty brothers and a few whites who have nerve enough to live as they damn please. An earth chockful of virgin wealth, and a few primitives prowling upon it. If they see anything they want they take it, and what the hell! Raw tastes and hungers and

31

desires let loose in a wild and opulent land. No law worth mentioning; no restraints; every man for himself. Queer and terrible things can happen. Almost every dark stretch of the forest holds its own grisly secret—"

"What," demanded Kit, "is all this about?"

Jerry's hard features for a moment relaxed in a wry grin. "I was just thinking," he remarked, "that Dad and Sergeant Bowman wouldn't have been skeptical or even astonished when this stranger and his beautiful sister arrived at the police cabin to tell them that they had found in the woods farther north a sledge stacked with gold nuggets in rotting caribou bags, and a man's tattered skeleton sprawled on top of it.

"These two gave the skeleton as nice a burial as they could under the circumstances, and then they hitched their own dogs to the sledge and came on south. Bowman says he himself saw the sledge, and he saw and hefted some of the nuggets. He said there must have been a quarter of a million—"

"Who was the poor devil?" interrupted Kit.

"The skeleton? Who knows? He may not have been the original digger. As I said, that sledge may have come by stages clear across from the Klondike—one man slaying the man ahead of him for its possession. The last chap, perhaps, died of the great northern illness known as 'nothing-to-eat.' That story is lost forever in the mists. We're concerned only with what happened afterwards."

Kit was somberly watching his brother's face. "Yes?" he breathed.

"The new owners of the sledge," said Jerry, "were a bit nervous about it. They had reason to be. Their guides, it seems, had turned out to be a bad lot, and they had parted company with them in a nasty row. These guides were loitering about somewhere in the neighborhood of *Saut Sauvage*. The truth was that the brother and sister were afraid to go on alone. It so happened that Inspector Bill Tearl was intending to go down to McMurray, and he volunteered to escort the sledge out of the woods. The three started off next morning in a snow storm—Dad and the two lucky finders." Jerry paused for a moment, and his lower lip bent up under his teeth as he gazed with moody eyes beyond the crackling fire.

"They said good-by to Bowman," he resumed quietly, "and set out for the south. And none of the three was ever seen alive afterwards."

The sergeant glanced at the crumpled cigarette in his fingers, and for the first time seemed to remember why he had rolled it. He pulled a blazing fagot out of the fire, puffed industriously for a moment, and then settled back at ease on one elbow.

"Two weeks later," he stated abruptly, "Sergeant Bowman made a little patrol southward. Not twenty miles below the police post, at a place called Great Owl Run, he found the woman with the lovely hair. She was lying face down in a deep drift with a .45 bullet in the back of her head. Her brother was nowhere to be found, nor Inspector Bill Tearl, nor the sledge load of caribou sacks."

Kitchener sat straighter, his dark eyes suddenly constricted with horror. "What had happened?" he asked.

"There had been two or three snow storms before Bowman took the trail," Jerry explained, "and there was not much left even for a schooled woodsman to read. No sledge tracks, no footprints. Between the spot where the woman lay and the high, steep bank of Great Owl Run, the underbrush had been broken and crushed down, as though a body, or perhaps two of them, had been dragged off and dumped into the creek. The stream runs deep and swift at that point, and seldom freezes over. Anything thrown into it would be swept down under the ice tunnels and probably carried all the way to the Arctic Sea."

"And you know no more than this?" Kitchener asked in a hushed voice.

"A little more, maybe. But the rest is pure guessing.

"At about the time that Bowman was finding the dead woman," Jerry added, "a man by the name of Simeon Bent came out of the woods at Fort McMurray. He had been in some sort of a fight a while before and had wounds about the head and face. I got wind of this man a couple of years ago and found out all about him that I could. One thing, he had been the head guide for the two musk-ox hunters.

"From McMurray this Bent bird went on down to Edmonton," Jerry continued after a brief interval. "He went a bit wild on whiskey blanc down there. In a rumpus in a back room he killed a man and was stretched a short term for manslaughter." The sergeant observed his brother fixedly. "He was splurging some in Edmonton, with plenty to spend, and I have it straight that his cash reserve was a bagful of gold nuggets."

"You mean—" said Kit, and stopped.

Jerry answered with a short nod. "Sounds that way, doesn't it? It was Bent who ambushed Dad and the two strangers. My guess it that he got the sledge, but for some reason he wasn't able to take it down country with him. Maybe the other guides were lurking near by and he didn't want to declare them in. He helped himself to one bagful of gold, and cleared out.

"It's my belief that he cached that sledge in the woods somewhere in the neighborhood of Great Owl Run," Jerry declared. "It's probably still there where he hid it on that ugly day twelve years ago." The sergeant tossed his cigarette into the fire and his muscular hands clenched tightly over one knee. "Bent served out his term in prison, hugging his secret. The minute they turned him loose he started for the north—"

"Carrying Dad's old gun," Kitchener cut in, his eyes suddenly grown as cold and murky as the wintry dawn.

"That sledge," asserted Jerry, "is still concealed in the forest up yonder, and Hell Bent is on his way to get it."

The sergeant raised himself to his feet and stood erect on the snowy hillside. "When Bent's time was nearly up I asked for the *Saut Sauvage* assignment, and Bowman sent me to take command of the outpost up there. I'm supposed to be on my way to that place."

"I understand now," said Kit, "why he'll kill you if he can."

"Of course," said Jerry carelessly. "I want to nail him when he gets that sledge, and he knows it." The policeman knitted his brows darkly. "The trouble is," he reflected, "I can't keep the assignment. Something else has turned up."

He contemplated his brother with shrewd eyes for a moment, and then faintly nodded his head as though he had made up his mind about something.

"Kit," he declared, "it's the luckiest thing in the world that you turned up when you did. I needed you frightfully. But you were always like that—an on-the-spot Johnny. You ready to carry on, Cocky-bird?"

"You know I am."

"Good! It's an outrageous and extremely hazardous business I'm wishing on you. But I have no choice. You're to go up there instead of me, and stick tight to this Bent, and get him."

"All right," said Kitchener. "I'd like to."

"I'm not going to report at all, Crowfeathers. I've got something else to do. But I don't want to be let out of the service for going A.W.O.L.—heading off on my own. I've disgraced you plenty as it is."

Kit watched his brother uneasily. "What are you going to do?"

"You and I don't look a lot alike," Jerry temporized. "I'm a darned sight better-looking guy than you, if it comes to that. But at the same time you approximate me enough to get by. Luckily the two constables up at *Saut Sauvage* have never seen me."

"What—?" Kit stopped, his startled eyes dilating as he began to gather the drift of Jerry's plans. "You don't mean—"

"That's why I introduced you to Diane as Buck Tearl," Jerry assured him with a bland smile. "The idea was beginning to ferment even then. I can't take the patrol, you understand, so somebody will have to go in my place. I'll put you in my uniform and give you my credentials, and you go north and tell 'em you're Sergeant Buck Tearl of the royal police. You'll take command of the outpost at *Saut Sauvage*."

CHAPTER VII
IN THE ROYAL SCARLET

As though his doubts and difficulties were completely settled, Sergeant Tearl moved serenely to his sledge and began dumping blankets and duffle bags off into the snow. Kitchener scrambled to his feet.

"Hold on!" protested the younger brother. "You're crazy!"

"You'll have no trouble," Jerry reassured him. "Constables Devon and Cross are holding down the *Saut Sauvage* trick, and they know me only by reputation." He turned with a deprecating laugh. "Just heckle them a bit and they'll never dream that you're not the sergeant."

"But, Jerry, the whole idea is absolutely preposterous."

"As for knowing police business," said the older brother smoothly, "you could have qualified for a sergeancy when you were nine years old." He came back to the fire, his features changed to an unwonted gravity. "You know I wouldn't ask you to do this, Kit, if I could see any way out of it."

"And you know I wouldn't hesitate," returned Kitchener, "if I really thought I could get away with it."

"That part's easy. Inspector Bowman isn't apt to come up this way this winter. You ought to get friendly enough with Cross and Devon to persuade them to keep their mouths shut if I come back in the spring and resume my job. If I don't come back all you need do is to slip quietly out of the picture, and the police can write another disappearance case in the records of the missing."

Kitchener looked sharply at his brother. "Where are you going?" he demanded.

"You remember the name of the Esquimau mentioned in the WBZ message?" Jerry asked.

"Kablunak, wasn't it? Kablunak's band of Ahiagmuit."

"Do you know what Kablunak means in the Ahiagmuit lingo?"

"No."

"White man," said Jerry.

"Well?" said Kit, and then caught his breath as he felt a peculiar significance in the other's manner. "What white man?"

"I wouldn't ordinarily pay any attention to a message like that, sent by nobody knows whom," said Jerry. "But it so happens that my own inquiries have brought facts to light that practically substantiate this information from WBZ. It came to me in a roundabout way from a Cree Indian, who had it from a Dog Rib, who had it from a Yellow Knife, who had it from a Bathurst Inlet Esquimau. It's funny, but you can almost always believe the stories that reach you by moccasin telegraph. According to this yarn, which really is more definite than mere rumor, there is a tribe of Ahiagmuit up on the shore of Queen Maud Sea, whose chief man is a white.

"This man," the sergeant added slowly and deliberatively, "is tall and lean, they say, and he has an eagle's nose and a snowy-white mustache, and terrible gleaming eyes, and under his *artikis* he wears a shining metal shield which, from its description, is the badge of the royal police."

"My God!" said Kitchener's lips, but his voice was suffocated.

"I don't know," said Jerry. "It may turn out to be a wild-goose chase. But I've got to go."

"But Jerry—" Kit was staring at his brother with awe-stricken eyes. "You don't think—you don't believe it possible—?"

"Who can say?" Jerry's weather-beaten face at that moment was tragic with wistfulness. "Most frightfully unbelievable things can happen to a man in the wilderness. It might be that this has happened."

"Wait!" gasped Kit. "You said that a body was dragged through the brush and dumped into the creek—"

"I said it looked as though that had been done," said the sergeant. "But we don't know whose body it was."

"You don't mean—you think there's a chance—?" Kit checked himself and faced his brother in a daze.

"Dad!" said Jerry. "Sounds improbable, doesn't it? But I know I'll never have a decent night's sleep again until I go and find out."

"It's impossible!" Kitchener burst out. "A white man living for twelve years with a tribe of Esquimaux! What conceivable reason could he have? Why would he go away up there in the first place? Or if he did go, why would he stay? Why would he hide from his family? Why never a word from him?"

Jerry laid a quieting hand on his brother's wet coat sleeve. "I can't answer any of your questions, Kit. Only this much I do know: there has been evil talk and sly, vile whispering—going the rounds." The sergeant's eyes were stony and expressionless in the reflecting firelight. "The woman was shot with a .45 bullet, which is the gun the police carry. Her brother may have been shot and thrown into the brook. Inspector Bill Tearl disappeared. The sledge-load of gold disappeared. And as you know, and others have found out, Bill Tearl's family have received from some anonymous source every January for twelve years an express draught for five thousand dollars."

"Jerry!" The cry was wrenched from Kit in an agonized gasp as the full, dreadful import of his brother's speech flamed into his brain.

"You know you could turn gold nuggets into an express draught if you wanted to." The sergeant's fingers closed tightly into the muscles of Kitchener's forearm, but his voice was restrained and very quiet.

"If anybody so much as hinted any of this to me, I would kill him. They're careful to keep their mouths shut when I'm near. But I know what has been said. Bowman and the other officers who used to know Bill Tearl—who knew what a clean, sweet, straight-shooting gentleman he always was—none of them has ever listened or allowed himself to believe anything except that a dark mystery was staged that day in the Great Owl woods. But others have had things to say. And none of us really knows what took place on that creek."

Jerry dropped his brother's arm, moved off restlessly for a few paces, and then came back again. "You know now, Kit, why one of us has to trail Simeon Bent and throttle the truth out of him if need be, while the other goes to Queen Maud Sea, where the white man with the police badge lives."

"Yes," said Kitchener. "Of course." He raised his head impulsively. "But why change jobs? You have your own assignment. Why not see it through yourself? Bent's going your direction. You stick with him. Let me find Kablunak's tribe."

Jerry regarded the younger man affectionately. "You're a great man, Old Crow, but what chance would you stand on the far northern tundras? In mid-winter. Living off the country. Did you ever stalk a caribou or run with the dogs for a thousand miles in the seven months' night? I'm an arctic man, my boy, and you—" He punched Kit in the chest with his thumb. "Our little five-mile breather almost did you in this morning."

Kit looked sheepish and ashamed. "Try me a week from now," he suggested.

"I'll be two hundred miles north of here a week from now," said Jerry, and unfastened the tie string of his parka. He pulled off his outer garment and started to unbutton his police tunic. "Strip!" he commanded.

Kitchener hesitated for just a second, and then with a wry grin he began taking off his clothes. It was so foolish of him to balk at his elder brother's decisions. He always gave in, and Jerry was always right.

"Will you be able to make it?" he asked as he shed his stag shirt.

"Ought to." Jerry's coat was in the snow and he was hauling his uniform shirt over his head. "There's only one thing can stop me. That would be the lack of meat. If I run across a caribou now and then I'll come back."

Kit had kicked out of his trousers and stood in his undergarments—a straight-backed, lean-shanked figure silhouetted against the curtain of falling snow.

"I'll give you all my police equipment," Jerry said—"sledge, blankets, guns—everything excepting the dogs. Those muts of yours would crumple up like paper, out on the barrens."

Kitchener drew on his brother's beautifully tailored shirt, stepped into the thick, warm trousers, and buckled the belt. With a feeling almost of reverence he slipped his arms into the scarlet tunic. He strapped on his side arm and stepped back to the fire. The coat was a trifle too roomy under the sleeves, yet Kit squared his shoulders with a sprightly sense of ease and self-confidence. Belted tight at the waist, the tunic seemed actually to fit, and with a queer, thrilling emotion he felt somehow that he belonged in it.

Jerry's eyes were full of mockery, but when he spoke there was a faint choking in his throat. He stiffened, and his hand went up in salute.

"Officer," he said, "may you never miss your man!"

His manner changed, and he curtly motioned his brother to sit down again. He squatted cross-legged and, with a stick in his hand, he began tracing a network of lines on the snow-covered ground.

"We'll say that this is our present position," and made a cross. "Strike northeast three days' march across the ridges, and you'll run into the Vermilion River. A swift stream, bowlders and rapids. Way back in the spruce hills. Follow it down past the mouths of one, two, three, four, five tributary creeks. The sixth will be Great Owl Run. It comes in from the northeast between two steep, granite banks. There'll be a tall, pine lobstick on the opposite shore that you can't miss. Travel up this creek about seven miles, and you'll reach the scene of the old tragedy. Twenty miles farther on is the police barracks at *Saut Sauvage*. Devon and Cross will probably be there. You go in and tell 'em the sergeant has arrived. You got it straight?"

He got up again and beckoned Kit to help him unpack the sledges. They exchanged almost all of their luggage, and reloaded and fastened down the lashings. They traded sledges, but each kept his own dog traces. Kit was driving tandem. Jerry used the fan hitch, which gave the huskies greater freedom on the open arctic prairies, and which was more easily slipped if a polar bear attempted to pounce upon the animals.

The older brother chuckled as he caught sight of the old, red, Hudson's Bay blankets. "Shades of the ancient mariner," he exclaimed—"I'm darned if you didn't bring granddad's last testaments with you. I'll sleep with a ghost to-night."

He looked around to make sure that nothing was forgotten, and then faced Kit with a troubled scowl. "You'll be all right, won't you?" For the first time he seemed to have misgivings.

"I'll be all right."

"I mean, take care of yourself."

"I hope you take your own advice," returned Kitchener.

"Don't stay long enough to go snow-blind," said Jerry. "I don't mean the eyes, but the soul."

Kit looked up alertly, on guard against one of his brother's flippancies. But this time he found no sign of laughter in the hard-lined face.

"Down in your country," Jerry resumed, "they call dope, 'snow.' Up here the snow is the dope. They get you the same way. There's something about the dazzling white country that worms into you and creeps around you and enslaves your heart and your brain like an insidious drug. We northern men are all of us a little cuckoo. You can come up here for a year and go back and forget. You can stay two years and still keep the will-power to break away. Three years, and you're lost.

"I call it going snow-blind." The policeman's voice was quiet and impersonal, but the corners of his mouth were drawn in jaded furrows and in that moment his depth of feeling was betrayed by his haggard, haunted eyes. "This frozen world becomes a part of you, and you a part of it. It blinds you to all save its own harsh, wild enchantments. You want to go out, but you can't stay out. You love it and hate it. You can't be happy anywhere else, and you can't be happy here."

He ended with a shortened breath and looked away, as though in embarrassment. "Finish your business here, Kit, and get out fast. One of us is enough."

Abruptly he changed the subject. "Take your time with Bent. After last night's stroll he won't travel far to-day. A man softened by prison. Cross the back lots as I told you and you'll strike his trail again somewhere along the Vermilion River. After that stick close. He'll be watching for you. Look out! But don't let him unearth that sledge without your being on hand to jump him. Got it all straight?"

"Perfectly," Kit reassured him.

"You'd better get some sleep then. If you and your dogs cork off for a few hours now you'll travel farther and faster in the end."

"When do you leave?" asked Kit.

Jerry had gone back to his sledge and he was stooping with his back turned. He did not look around. "When you're ready to go," he mumbled.

Kitchener unrolled the blankets of the service issue which, in the future, were to be his own. As he passed the sledges on his way to pick a sleeping place in the lee of the rocks, Jerry stood up and without warning clamped his brawny right arm around his brother's head.

"It was good to see you once more, old pioneer," he said in a thick, gruff voice.

Kitchener waited motionless, feeling a lump come into his throat and almost choke him. There were a thousand things he wanted to say, but he was abashed by his own sentimental longings, and he stood tonguetied, and said nothing.

"Remember the last time we changed clothes?" asked Jerry—"the day I induced you to put the kitten's collar on the little black and white striped animal, which the scientists call *mephitis mephitica*, and the Indians call *Sikak* the skunk? And Dad made me wear your clothes and sleep out in the woods."

Jerry laughed gently. "Go to sleep, Cocky-bird. It'll all come out right in the end."

"See you later, Jerry," said Kit. He stumbled off behind the rocks, rolled up in his blankets in the gray, snowy dawn, and within three minutes was soundly slumbering.

The snowfall had almost ceased when Kit awakened. It was a dull, sodden day, windless and utterly quiet. The clouds were hanging low over the forest, black and ominous, overcasting the wilderness with a strange, uncanny twilight. For a minute or two after his eyes were open Kitchener lay in warmth and drowsy comfort. But all at once it occurred to him that there was something foreboding in the complete absence of sound.

His body went taut in the middle of his langorous stretching, and he threw off the blanket and sat up. The campfire was still smoldering, and somebody was bending over it.

"Hello, Jerry—" he said, and then stopped short. The figure in the smoke had turned, and he saw that it was not a man. He scrambled to his feet, rubbing his eyes, staring in astonishment. The fire-tender was a woman—Diane Durand.

"Good morning," said the girl coolly. She emerged from the suffocating haze of the fire, which she evidently did not understand how to manage, coughing and shaking her head as though to rid herself of the smoke.

In the daylight he noticed that her touseled hair was not the flaming red the fire reflections had imparted last night, but verged into softer tints of bronze. The eyes which regarded him steadily were deep and luminous and flecked with a golden brightness. There was something impudent and unflattering in the way she looked at him.

He regained his breath and faced her suspiciously. "What are you doing here?" he demanded.

"It's not my fault," she returned. "I came back because I had to. Blame your friend's high-handed interfering. By the time I had reached my uncle's camp he was gone."

"Gone where?" exclaimed Kit.

"On northward. Without dogs I can't hope to overtake him. You're going up that direction, aren't you, sergeant?"

Unwittingly Kitchener's shoulders straightened. It gave him a queer, uplifting sensation to have her think that he was an officer of the Royal Canadian Police.

"Yes," he said, "I'm going north."

"Then you'll have to take me with you," she announced calmly. "When we catch my uncle you can get rid of me."

Kit looked around uneasily. "Where's my—my friend?" he asked.

"He's gone," said the girl.

"What?"

She fumbled in the pocket of her mackinaw and brought out a folded slip of paper, which she handed to Kitchener. "Here's a note he left for you. I picked it up and read it."

With a sense of impending evil he opened the sheet and found a few lines of pencil-script in Jerry's careless scrawl. He read:

Dear Kit:
Don't forget there are a million of 'em as pretty as this Diane. I saw a funny look in your eye this morning. I'm just warning you, that's all. Don't let her make a sap out of you and I have no fear about anything else. So long, old crow. The things I like least about life are its repetitions. You get your hair cut or mow your lawn or paint a house or cook breakfast or shave or wash a shirt or kiss a girl, and it's all to be done over again to-morrow or next week or a year from now. The only thing I know that stays done is to have your teeth pulled. Cheerio, Cocky-bird. Always exit on a laugh.

Jerry.

With eyes grown suddenly misty Kitchener turned and gazed around the glade of evergreens. On the opposite hillslope he found the trail left by sledge runners and trotting dogs' feet and a pair of big, slashing snowshoes. The tracks ran straight north and apparently were several hours old. Jerry was well on his way towards the dreadful darkness of Queen Maud Sea.

CHAPTER VIII
FOLLOW ON

It was like Jerry to vanish lightheartedly as though he were dropping off somewhere for a frivolous week-end, instead of undertaking a journey that would have appalled the most hardened *voyageur*. His comings and goings had always been thus casual and unexpected. He hated to say "good-by." Kit had found his astonishing brother once more, only to lose him. They might meet in a year, or in ten years, or perhaps never again.

As Kit turned the paper over his finger he was stricken by a sudden recollection. He glanced sharply at Miss Durand.

"You say," he asked, "that you read this note?"

She nodded her auburn head. "*Uhuh!*"

In spite of himself Kit felt an uncomfortable warming of blood under the skin of his face. "I wouldn't pay any attention—he doesn't mean anything—" He caught his breath in embarrassment. "He's a lunatic."

"He must be a good friend of yours to give you so much good advice," said Miss Durand.

"He's an old friend, anyhow," agreed Kit uneasily. "We've known each other for years. Just the same, he's an idiot."

"Anything else you want to call him—why, yes," she returned mildly. "But he's no idiot. I think it was very smart of him to warn you."

Kitchener shifted his feet. "I don't know what he was talking about. Warn me about what?"

"Against anybody named Diane," said the girl serenely. "Look at Diane d'Angoulême and Diane de Poitiers, just to mention a couple. There were a lot of 'em in history, and they all were sly and tricky and full of the old Nick. It pays to be careful in your dealings with the Dianes."

"Those two are dead," remarked Kitchener. "And I don't need Jerry to tell me what to do about their successors."

The girl moved to avoid the drifting smoke from the camp fire, and then tilted her head sidewise as she examined him impersonally from under the curve of her hazel eyelashes. "What was the funny look in your eye your friend Jerry noticed?" she asked.

Kitchener stared at her. The audacity of her asking him that! There was an impish suggestion about her mouth and lips that did not quite approach a smile. He found himself feeling bitterly resentful towards Jerry. He might at least have left the nonsense out of his note.

"Does it look funny now?" he asked stiffly.

"Well—no," she answered judgmatically, and half closed one of her own bright eyes, as though to see him better with the other. "Not noticeably."

"What Jerry meant," he remarked, "is that I might fall for you because you're so pretty. You are, you know." He was trying to appear as nonchalant about it as the girl herself. "But he also said there were a million of 'em. So what does that amount to?"

"Not a thing," she said.

"Certainly not. I've met a good many of the million myself—Daphnes and Delilahs and Dulcys, and maybe even a Diane or two. Darned pretty, some of 'em—but what of it?"

"We haven't anything to worry about," she assured him—"anyhow you haven't. I can see you're too well insulated." She looked at him demurely.

"I know now," she suddenly declared, "why he calls you Cocky-bird. When you push up your left eyebrow, it makes you—you're just like that."

He hastily drew his eyebrows straight, and scowled at her.

"I think it's cute," she said, and the smile grew definite, and wicked.

He confronted her furiously. "Listen here!" he said: "I suppose you expect to go along with me?"

"I sort of took it for granted."

"Why don't you go down to Port-o'-Prayer and get the old Scotch factor to ship you out? It isn't far from here."

"Because I don't want to. I came to find my Uncle Jim, and I'm going to find him. If you won't take me with you I'll tag on your trail. Anyhow I will until I freeze to death or die of hunger." The girl extended her empty hands for his inspection. "I haven't any outfit or anything."

"You wouldn't be able to keep up with me," he objected.

She tossed back her head and her face looked childishly bewitching under the tousel of ruddy hair. "I'll keep up," she promised. "I've snowshoed a lot," she said—"for sport. Saranac and Banff and St. Moritz."

"How the deuce did you happen to lose your uncle in the first place?" he asked her ungraciously.

"I didn't exactly lose him," she replied. "I was visiting friends in Ottawa, when he wrote me that he had decided to spend the winter in this country. I thought it would be nice to be with him, and telegraphed him to wait for me. But he was gone before my message reached him. However, I supposed I might overtake him, so I caught the next to last boat down the Slave River and went ashore at Fort Smith. But for some reason Uncle Jim had changed his mind and struck off from farther down country."

"Yeah?" said Kitchener. "What does he want up here?"

"He thought he'd spend the winter trapping," she answered as glibly as though she had learned a formula by heart. "His lungs are not good and the doctor ordered him to spend a few months in the open."

"Oh, yes," said Kit expressionlessly. "This is a good place for the lungs."

"While I was marooned at Fort Smith, wondering what to do next," the girl went on regretfully, "a couple of Indians told me of a man who had outfitted at Port-o'-Prayer for a trip north. From their description I knew it was Uncle Jim. I thought there was still time to intercept him, and I persuaded these Indians to guide me east from Fort Smith to cross the trails above Port-o'-Prayer. They brought me safely as far as the Dog-

Rib country, and then got frightened about something and said they were going back. They were stubborn about it, so I had to let them go, and came on the rest of the way alone."

Kitchener was watching the girl sidewise. Her manner was so innocent and confiding that it was hard to disbelieve her. But he was certain that in most of its details the yarn was pure fiction. According to Jerry Tearl—and Jerry usually knew what he was talking about—the uncle's name was not Jim Durand, but Sim Bent. At the time he was supposed to have written to his niece and started into the woods he was still serving time in the Ottawa prison.

The girl's excuse for entering the wilderness was unbelievable. A woman so obviously fastidious in tastes and habits certainly would never submit voluntarily to the rigors and hardships of an arctic winter, unless she were actuated by exceptional motives. Kit felt sure that she was acting with Durand, or Bent, in an attempt to sledge a load of stolen gold nuggets out of the forests. Her story of being "lost" was probably only a pretext to bring her into contact with the police of the district, so that she might spy upon their movements and attempt to throw them off her companion's trail. She was clever enough and daring enough to hoodwink the entire force of the mounted.

Kit turned suddenly to rescue a skillet of beans, which the girl had appropriated from his pack while he slept, and set on the fire to burn.

"Sorry!" she exclaimed. "I just simply forgot 'em."

As he glanced around at her lovely, contrite face the line of Kitchener's jaw molded unconsciously into a harder line. The notion had struck him that it would be a good idea to keep her with him. If she were playing a subtle game at his expense, it would be a good job to have her where he could watch her. He felt a strange premonition that through Diane he eventually would be brought to his reckoning with the man who brazenly carried his father's service revolver.

"You might have known about Indian guides," he remarked to hide his inward thoughts. "Unless you arrange ahead of time for regular, listed men, you're out of luck. You pick up these fly-by-nights of the bush and they're sure to ditch you at the first hard portage."

"I'd have been all right," she said, "if my dogs hadn't chased a rabbit and run away with my sledge and everything I owned. And then your friend Jerry came along with his high-handed performance."

Her manner changed and she grew wistful and dangerously appealing. "You owe me something if you're his friend. You're going to take me with you, aren't you?"

"I'll take you," Kit consented.

They lunched on what Inspector Bill Tearl used to call the "ABC's" of the wilderness, ashes, beans and coffee. Then, as soon as they had cleaned up and repacked, Kit harnessed-in his dogs, and they started off together upon the northward trail.

It was a gloomy day, with only a few hours of the short daylight left. The snow had stopped falling, but the clouds that they saw through an occasional rift in the spruces were black and low-riding, portentous of trouble.

For a little distance Kitchener followed Jerry's plainly marked trail. Jerry was wearing a pair of big, broad-toed Chippewyan snowshoes. At one place he had plowed unawares over a sharp root hidden under the snow, and by the subsequent tracks it was seen that the webbing of the right raquette had been torn. The small mishap had not halted him. He had kept onward with enormous energy, and apparently would not bother to make repairs until darkness forced him into camp.

It somehow was comforting to know that Jerry was not many hours ahead and that the future and the past were still tethered together by a visible line of footprints. As long as he clung to the trail Kit was warmed by a feeling that some part of his big brother still lingered companionably with him. But he had reached the time of final parting. After a few hundred yards he resolutely turned leftward, and would not look back at the forking of the trails. He set his eyes on the clean, new snow ahead, which, to his misty vision, was like a freshly turned page that had been assigned to him alone. Jerry had crossed out of his life again, and he was left on his own resources.

Kitchener's attention was fixed on the snowy aisles of the forest in front of him and the compass that he wore on his wrist like a watch. Jerry had given him the compass with the injunction: "Read it often and believe it absolutely, even though you know it lies."

Presumably Miss Durand was trudging behind the sledge. Kit did not glance around. He felt a malicious satisfaction in imagining that she was having difficulty in keeping up. Although he was rather sore from yesterday's travels, he was beginning, nevertheless, to find his snow-legs. He fancied he was setting a stiff pace.

There is nothing so deathly quiet as the deep woods in winter. In the lull between storms the trees stood lifeless as pillars supporting a roof thatched solidly with snow. The chinking was constantly slipping, falling as softly as feathers on heads below. There seemed to be a complete absence of life. Through long stretches of the darker valleys not a tiny, clawed footprint disturbed the white surface of the ground. Even the shy, wild things of the forest shun the places of the deepest gloom.

Early in the afternoon Kit emerged suddenly from thick cover to skirt the edge of a frozen swamp. He lifted his head to look at the open sky and breathed more freely, feeling that a great oppression had been lifted momentarily.

Among the sedges that stood like broken spears in the swamp there were millions of rabbit tracks. Where rabbits make their homes their hunters likewise live. The padded prints of mink and otter and fox were seen on all sides. The muskegs of the wilderness are bloody carnival grounds. But to-day there was a strange brooding quiet everywhere. Not even a jay or a whiskey-jack flew down to mock at the travelers.

Kit traveled on to the northwest and trusted in his compass. And a while before the breathless twilight set in he crossed the base of a long, timbered slope and came out on the banks of a river. At the place where he struck the stream it was sheathed solidly in ice, but farther down he saw ugly rocks and caught the mutter of wild, white water. From Jerry's description he knew that this must be the Vermilion River.

Miss Durand left her place behind the sledge and came forward among the panting dogs. Her hand was pressed against her ribs, as though to hide her rapid breathing. She grinned cheerfully at her fellow traveler. "You can take it faster if you feel like it," she remarked.

Kit laughed ironically. This was simply bravado. She probably knew that he couldn't go much faster, even as he was aware that she never could hold the pace if he did.

Along the curve of the river bank ran a scuffled trail. A sledge and dogs and a solitary man had passed here sometime during the day. Kit called the girl's attention to the peculiarities of the snowshoe tracks, their waffle-mesh packing, the wide-spread gait, the deep drag of the heels. These same snowshoes had broken the path for him yesterday, and there was no question of their wearer's identity.

"It's your uncle," he said.

She descended the sloping embankment to look with quickened interest.

"How long ago?" she asked.

"Since the snow stopped falling. He can't be many hours ahead."

Kitchener hied-on his drooping dogs and the sledge once more got underway. Night was approaching under a lowering sky and the reaches of the river valley and the spreading hills of spruce had begun to fade into a purple-stained haziness. Again Kit moved on in the advance, his eyes strained ahead as he made use of that last half hour of twilight.

He was a hunter pursuing a human quarry. In the dim miles somewhere ahead a tall, furtive figure was moving along with a train of dogs, crowding a little more distance on the end of a hard day's march. If Jerry had guessed correctly, this man held in his guilty keeping the secret of the old tragedy on Great Owl Run. Presumably he was on his way now to regain the spoils of an earlier crime. The sledge with its fatal lading undoubtedly had been cached near the place where the woman was shot and her brother and Inspector Bill Tearl had vanished—one, perhaps two days farther north.

Kit hoped to be on hand when that rotted sledge was unearthed. He had the trail now, and he would hang on, wherever it led him. By the freshness of the prints he estimated that at this moment his man could not be more than ten miles farther down the river. After this evening he must be wary, neither lagging too far behind, nor closing-in too soon. Above all else the man must not be allowed to suspect that a pursuer was following the river route.

Beyond his anxiety to surprise the ex-convict red-handed in possession of the long-lost sledge, Kit's plans were still somewhat indefinite. He probably would arrest his man, and, posing as Sergeant Buck Tearl, hand his prisoner over to the police at *Saut Sauvage*. With the new material evidence backing the circumstantial facts that Jerry had gathered, it might be possible to convict the man of an ancient crime. For one thing he would be hard pressed to explain how he happened to be armed with a revolver that at one time had belonged to the missing inspector of police. Even if conviction failed, there still would be a chance of forcing out the truth concerning Bill Tearl's disappearance and hushing the scandalous rumors that had sullied his memory.

For the immediate future Kitchener held no misgivings. He wore a policeman's coat and carried a policeman's gun, and unless somebody discovered that he was an impostor, he held the authority of the law in this gloomy neck of the woods. If his man showed fight the former intercollegiate pistol champion would have no need of begging quarter.

His present doubts concerned only Diane Durand. She perplexed him and worried him more than he admitted even to himself. She was a vivid young woman, fearless and humorous and intensely human, with a queer strain of sweetness underlying the dominant qualities of recklessness and willfulness. He liked her in spite of himself. There was danger of his liking her much too well if he failed to heed his saner judgments.

Luckily, he had been forewarned. She was associated with the scarfaced man, towards whom Kit was beginning to feel a strong personal enmity. In the final reckoning, she too would be his enemy. And a perverse, highly organized woman is so often more bitterly implacable than the ugliest tempered man. He feared her, almost as he feared himself and his own sentimental weakness. For that reason he had set his face and his heart against her. His brother had trusted him, and whatever else he might do on earth, he could not fail Jerry.

He drove his weary dogs down river until darkness finally hid the trail of the sledge that had gone before him. Then he called a halt for the night. The lee side of a great spruce windfall served well enough for a campsite. He unhitched and tossed each of the dogs his evening's portion of ice-stiff fish. Then he pitched the Burberry tent, which he had inherited as a part of Jerry's luggage. He built a tiny fire screened behind the river bluff, and, with the girl's help, he scrambled together a hot supper.

They kept awake only long enough to eat. Then with a faint, tired "good night" the girl crept into the tent.

"'Night," said Kit curtly. He rolled up by the fire in the spare fur robes and was asleep before the dogs had finished burying themselves in the snow bank beside him.

At the hour exclusive to milkmen and the rounders of night clubs in milder lands farther south, Kit aroused himself in the frigid darkness. A stiff breeze had sprung up in the north and sleet was rattling among the gaunt branches of the willows and alders that hedged the riverside. There was something in the wild sound of the wind and the feel of the raw, tingling air that filled him with unpleasant foreboding. A native could have told him that one of the dreaded northeast storms was gathering forces to sweep down from the polar regions. It was nearly the end of the year, three days before Christmas.

He raked up the dying embers of the fire, fed on new fuel, and started breakfast. Then he shook the tent flap and awakened Miss Durand.

The girl pushed a reluctant head out into the cold, glanced heavy-eyed about her, and yawned impolitely in Kitchener's face. "What time is it?" she demanded.

"It's an unearthly hour," he said.

"I haven't had half enough sleep," she protested.

"Neither have I," he returned unfeelingly. "Get up. I'm pulling out of here in twenty minutes and taking the tent with me."

They were both too drowsy and too cross even to pretend to be good-humored, and they ate breakfast without talk, and then struck camp and reloaded the sledge like a pair of automatons. While the girl was pulling on her green parka and mittens, Kit served the dogs their fishy portion and hustled them into the traces. The man and woman then slipped into their snowshoes, fumbled at the lashings with numbed fingers, and started the day's march as the sullen dawn was beginning to break.

They traveled as they did yesterday, Kitchener acting as pioneer, and the girl tramping behind at the "gee" pole of the sledge. The new light revealed the partly obliterated trail of the man who had proceeded them down the river.

Kit followed with his head bowed to the cutting sleet, pushing on remorselessly, and not always remembering the slender, frost-whitened figure that trudged at his heels. Some time in the morning he came to a sheltered place where the remnants of a campfire had been snowed under, not many hours earlier. The ex-convict had spent the night here, and had gone on again, probably at daybreak.

From this point the trail was fresher and, for the present, very easily distinguished. The man was staying with the river. He had crossed the ice of a tributary creek and still continued down the course of the main stream. This creek was the first of the branches that Jerry had mentioned. The fifth would be Great Owl Run.

Kit did not wish to overtake his man until after he had turned into the Great Owl country. Late in the morning he discovered that the tracks of snowshoes and sledge runners had a cleaner demarcation at the edges, and he realized that he was closing up the gap too quickly. Thereafter he moved more leisurely and kept a sharper look-out ahead.

He and the girl halted at noon for lunch, and later they again stopped for a few minutes to give the dogs a breathing spell. The afternoon was beginning to fade when they reached the second of the creeks that flowed from the east into the Vermilion River.

The small stream entered the larger waterway between sloping, timbered banks. Kit descended through the willows at the head of his dogs, started across the thick ice, and then stopped as short as though an alarming voice had challenged him. In the snow along the north margin of the creek he saw a new trail—dog tracks, the twin grooves of a heavy-laden sledge, and a pair of big raquettes crushing through the snow.

Kitchener brought his team to a standstill and curtly signaled Miss Durand to halt. He strode forward to investigate, and then stood in wondering silence.

The newcomer evidently was a heavily built and energetic man. His snowshoes were of the two-bar type, remarkably broad at the toes, but in spite of their sustaining spread they sank deeply under his hard-cruising weight. The webbing of the right shoe had been torn, and afterwards roughly repaired. The imprints were too familiar to leave any possibility of doubt. Kit yesterday had examined a line of tracks that were identical with these, and he knew that he could not be mistaken. The new arrival was Jerry Tearl.

Kit beckoned on his companion and crossed the brook to regain the embankment of the main stream. The broad-toed prints ranged down to the river's edge, and there turned northward to meet and run parallel with the trail that Kit had been following all that day. Jerry and the ex-convict were traveling the same direction, and by the recent appearance of the two trails they could not be many minutes apart.

It was incredible that the pair had actually encountered one another and were cruising in each other's company. One must be following the other, with not more than a couple of miles separating them. Kit anxiously inspected first one snowshoe depression and then another, trying to decide which held the deepest film of sleet. To his untrained eyes there was no appreciable difference in the trails. One man probably was a little ahead of the other, but which was the pursuer and which the pursued, Kit was unable to determine.

CHAPTER IX
GRANDFATHER'S RED BLANKETS

What change of plan or error of reckoning had brought Jerry into the Vermilion River country, when he should have been miles from here, heading due north, Kit at this moment was unable to imagine. He wasted no time in futile speculation. It sufficed him to know that Hell Bent and his brother were cruising on the river route, almost within rifle shot of one another, while he and Diane Durand were trailing close behind. He did not need the gift of prophecy to realize that events were rapidly shaping themselves towards some sudden crisis.

The girl had come down the river slope to look curiously at the juncture of the trails. For a moment Kitchener lifted his icy eyelashes, trying to discover from her face whether she recognized the pattern of Jerry's raquettes. She did not enlighten him.

"Funny there'd be somebody else along here on a day like this," was her only comment.

"Oh, I don't know," said Kit carelessly. "Maybe some trapper finishing his rounds. You find fur-hunters' shacks scattered here and there all through the wilderness. Come on. Let's go."

They took advantage of the last of twilight and hurried on after the two who had gone before. Kit had no expectancy of closing up the distance to-night, and the best he could hope was that conditions to-morrow might remain favorable for tracking. At this moment, however, the prospects were disquieting. The sleet was changing to snow—stinging, dry flakes that had begun to eddy into drifts along the exposed banks of the river. As he pushed onward he cast many dubious glances towards the northern sky, worried by the auguries that spelled heavy weather and smothered trails.

When darkness finally hid the ground underfoot he had no choice but to go into camp. This night they were lucky enough to find an overhanging bluff by the river which served both as a windbreak and a sheltering roof. By the time the tent was up and supper had been cooked, their fire was almost blotted out by flying clouds of snow. Kit shoved the smoldering fagots closer to the cliffside, and then groped his way along the cracking edges of river ice and dragged in enough down-timber and driftwood to last through the night.

Diane Durand left her tent flap open to catch the rays of heat, and Kit snuggled down by the snoring dogs, where the reflected warmth reached the wall of rock. A dozen times during the night he awakened to replenish the fire and to listen with gloomy forebodings to the wind and the rush of snow down the river levels.

At daybreak he and the girl aroused themselves in a world of swirling whiteness. The moment he had cast off his robes he wallowed through the drifts to the river bank. It was as he had feared. The landscape stretched away into ghostly backgrounds, an unbroken monotony of snow. This was to-day, and all of yesterday's records were buried under the great downfall of the storm.

Kitchener felt reasonably certain the ex-convict and Jerry both were heading for Great Owl Run. The trails had disappeared, and there was little prospect of picking them up again. But as long as he held the guidance of the river and kept count of the branching streams there was slight danger of his going astray. Diane Durand did not seem to be much alarmed by the burying of yesterday's tangible paths.

"Uncle Jim'll be up there somewhere," she said serenely, "and if we keep on the way we're going we'll surely find him."

"Shouldn't doubt it," said Kit.

Through that brief, blustering day they struggled forward in the welter of snow, like specters in a world of death, seeing no living creature, walking in a vast blankness. They crossed the mouths of a third and a fourth creek that ended their ice-choked careers in the Vermilion River. As night closed in at the end of the ghastly daylight they struck the fifth branching stream.

On a high promontory, barely discernible in the hurly-burly of the storm, Kitchener made out a tall, gaunt fir tree that had been stripped of its middle branches and left standing above the river, a beacon for all passers-by. This was a "lobstick" which the Indians had trimmed fantastically to commemorate some noteworthy tribal event. The ancient marker, Jerry had said, would indicate Kit's turning point. This creek must be Great Owl Run.

Whether Diane Durand knew anything of local geography Kitchener did not know. But she offered no protests when he quitted the river here and turned up the side stream.

In almost any other land Great Owl Run would have been called a river. It was thirty or forty feet wide between its sheer banks, a deep, swift-running stream coming out of the high hills in the northeast. For stretches the course was closed solidly from bank to bank, but along the narrow races the water poured out thunderously from under the ice tunnels, and would not freeze even in below-zero weather.

There was no sign of human footprints along the sheltered shores. If anybody had come this direction during the last twenty-four hours the trail was blotted out under the heavy snowfall. Kit moved furtively and as long as he could see he kept a restless lookout among the gloomy coverts. Bill Tearl and the two outlanders had met with a strange and terrible fate not many miles farther up this stream, and Kit was conscious of a haunting oppression of mind and spirit as he neared the scene of the old tragedy.

Darkness came, and he continued to grope his way up the winding watercourse. The dogs were sagging in the traces, staggering belly-deep in the snow. Behind the sledge Diane Durand stumbled and floundered in the drifts, almost at the end of her endurance. But still Kit would not halt.

As they advanced the forest grew blacker and denser. The gale still raged overhead, but in the timber-smothered depths of the creek bottoms scarcely a breath of wind reached them. Evergreens do not rustle like deciduous trees, but moan and sigh in living anguish. There are few sounds more dolorous than the wailing of a spruce forest at night.

Kitchener was groping his way through a tangle of snowy underwood, when he was conscious of a shadowy movement at his elbow. Startled, he turned his head to see a slight, wraith-like shape hurrying at his heels. It was Diane Durand. In the darkness he could just see the blur of her lifted face.

"What's the matter?" he asked as he resumed his weary stride. There was no reason why he might not have spoken in a natural tone, but through the warning of some vague instinct he pitched his voice to a whisper.

"I don't know," she answered. "I— How much farther must we go?"

"Not far now," he said.

He expected her to drop back to her place with the sledge; instead she kept at his side, pressing even closer, as though something had frightened her and she was seeking the reassurance of human fellowship.

It was curious. Until this moment she had never betrayed any symptom of timidity.

"I've never seen it so dark anywhere," she complained. "It isn't like being out-of-doors, but feeling your way in a strange—" and hesitated for the word—"cavern. Everything is so—shut-in."

Kitchener had nothing to say. He was forcing his way doggedly through the low, jungle-like thickets, when suddenly, unreasoningly, his breath was quenched in his lungs and his heart stood still.

Something soft and silent and somehow horrible, seemed to move through the air just by his head.

He was not aware of any sound, nor of actual motion. Yet without seeing or hearing he knew that something alive had passed through the darkness and stared at him.

And Diane knew, and the dogs knew. The girl's hand was clutching the muscles of his forearm, trembling. The dog team scrambled forward to slink at Kitchener's heels. Like the girl, the beasts also had discovered a sudden need for human companionship.

Kit had pulled up short, listening, his eyes striving vainly to penetrate the stifling gloom.

There was nothing, only the sighing of the spruces and the cracking of frost-brittle branches along the hidden creek. His common sense tried to tell him that he was deluding himself with overwrought imaginings, but his high-keyed instincts knew better.

As he waited, tense and breathless, with the girl clinging to him and the dogs cowering at his feet, it came again. For an instant he fancied, or rather, felt, that a ghostly shape, blacker than the blackness of the night, had soundlessly crossed his line of vision. Similarly, he was conscious of a wavering in the darkness behind him.

Kit felt a cold tingling creep up his backbone to the base of the neck, that queer, atavistic sensation that modern men probably have inherited from furry forebears, who bristled in moments of danger and dread. The girl was standing close, her slim young body as taut as though she had suddenly passed under a mesmeric spell. Without thinking what he did, Kit's arm slid around her waist, and she did not try to move.

Again he was aware of a shady stirring, as though a grotesque and impalpable substance had stooped his direction and brushed him by. For just that moment the dead air was disturbed and he had the impression that a soft, monstrous form had swept past his face. And all at once the awful silence was disrupted by a harsh, snicking sound—like a pair of steel scissors' blades that had sharply clashed.

Kit caught his breath, and then his drawn muscles relaxed and he laughed feebly with the letting down of over-strained senses. "Oh, gosh!" he moaned. "What a pair of idiots we are! Scared—"

"Of what?" the girl gasped. "Oh, what?"

"Do you know the name of this place?" Kit's voice sounded more as though it belonged to him. "Of course! I never thought!"

"This place—?" she echoed.

"Great Owl Run. There must have been a reason for the name." He released the girl and looked shamefacedly into the darkness. "Owls!"

Something glided past them so close that they felt the fanned wake in the atmosphere.

"It's an owl pit in here," explained Kit, who had become his own man again. "There must be dozens of 'em. They're just swooping to look at us—"

The girl shuddered and threw up one arm to defend her face. "How terrible!" she faltered.

"A puppy or a wolf cub would never get out of here alive," he told her. "But a man and woman and grown dogs are perfectly safe."

The girl strained forward as his eyes tried desperately to fathom the obscurity. "I can feel them about us," she whispered. "They must be enormous."

"Great Northern Owls!" he said. "I saw one once that had wandered south. He was six feet across the wings. Bloody night pirates! Fiends! This must be a fearful pocket of the woods. Where the owls live nothing else ever lives." He touched her hand. "Let's get on."

Miss Durand was somewhat reassured, but the dogs did not like this place at all. Thenceforward Kit had no worries about the jaded animals keeping up with him. They were nosing his heels at every step.

As he crunched over a carpet of spruce needles, which in places was bare of snow, vague, feathery flutterings wove invisible orbits about his head. Once something croaked above him, and later one of the fearsome nightbirds sent out his hunting call, a voiceless, disembodied sound, like a despairing groan floating out of an insatiable emptiness. He knew it was only an owl, and yet his blood was chilled by the unearthliness of the cry.

He had no idea how far he followed the windings of that ill-omened creek. For hours, it seemed to him, he groped his way among shaggy tree trunks, around rotted windfalls, through tangling, flesh-tearing thickets. And then, without warning, he found nothing in front of his outreaching hand. He stopped and peered blindly, and knew only that the dense forest had abruptly come to an end and that there was open space before him.

Gingerly he moved forward again, and barked his knee on the sharp edge of a stump. There were other snags and stumps sticking up from the ground. He brushed the snow from one of the old stubs, and found the scars of ancient ax-work. Here, apparently, was a man-made clearing.

Diane Durand had pressed up behind him with one unquiet hand touching him as she tried to see past his shoulder. The dogs squatted on their haunches and sat in an uneasy line, their noses and sharp ears cocked to the fore. And then, before anybody could stop him, one of the beasts flung up his head and let forth a long, lugubrious howl.

The sudden eruption of sound in that hushed closure of the wilderness was indecent, uncanny, frightening. Kitchener caught the animal's throat and choked off the last echoing quaver. "Shut up!" he commanded under his breath.

The girl had ventured a few paces forward, and he straightened and stole up beside her.

"I think there's something there," she said close to his ear. "I can just make it out—square and black."

Kit lifted one eyebrow and stood at straining attention. Gradually a dim, dark outline took shape in the gloom. "It looks like a house," he mused.

A mutual curiosity drew them on, and after several cautious halts, they arrived before a low-roofed, dismal-looking structure of hewn logs, that stood, apparently, in the middle of an abandoned clearing. There was no sound within, no glimmer of light; the place smelled of emptiness, desolation and decay.

Kit moved under the dank front wall, and waited with his mouth half open and his head alertly tilted. The open doorway yawned at him and the puncheon door hung on one rusted hinge that creaked faintly with the pressure of the wind. At the right and left loomed the dark squares of two broken-shuttered windows. In the faint odor of must that emanated from the interior murk he caught no scent of smoke nor savor of recent cooking. The one-time occupants of the cabin must have been a long while absent.

Kitchener's sense told him that he might enter the place openly, and that there would be no one to deny him the right. But something more than mere instinct of caution urged him to hesitate. His hand went down to unbutton the flap of his pistol holster, and that simple, unthinking act made him bold. He shouldered aside the swaying door and stepped into the cabin.

Something squeaked and scuttled away overhead, and became silent. The old roof evidently sheltered squirrels, or rats. There was something else. It was a low, measured sound, lifting and falling, like a man breathing in the dark.

The dead air within seemed many degrees colder than the zero weather outside. Kit found himself shivering as he stared into the frigid obscurity, striving with every nerve aquiver to locate the source of that strange, breathy heaving.

Diane Durand had come into the cabin and remained a stilled shadow at his side. The dogs were cowering in their tangled traces at the doorway, snuffing audibly at whatever it was the darkness hid. It might have seemed that they were afraid to stay alone outside, and fearful of coming in.

Kitchener had his flashlight in hand, his thumb irresolute on the button. He drew a quick breath and suddenly pressed the contact. A spot of light danced on the farther wall, and he swung it in a circuit of the room.

His swift reconnoitering disclosed nothing immediately alarming. The brilliant bull's-eye flicked from wall to wall, illuminating bare, peeled logs, warped and moldy and showing wide cracks at places where the chinking had crumbled. The first hurried survey revealed a clay fireplace choked with stale kitchen litter, a greasy iron pot hanging on a crane, a broken-legged table covered with tattered oilcloth, a slab bench, a trash heap of empty tins and battered cooking utensils, a sheet-iron stove and stove-pipe flaked red with rust, a disused ax driven to the hilt into one of the sill-logs, and a double-decked bunk made of poles and stuffed with withered balsam branches and frowsy-looking bed clothing.

The single, four-square room held no visible habitant, and yet, deliberate and rhythmic as tick-tocks, the breathing sounds continued. Kitchener felt his eyes growing bigger as he switched his light back to the bunk. There was something in the lower section, a shapeless bulge hidden by a red blanket.

For lengthening seconds he watched and listened so particularly to the other breathing that he himself forgot to breathe. At first he thought the blanket had shifted slightly, but as he eyed it closely he changed his mind and decided that nothing had moved. But still the strange, bellows-like pulsations filled and expired, lifted and died again.

Slowly his glance turned upward, and then he shot his light towards the ceiling beams. There was a gaping hole in the roof, where a patch of shakes had rotted through; and one of the rafters had loosened at the eaves. A current of air sucked through the door and drew out through the vent overhead, causing the sagging roof to billow at intervals like a tent-top in a wind. It was the cabin that was breathing.

Kitchener should have been relieved when he traced the source of disturbing sound. But he wasn't. There was something wrong about this place. He felt it. He knew it. He felt it in the air, in the chilling darkness, in his blood and nerves and in the marrow of his bones. The light flickered back to the bunk. He looked, took a couple of steps forward, and looked harder.

The red blanket was an old Hudson's Bay Company four pointer. He saw the marking stripes at the corner that hung off the edge of the bunk, and also he saw a charred spot in the fabric, down near the border. A spark had hopped out of the camp fire his first night in the woods and scorched that hole in the wool. It was Grandfather Tearl's old red blanket. There was no mistaking it. He had given it to Jerry when they traded clothes and equipment, two days ago. Jerry was here, or had been here.

With misgivings that he could never have explained, Kit moved to the bunk and pulled at the edge of the blanket. He tugged tentatively, and then jerked it to the floor. In the middle of the bunk was a crumpled garment—a gray stag shirt—and nothing else.

Kitchener stood like a torpid man, staring senselessly at his own bare hand. His fingers were wet and sticky. He turned the light towards himself and felt weak and sick. The blanket had left a gory smear across his palm.

As though he had suddenly aroused himself from a stupor he snatched up the shirt from the mattress of browse. He looked at the label under the neck band. It was the shirt he himself had purchased not long ago at a New York store of outfitters. His brother had it when they last saw each other.

In an access of horror Kit spread wide the garment and brought his lamp to bear. And then his eyes shut as though with an anguish that was almost too great to bear. In the center of the back, where the cloth would stretch over the wearer's shoulder blades, he found a small, round hole, soggy to the touch and stained an ugly crimson.

"Jerry!" The name stuck in his throat, choking him.

He whirled with his light to see Diane Durand standing behind him, her lips apart, her eyes wildly gleaming as she stared at the bunk. "What is it?" she gasped.

Kit said nothing. His spot-light was a will-o'-the-wisp, darting about the room. A bare floor of hard-packed earth; bare, log walls; naked timber-rafters supporting the roof: there was no hiding-place here. He heard nothing except the thumping of his heart, the sighing of the old cabin, the horrible sniffing of the dogs in the doorway.

The snow had swirled down through the hole in the roof, whitening the floor in the middle of the room. In the snow Kit discovered the pattern of a man's boot-sole fouled with red. The light blazed a path through the darkness as he moved forward, crouching almost to his knees. There were other bloodspots on the floor, a spattering trail leading to the broken window at the far end of the cabin.

On the floor beneath the casement there was an ugly, dark pool and the windowsill was similarly bedabbled. He stood up, looked into the outer darkness. Shrinking from contact with the red-stained sill, he thrust his head out of doors and turned his lamp downward. His breath stopped short as he peered after the piercing light beam.

The cabin, he discovered, had been erected on the brink of Great Owl Run. The embankment descended in a sheer drop, straight down to the stream, twenty or thirty feet below. In the flash of his lamp he caught the gleam of black, open water racing under a yawning ice-tunnel a little farther downstream.

He turned away, his eyes in a stinging mist, conjuring the image of his lusty brother: the dauntless Jerry who had started with such supreme self-confidence on his journey to Queen Maud Sea.

Kit needed to search no farther. He knew what had happened. Jerry must have been in the lead, traveling down the Vermilion River and up the course of Great Owl Run with Hell Bent only a mile or so, a couple of hours, behind. Jerry could have had no warning that he was being followed. Tired out after bucking the blizzard all day he had crept into the bunk with his clothes on, rolled up in Grandfather Tearl's blankets, and slept.

It did not take a morbid imagination to visualize the rest. The second man arrived stealthily under the cover of the storm. He would have paused outside for a moment to remove his waffle-meshed snowshoes. Then he tiptoed into the gloomy cabin, pausing to listen and searched out the location of the bunk.

Probably the rats squeaked and scuttled away in the rafters. Silence after that, save for the sighing of the cabin and the breathing of the sleeping man. A furtive approach; a shot fired at close range. Utter quiet then. Only the wind drawing softly through the cabin roof.

The valiant, resourceful Jerry had been caught asleep with his boots on.

Kit could visualize only too vividly the subsequent horrors: the stripping off of blanket and shirt, the search of pockets; a limp shape toppled off the bunk, dragged across the snowy floor, boosted to the window sill and dumped overside. A plummet-like drop, a cold splash in the darkness below.

Kitchener's gun was in his hand, but he was not thinking of himself or of lurking dangers. He was staring in direful fascination at the black window opening, hearing only the swirl and gurgle of Great Owl Run, the downpouring waters that ran under ice to empty their flotsam at last into the frozen wastes of Queen Maud Sea.

CHAPTER X
ALWAYS FIRE FIRST

The soft stirring of footsteps jarred Kitchener out of his hideous reverie. Diane Durand had stolen past him in the darkness, and with reaching hands she leaned forward to look out the window. He grabbed her and flung her backwards so violently that she cried aloud, clutching at the finger-marks on her wrist.

"What are you doing?" she demanded, amazed and angry.

"Keep away from that window!"

"What for?"

"There's blood on it. It's everywhere."

He had switched off his light and was unable to see her face, but he heard her draw a shuddering breath and felt her dynamic glance fixed upon him. "It's—what?" she said in a small, muted voice.

"It's murder," he said, wondering what made his own speech sound so strange. "That's all. Just a nicely planned shooting in the back."

"Who?" gasped the girl. "Who?"

"My—" Kit stopped so abruptly that he bit his tongue. "An old friend of mine. He was worn out and trying to get a little sleep. I guess he didn't know that it happened. I—I hope he never knew."

"You—what makes you so sure?" she asked in a chilled whisper.

"I'm as sure as though I'd seen it." His short, ugly laugh did not have quite the ring of sanity. "His shirt with a bullet hole in the back, all smeared. The blankets he died in. The dripping across the floor—right there—right at your feet. A body lugged to the window. Overboard and into the creek. That's how it was done. A pretty little job. A neat piece of work from behind. Your uncle Sim or Jim or whatever you call him. A straight-shooter—a straight-shooter-in-the-back! A nice, sweet boy he is!"

There was a dead silence for a space, and then a harsh, choking sound in the darkness. Then Diane Durand's voice, icy and level and dangerously restrained: "I can't believe I understood you. Will you say that again?"

Kitchener was so stunned by the tragedy that he was unable at present to think clearly or rationally. All that could matter to him was the aching certainty that Jerry was gone. Funny old Jerry! He had been done out of life and disposed of like a trapped, helpless animal. Stalked in his sleep and brutally killed! The numbing realization left Kit without any sense of discretion. He wasn't caring about anything now, what he did or said or what happened next.

"I said that your uncle came in here and stood over him while he slept and put a bullet into his body."

He felt the girl flinch, and he was conscious of her eyes staring at him. "That's a lie!" she panted.

"Killed him with the old ivory-butted gun!" Kit laughed insanely. "Of course! The beautiful, engraved six-shooter that stood for law and order! How things work out! God, what a joke everything is!"

The girl turned on him in a flash of savagery. "What a beast you are! You don't know. You make a wild and wicked guess, and accuse a man of murder. With nothing whatever to go on except your own crazy notions of what might be—of what you seem to want it to be. You policemen! No wonder people are afraid of you. That's your idea: get somebody, no matter whom. It doesn't matter whether he's guilty or innocent. Get him! Frame him! Bring him in! Swear his life away! Get your man—any man—"

"Listen, baby!" Kit cut in fiercely. "I don't need your advice—or criticism. That sort of talk isn't helping any. I've seen what I've seen. That's plenty. The waffle-mesh tracks we followed down the river. You know who those belong to. Stalking the two-bar shoes through the storm, right to this place. Don't think I don't know the ins and outs of this business. I know whom to look for, and I know he can't be far from here right now—"

"You haven't a shred of real evidence!" she interrupted passionately. "And to say what you've said, without being sure—it's cruel, it's criminal!"

"Yes?" he retorted. "Well, let me tell you—I'm going out and find the bloody prints. There'll be tracks somewhere around here. And they'll show the waffle marks. I'm just that sure of that. If they shouldn't I'll apologize. I'll beg your pardon on my hands and knees. You can't ask anything fairer than that."

Kit swung around to face the open doorway. It was snowing heavily outside and the wind still moaned through the firs. In the black forest farther down stream the frightful cry of a giant owl quavered in the night—a hideous, hungering sound. He couldn't forget the name of this place. Great Owl Run. His father had been finished here twelve years ago. And now his brother! A fateful spot for the Tearls. It wasn't just coincidence—it was kismet. This place had haunted his imagination since childhood. Now he had found it for himself. And Bill was gone and Jerry was gone, and only Kitchener was left.

Perhaps Kitchener would go next in turn. That would be consistent. And he didn't particularly care. Little Jane would carry on. It was queer how his thoughts kept going back to Jane now, and he could smile tenderly to himself, thinking of her. She was the best of the lot. It didn't matter about himself. He wasn't afraid of the owls or the mysterious forest or the red-handed murderer who undoubtedly was skulking somewhere in the neighborhood.

His pulse had slowed to a sober, steady beat, the fever of his blood had simmered down to an ominous coolness. There was something he had to do, and he was ruthless and reckless in the zest to see it through. Whatever happened, he asked only that it might be swift and decisive.

He started towards the door, but a hand reached in the darkness to grab his sleeve. "What are you going to do?" asked Diane Durand in sudden panic.

"Find him, and arrest him—if he doesn't try to resist."

"Oh, no!" The girl's tone had changed. She was frightened and desperate. There was frantic appeal in her voice. "No! Wait! You've got to wait! Something terrible will happen! Don't. Please don't!"

"You seem to think he will resist." Kitchener's laugh sounded unfamiliar in his own ears. "Well, he probably will."

He shook off her hand and started again to leave the cabin. But at the doorway he changed his mind and halted. He thought he caught a sound behind him—not where the girl stood, a little to the left—but straight back, over near the fireplace. He had thoroughly searched the room. Nothing was there. And yet—

Again he heard it. Unquestionably! A soft, whisking sound—higher up—near the roof—like snow sliding. He turned, and his pocket light again found its way into the hand. He didn't touch the button, but was ready to shoot on the flash at an instant's notice.

In his loosely gripped fist the butt of his pistol rested comfortably. The expert marksman gave no conscious thought to the weapon. It was as much a part of himself as the hand that held it. The safety slipped off with the reflex of the thumb. His whole attention was centered towards the ceiling beside the chimney, where he knew there was a wide hole opening through the roof.

It was too dark within and without to differentiate between the solid part of the roof and the open sky. But a prescience more astute, more sensitive than mere eyesight, appraised him that something was blocking the gap above, staring into the cabin.

All was still now, save the slow, gentle shifting of the rafters, but Kit was positive that somebody or something had climbed onto the roof—that a face was peering down.

He was waiting with every faculty straining to catch the least hint of sound or movement, when, as sudden as lightning, a white, blinding ray flashed downward to cut the darkness like a shining blade and hit the farther wall in a dazzling bullseye.

Kitchener's reactions were as spontaneous as it is to live or to breathe or to fight back from a corner. He saw the hard, round spot of light at the upper end of the shaft—the focus point of the searching beam. The light was swinging his direction—reaching for him—

There was no volition on his part. It was as though his pistol lifted and sighted itself and went off on its own responsibility, regardless of his own will or intention.

Flame spurted, the butt kicked back in his fist, the log walls were jarred as though by a sledge-hammer blow. At the same instant the light winked out, and some broken, clinking object dropped and struck the hard clay floor below.

The room was still filled with the first explosion, when a fiery streak stabbed down at Kitchener from the darkness of the eaves. A chunk of lead hit the wall just behind his neck and plunged deep into one of the logs. The man on the roof had fired at the flash of Kit's gun, and missed him by inches.

As the report of the return shot jarred in his ears, Kitchener side-stepped and ducked towards the floor. His bullet had shattered the lense of the intruder's lamp. He was safe enough, as long as he kept his thumb off his own switch-button.

But Kit was not playing for safety. This blind-man's work irritated him. On the roof crouched the man who had assassinated his brother Jerry, and who also must have had a hand in the ambushing of Inspector Tearl. Kitchener was troubled by no scruples of chivalry. He grinned dourly to himself in the darkness as he realized how he had met his first test in police uniform. He hadn't even thought of the traditions of the service, but fired instinctively and beat his man to the shot. So Jerry undoubtedly would have done in his place. There was no sense in dealing politely with a dangerous criminal who knew no code.

At this moment Kit's only regret was that he had shot too accurately. He had sighted for the man's electric lamp and smashed it. If his bullet had only been a little off the line he might not be crouching in the darkness now, with a live murderer at the roof hole, ready to plug him the instant he revealed his whereabouts.

The sweetly pungent reek of picric acid was a familiar scent in Kit's nostrils. It reminded him of the target gallery where he used to put in an hour every afternoon following the dismissal of the class on torts. In law a tort is an evil or injury done one man by another, and the professor had taught his students that the wronged party was entitled to complete redress. Kitchener was thankful to-night that he had learned something in college beyond the theories of books. If he caught a single glimpse of his man no court of law would ever need to settle this affair.

He turned his light-stick upward and pushed the button. A luminous streak splashed to the ceiling, limning brilliantly the jagged hole in the roof-shakes. In the opening he saw a bulky shoulder and an arm and a man's big fist clenching a revolver. His own gun went up. Eyes and finger synchronized to their business, but in the fractional second required to make sure of his aim, a living, gasping weight landed on him from behind.

Kitchener had no warning of the attack. The shock sent him down on one knee and his flashlight was knocked out of his hand and went flying across the room in a twisting, white arc. He was unable to check the pressure of his forefinger in time. A jolt of sound hit his eardrums as his pistol exploded haphazard to send a bullet on a ricocheting course from the chimney to the side wall and across the splintering door-slabs.

His assailant was Diane Durand. He had forgotten her in those few seconds and had allowed her to get behind him. And now she had both arms around him, clutching his pistol-hand, clinging to him with an amazing strength.

Kit had often heard the phrase about female deadliness, but he never thought it really meant anything—not until now. Under their silken softness her muscles were almost as strong as his, and at that moment she seemed twice as agile. He regained his feet and tried to wrench his arm free, but small fingers and sharp nails were digging into his wrist with the force of desperation.

The girl was hanging on his back, and whichever way he turned he swung her with him. Her face was pressing his neck and he could feel the breath come and go harshly from her open mouth. "Let go!" he muttered, and tore furiously at her hands.

On the roof overhead he heard a slipping, sliding sound, followed by a heavy thump in the snow behind the cabin. The man outside evidently was dissatisfied with his peek hole, and had dropped to the ground. Either he had decided to run away or had started around for the cabin door.

Kit was in too tight a situation to hold any false punctilios in the distinction of sex. Courtesy towards women is a nice trait, but it was absurd to be gallant with his life at stake. The beautiful gestures of life are outmoded. There are no gentle disciples of Gautama left in the world to feed themselves to female tigers.

This girl was fighting him like a man. He locked his fingers under hers and wrenched backwards with his full strength. Her breath grew short and sharp and he felt her supple tendons cramp themselves convulsively. He was hurting her badly, but she still clung to him, trying to plow her nails deeper into his flesh. Fiercely he tore her grip away, and whirled to fling her from him.

But she was a shade the quicker. One slim, tenacious arm crooked itself around his neck and tightened under his chin to choke back his breathing. The second hand darted around to clutch him across the mouth, trying to twist his head off his shoulders.

"Drop that gun!" a voice sobbed in his ear. "I—I'll make him quit if—if you'll—quit!"

"Quit!" Kit laughed truculently against the warm hand that was stifling him. "Quit, Hell!" He jerked his head aside at the price of a furrow of skin gouged from his upper lip. Then, with a contortionist's movement he dropped to one knee, taking the girl with him and attempting to fling her in front of him.

His pistol was in his fist and he did not dare to put it away or drop it. At any minute the expected footsteps might cross the threshold from without. He only had the use of one hand, and his attacker was as active and lithe and stubborn as a pouncing cat. He almost threw her by the unexpectedness of his ruse, but not quite. She recovered her advantage with a surprising shift of her wiry body, tumbled across his shoulders, twisted a rounded leg behind his knee, and wrapped both flexible arms in a tightening strangle-hold against his wind-pipe.

Both were panting in the darkness, and Kit could taste a warm salty trickle on his lips. He was furious. It stung him to the depths of his masculine complacency to realize that this slender, boyish-built girl was quite as able-bodied as he. At that moment, if his thumbs had been able to reach her pretty throat, he could have throttled her cheerfully.

But she was like a leech, a fierce little incubus, hag—riding his back. He set his teeth and, with a sudden effort of exasperation, he heaved himself erect, wrenched his shoulder around and threw back his head.

His skull hit something soft and yielding with an impact sufficient to hurt through the hardness of his cranium. He heard a broken little cry behind him, and the girl's tense body relaxed a trifle, and for an instant her arms loosened their clutch. She tried to grab him again, but this time he evaded her hands and tore himself free.

He did not linger to find out what had happened. He felt the draught of the open doorway, and turned leftward to plunge out into the snowy night. Groping blindly, he sprang through the door, stumbled over something that yelped and snapped at his leg. He tumbled sprawling into the middle of a shrieking, struggling heap of dogs.

His team of huskies had been sitting in an uneasy circle at the cabin entrance. It was too dark to see, and he had completely forgotten them. The reminder was so sudden that he did not quite know what had happened until he found himself flat on his stomach in the snow, the center of the writhing, howling pack. A wet, furry body fell backwards and sat on his head. A second shape bounded across him, tangling him in the sledge traces. One of the beasts snarled in fright, and something slashed his pants and nipped the flesh of his calf.

Fighting with both hands, he warded off the milling shadows, and managed to lift himself to his knees. A set of sharp teeth clicked in his face, and as he threw out his arm to protect himself his pistol slipped from his grasp and went spinning away into a snow drift. He righted himself somehow, and scrambled to his feet. Kicking the dogs away, he disentangled himself from the twisted harness lines and stooped forward to plunge his arm shoulder deep into the nearest snow bank.

Frantically he groped about with his bare, chilled fingers, and gasped with relief as his hand closed over the icy butt of his lost gun. This was sheer good luck. He might have spent an hour in futile search for the weapon. He examined the gun critically to make sure that the action was not clogged, and then stole around the cabin, closely hugging the walls.

There was nobody in sight. He wedged himself into the angle of the chimney and waited with every sense keyed to hair-trigger alertness. The dogs were raising such bedlam in front of the shack it was impossible to hear any other sound. He gaped right and left in the darkness. The man on the roof had jumped down on this side, but there was nobody here now. Perhaps he was ambushed in the neighboring timber; perhaps he had fled.

Kit ventured out of his sheltering nook and pushed around to the side of the cabin overlooking the high embankment of the brook. Still he saw nothing, heard nothing except the gurgle of water and the raving of the dogs around in front. He retraced his steps, waded through the animals, and looked in at the doorway. His electric lamp was still blazing in the corner of the room where it had fallen. All the rest of the interior was shrouded in darkness. He did not see the girl and did not stop to search for her. In three strides he crossed the room, snatched up his lamp, and again ran out of doors.

His light cast strange, ghostly patterns among the sheeted stumps and along the ragged, white fringe of the forest. The higher plumes of the firs swayed and moaned in the wind, but everything was deathly still in the underwoods below. He made his way around the cabin, boring the darkness in all directions with his flashlight, steeling himself for the crashing shock of a bullet.

He reached the rear of the cabin, and nothing interrupted his wary advance. The lamp was brought to bear, and he paused to read the story in the snow. Here were a pair of big boot prints. The intruder had removed his snowshoes at this spot and climbed to the roof. The eaves were only hands'-reach high, and he had boosted himself upward from a convenient windowsill. Farther out were two deeper bootmarks. This was where he had jumped off the roof. There was a circle of scuffled tracks at this point. He had donned his snowshoes here.

Kit flashed his light outward and saw a line of webbed tracks, heading across the clearing to the forest. Great, long strides—almost running. The murderer evidently hadn't cared for his enemy's marksmanship and decided that he had had enough.

There was nothing else that Kitchener needed to see. He switched off his light and returned to the cabin doorway.

"Hello!" he said to the darkness.

There was no response.

"You there, Diane?" he demanded. "You might as well know it. The waffle-mesh snowshoes. Your lovely uncle! He was here and took a crack at me, and beat it, and left you to the wolves."

"You fired first!" an unsteady voice spoke out from the shadows. "And nobody left me. He didn't know I was here. I was careful that he shouldn't. If he had he'd have come in and got me. You may not know it, but I saved you—"

"Or him," interrupted Kit. His sore lip yielded to a battered grin. Somehow he bore no malice towards the girl. Nobody could blame her for fighting for her own. That was the sort of blind, unreasoning loyalty that he himself understood only too well. He turned on his lamp again and switched the light around until he found the slight figure standing lonely in the middle of the room. She faced him unflinchingly, and apparently was trying to check her labored breathing.

As he looked at her he felt a queer catch in his breath. Her shirt was torn at the collar, her ruddy hair was flying at wild ends, a bruised, bare arm emerged from a sleeve ripped to the shoulder. But her pert nose was the worst. It looked a couple of sizes larger than he remembered it, and was frankly bloodied.

"Ah, gee!" he exclaimed contritely. "I'm sorry. Honestly, I didn't mean to do that."

"Is it bad?" she asked, and crooked her arm across her face.

Kit hastily dug a clean handkerchief out of his pocket and gave it to her. "Gosh!" he muttered. "I never hurt a girl before in my life."

"I don't think it's broken," she assured him through the crumpled handkerchief. "What did I do to you?"

"You skinned my wrist and half ripped off my lip, that's all."

"Well, that's something, anyhow!" Her dark eyes brightened with satisfaction. "That makes us quits, doesn't it?"

Kit drew a deep breath of relief. It was wonderful of her to take it that way. "You're a good sport!" he ejaculated. "Darned if you aren't! The Dianes! Hellcats, maybe. But that's all right. I hope I always have a Diane for an enemy."

"You will," she returned evenly.

He cast a sharp glance at her, started to say something, but changed his mind and turned away. From his pocket he produced a match and ignited the litter in the fireplace. "Might as well make it comfortable here," he said as a cheerful blaze crackled up in the darkness. "I hate to leave you alone, but there's no way out of it."

"You—where are you going?" she faltered.

Kit did not answer. His thoughts were out in the dark forest, pursuing the trail of the waffle-webbed snowshoes. In a few minutes he would be on the march again. The other man would be very tired too. Wherever he went fresh his trail would be easily followed. He couldn't stay on his feet forever. Kit could keep going as long as the other man did, and he had no intention of being shaken off now.

"I'm going with you," the girl announced.

"You!" he countered. "What chance would you stand? I'm traveling tonight. I'd leave you miles behind."

She started towards him, tottered uncertainly, and caught at the table. "I'm all in!" she said piteously.

"Of course you are," he assured her. "You stay here and get some sleep and rest. I'll come back for you when I can."

Kit went outside, unharnessed and fed the dogs and turned them loose to find their own sleeping places. An ax, two blankets, matches and a few packages of provisions were strapped together into a small back-pack. The remainder of his equipment he carried into the cabin. He dragged in several armloads of down-wood and stacked it in a pile by the fireplace. Then he drew the old ax out of the cabin sill, spiked the door back on its hinges and refastened the shutters over the broken windows.

The girl had watched him in gloomy silence, knowing it would be useless to try to dissuade him from his plans.

"I've fixed you up as well as I can," he said. He shouldered his pack-sack and picked up his rifle. "Good night, Diane."

The girl was standing by the fireplace, dejectedly. "I hope—" she began, and stopped.

"What?" he asked.

"Nothing," she said drearily. "Good-by."

Without a backward glance Kit passed out of the cabin and strode off alone into the blustering night.

CHAPTER XI
/SAUT SAUVAGE/

The police shack at *Saut Sauvage* was buried in the snows of the remote wilderness. A fitful storm of sleet was lashing southward from the arctic barrens. It was December 24, a squally, gusty evening, bitterly cold. The wind was many things that night: a child sniffing and sobbing outside the batten door; a scolding old woman; frightened puppies whimpering in the darkness; a pack of wolves raging howling around the ice-banked walls; a gang of bad boys, laughing and throwing missiles against the rattling windows.

Inside the plank and tar-paper building the confined air was close and oppressively hot. The sheet iron stove, big enough to take a pine stump at a gulp, was stoked until its round sides looked like a red apple and its tin chimney shot a column of sparks above the drooping, stunted trees without.

Constable Joe Cross was at home, spending Christmas Eve in his most civilized manner. He had combed his sandy hair and trimmed his stiff, blond beard and put on his best necktie and the clean flannel shirt that he had washed and mended for this occasion. At the present moment he sat astraddle a slab stool before a packing-box table, which held three dry-batteries and a small radio receiver. He held a pencil in his huge fist and a pair of ear-phones were clipped over his crimson, frost-bitten ears. A lantern, hanging overhead, helped the glowing stove to furnish the light for his writing.

The great radio stations at Springfield, Massachusetts, and Lincoln, Nebraska, both were ranging the continent to-night with Christmas messages for the boys of the Arctic Patrol. Constable Cross was switching the dials first from one wave length to the other, waiting breathless and expectant for his own name to come out of the stormy night.

Meanwhile he was picking off the greetings intended for luckier men. Sometimes he would jot down a line or two to be read over again to-morrow, sighing with vicarious satisfaction in the knowledge that Corporal Somebody's sweetheart still loved him or that Constable Some One-else's family was thinking of him somewhere at this very instant.

A couple of trappers, Jean Bruyas and Giffard the Runt, who kept hunting shacks somewhere in the neighborhood, had wound up their circles at the police post where they knew the radio would be working and a Christmas Eve mulligan would be stewing on the stove.

Bruyas was a great tree of a man, black and hairy, slow and thick of body and wits, unsmiling, unfriendly, utterly fearless, with remorseless slits for eyes and a loose-lipped mouth from which half the front teeth were missing. In contrast Giffard was small and wizened and active as a sparrow. At times he was overly talkative and too ready with his laughter, and again he went into long spells of sulky, touchy silences. The Chippewyans called him Giffard *Noondea*, which in their language meant "the weasel," and was not a complimentary nickname. It was suspected that he would sometimes lift a fur from another man's trap if he were absolutely certain that the other man was nowhere about.

Giffard and Bruyas had been running their trap line along separate branches of Great Owl Creek for a decade or more. They were well acquainted and kept out of each other's way as much as possible.

Earlier in the evening three Yellow-Knife Indians had walked into the post. The Indians, as a rule, avoided the police when they could. But these three were civilized and Christianized, and wore neckties. They were known severally as Tom Salmonfish, Athu, which was short for *Athulejeray*, the musk-ox, and Pete Tomorrow. Salmonfish and Athu had been converted to two religions apiece, besides still keeping their faith in the old tribal gods. All of which, Constable Cross had remarked, should make them good enough to die young, and he hoped they would.

The three of them squatted together on a corner of the floor, uneasy and furtive in the presence of the law, muttering mysteriously to one another, while they waited for a hand-out.

At eight o'clock in the evening Constable Mark Devon returned from a short patrol he had undertaken during the last few days into the Slavey hunting grounds. Devon blew in with the storm, enveloped in a gust of snow that battered its way into the room as he opened the door and hastily shut it behind him.

It was impossible to see anything of Devon because of the sleety snow that clothed him from head to foot. He looked more like an icicle than a man.

"Well, boys, we're going to have a white Christmas!" he announced as he limped to a stool in the corner and sat down to tug off his frozen boot-pacs. "Ain't it nice for the kiddies?"

Constable Cross turned momentarily from his radio. "'It snows!' cried the schoolboy," he sang out boisterously. "'Hooray!'"

"Froze my foot again this morning," remarked Devon as he tenderly peeled down his thick-ribbed sock. "Same as a year ago. I always lose a couple of toes for Christmas."

"Are you maybe hangin' your stockin' to-night for Santa Claus?" inquired Jean Bruyas with his twisted, broken-toothed grin.

"Nope," answered Devon. "I'm through. I hung it last Christmas and all I found in it next morning was the two toes that had come off with the sock."

Cross started to make some remark, and then checked himself, raising his head and listening intently in the ear phones. Slowly his startled, incredulous expression yielded to a look of utter beatitude.

"It's for me!" the others heard him gasp.

His pencil was feverishly writing on the paper. Presently he stopped, swept off his head clamps and stood up to flourish the scribbled sheet. "From my sister!" he announced breathlessly.

"Yeah?" said Devon.

"Two or three thousand miles through sleet and darkness," the first constable declared proudly. "Can you beat it? And think of all the people who must have heard my name mentioned!"

"After that one big experience," remarked Devon, "anything else that comes over the radio to all those people will just be a lot of applesauce." The tall policeman was very cutting about his comrade's Christmas message, but he could not quite hide his envious look as he eyed the slip of paper. "Well," he asked grudgingly, "what'd your sister say?"

Constable Cross threw out his chest and moved closer to the lantern. Wrinkling his forehead over his own scribbling, he read in a loud voice:

> Constable Joseph C. Cross,
>   Royal Canadian Mounted Police,
>   *Saut Sauvage*, Saskatchewan, Canada.
>
> DEAR JOE: WE ARE ALL WELL AND HOPE YOUR HEALTH IS GOOD TOO. WISH YOU WERE TO BE WITH US AT OUR BIG TURKEY DINNER TO-MORROW.
>
> Your affectionate sister,
>   ELEANOR.

"Humph!" said Devon. "Is that all?"

"That's enough, ain't it?" said Cross contentedly. "It's just supposed to be a greeting."

"Seems to me like they're sort of ritzing us with their turkey." Devon sniffed the savory atmosphere of the police shack. "What are we having?" he demanded.

"Ptarmigan and moosemeat all mix' togedder," said Bruyas.

"No rabbits?" asked Devon with a suspicious glance towards the singing pot.

"On Christmas Eve!" exclaimed Cross. "Rabbits?"

Constable Devon pulled off his steaming parka, and then turned back expansively to face the other men. "Turkey!" he snorted contemptuously. "Can you imagine anybody wasting radio juice to blow about a turkey, and here we got moose and ptarmigan and no rabbits!"

Giffard the Runt had sidled over to the packing-box seat the moment Cross vacated it, and was listening in the ear phones. Suddenly he looked around with a wry expression. "I don't hear no voices," he declared. "It sounds more like mosquitoes in a muskeg."

"Mosquitoes?" Constable Cross turned questioningly.

"Maybe somebody's cut in with a key," suggested Devon. "It might be C.W. stuff from Edmonton."

Cross pushed Giffard off the box and resumed his place at the receiver. "It is!" he said after a moment, and turned his dial knobs. "Edmonton official calling for somebody. From Inspector Bowman." He cocked his head on one side, and those who were watching saw his eyes blink. "It's for us!" he cried.

Constable Devon hurried across the room and shoved a pad and pencil under his comrade's fist.

Cross was able to read code if the sending did not come too fast. He was writing painstakingly, with his tongue stuck in the corner of his mouth. The message was coming through slowly, and from the look of his face the news must have been somewhat disconcerting. Once he frowned and shook his head.

"What is it?" demanded Devon when the pencil finally stopped moving.

Constable Cross pushed away from the receiver and looked uneasily at his comrade. "It was sent," he declared, "to Sergeant Buck Tearl, *Saut Sauvage*."

"What?" demanded the other.

"It must mean he's on his way here to take command," said Cross limply.

"Gosh!" mourned Devon. "Why can't they let us alone?"

"What did you expect?" returned Cross. "That they'd let two bum constables loaf here through the winter without sending somebody to boss 'em?"

The pair exchanged a sobered glance. It was no light matter for two men to be snowed-in together through long months of blackness; and the arrival of a third man would multiply the dangers of friction and discord: particularly when the newcomer held the authority to make the lives of the first two as disagreeable as he pleased.

"What's he like?" groaned Devon.

"Tearl? I don't know. He was on this side when I was in Alaska, and when I was in Alaska he had been sent somewhere else. It just happened that way. So far we haven't run across one another."

"I have heard o' dis Sergean' Tearl," put in the bearded Bruyas. "Dey say he is wan bad feesh."

"Everybody's heard of Tearl," said Cross.

Giffard's squinty eyes turned maliciously from one policeman to the other. "They say he's a devil," he remarked.

Constable Devon silenced the runt with a lengthy stare. "I've heard myself that he's bad medicine for trap thieves and whiskey blanc peddlers and other little slinking ferrets of the woods." He turned back casually to Cross. "On the other hand," he added consolingly, "he may not be so bad. You know Jimmie Poe? Poe says he's all right."

"Weren't they up at Herschell together a couple of winters ago?" asked Cross reflectively.

"Yes. The two got caught in a storm and had to coop-up in an igloo for three weeks. Each had a quarter's pay in his pocket and nothing much else. They were eating mittens before they got out, and on top of it all, Jimmie Poe had gone snow-blind."

Devon grinned. "But Buck Tearl kept him entertained. The sergeant—he was a corporal then—had found a walrus tusk somewhere, and he carved out a set of ivory dice. And the two spent three weeks in a snow-hut shooting craps by the light of a blubber lamp—"

"And Poe was snow-blind?" interjected Cross. "You mean he couldn't see anything?"

"Nothing at all. He couldn't see Tearl or his own bank roll or the dice or the spots on 'em. Maybe Tearl didn't even bother to draw the spots on 'em. Maybe he left his dice blanks. I don't know. What I'm getting at is to show you what a good guy he was."

Cross licked his lips meditatively. "I'd have liked to have been in that game."

"Sure you would," returned Devon. "You'd have made your killin' in about fifteen tosses. But not Buck Tearl. He'd call out the numbers that Jimmie couldn't see. 'Seven', 'eleven', 'big-Dick', 'box-cars', 'little Jodie', and sometimes they'd roll up right for Jimmie."

"Now if it had been you," mused Devon, "you'd have forgot Jimmy was playing too. Then he would have had nothing but time left on his hands for three weeks."

"You don't mean," broke in Cross, "that Jimmie won?"

Devon ignored the interruption. "For twenty-one days Corporal Buck Tearl sat there helping Jimmie to amuse himself. In the end, just before the storm broke and they were able to travel again, Tearl had a phenomenal run of luck and made forty-two passes and cleaned Jimmie for the works. But where another man would have mopped up in an hour Tearl squatted patiently and let Jimmie have his three weeks of fun. That's the kind of a pal Buck Tearl was."

Devon lifted the pot lid to peer into its bubbling interior, sniffed once or twice, and turned back to Cross. "What was that message about?" he suddenly remembered to ask.

"About a Yellow Knife up yonder being murdered a while back. The word must have gone down the other direction through Fort Resolution and Simpson, and finally reached the inspector. He was just telling Sergeant Tearl to send somebody to investigate."

"Is that all?" said Devon. "And I suppose Tearl'll be sending you or me up through a blizzard to make notes on a dead Boogie."

Cross looked resentfully towards the three Yellow Knives in the corner of the room. "Any of you know about a murder up your way?" he asked.

The Indians exchanged solemn glances and said nothing.

"You, Tom Salmonfish!" exploded the constable. "You know anybody who was murdered?"

"Nop," said Salmonfish indifferently.

Cross dropped his head menacingly and was about to start the tortuous process of extracting information from an Indian, when something arrested his attention. He raised his head and looked towards the frosted window, listening.

For five seconds he held motionless with one ear tilted upward. His companions likewise had frozen to silence and were watching Cross. There were no audible sounds save the howling of the wind outside and the bubbling of the kettle on the stove within. But the constable's companions waited expectantly, knowing that his woodsman's instincts had apprised him of some unusual note in the bellowing of the storm.

All at once Cross' alertness was backed up by a dog coming to life and sending a challenging bark through the outer darkness. The first husky was joined by a bass-throated friend, by a dozen, by forty savage, yelling brutes that aroused themselves from their nests in the lee of the barracks wall to fill the night with their frenzied babel.

"Wolves?" suggested Devon.

"Don't think so—" Cross stopped his speech and lifted a silencing finger.

In the other direction, from somewhere to the southward, they heard something breaking its way through the underbrush. Then, for a full minute, the wind sank fitfully and almost died. In that brief lull the sounds of a man's voice reached the shack. He was crossing the clearing in the storm. And then they heard him raise his tones higher, and a queer, sing-song tune came to them out of the night:

"Down in the woods lived a squaw and her old Injun.
Their only blankets were the cold frost and snow—"

The words of the song drifted to the shack in a melancholy baritone, and then the singer changed to a lugubrious minor key and repeated his dismal refrain, this time with full tremolo effects:

"Down i-hin the woods li-hived a squaw and her old In-jun.
Their o-honly blankets we-here the coooooold frost and snooow."

The crowd of huskies had charged around the barracks, flinging themselves at the stranger in a raving circle. But, whoever he was, he would not let the dogs flurry him until he had rounded off the full, last period of his song. Then he turned upon them with violent words, and the men inside heard the thud of something on hollow ribs.

The two constables stared at each other, and Devon moved towards the front entrance. But the newcomer was quicker. The latch rattled, the draw bar was pushed up, and an icy blast of weather filled the room. A muffled figure stumbled across the threshold. He was a slender, rangy, easy-moving individual, who had turned negligently to force the door shut behind him. As the latch caught he swung around to confront the occupants of the shack, and he appeared to take in every detail of the place with a single, flickering glance.

His head and shoulders were covered with drifted snow and a beading of ice had formed upon his eyelashes. The austerity of his features, the severe line of his mouth and his ascetic, high-bridged nose, was relieved by the mocking glimmer of his dark eyes and the sardonic expression of one upcrooked eyebrow. He ignored the Indians and the trappers as he curiously inspected one and then the other policeman.

"Which is Cross and which is Devon?" he asked.

Without waiting for a reply he bent flexibly at the hips and proceeded to pull his hooded parka over his black head. He dropped the white encrusted garment to the floor and stood erect, a trim, nonchalant figure clad in the royal scarlet of the Canadian police.

A glimpse of the chevrons on the tunic sleeve sufficed to wipe every vestige of expression from the faces of the two constables. They drew themselves up, stiff and soldierly, before the ranking uniform.

"I'm Cross," said the shorter, lighter-skinned man. "You're Sergeant Tearl."

"Right!" The newcomer broke into the constrained moment with a quick, infectious grin. He pulled off his mitten and impulsively held out his hand. "I've been looking forward to seeing you boys," he said. "How are you? Merry Christmas! When do we eat?"

CHAPTER XII
SERGEANT IN COMMAND

Kitchener faced the constables in his scarlet tunic with easy confidence, swaggering a little as Jerry might have done if he had stepped in to take command of the outpost at *Saut Sauvage*. Inwardly he was not so sure of himself.

He watched the pair warily. Jerry had said that he was not acquainted with Devon or Cross. But there remained the danger that one or another of the constables had seen him somewhere without his knowing. Both officers must have heard of the sergeant, and possibly carried mental pictures of him. Jerry was too vivid a personality not to leave strong impressions upon the people he met.

A guilty conscience may have made Kit oversensitive. The constables studied him critically for a moment, and then exchanged sidewise glances. For an instant Kit held his breath. What thought had struck them? Did they suspect something was wrong? It was an anxious moment. To be unmasked now would be calamitous.

Whatever his secret doubts he put up his boldest front. And all at once the tense atmosphere seemed to clear. The constables grinned at him in apparent comradeship and shook hands with him. If their suspicions had been aroused they evidently wanted to be more certain of their ground before they denounced him.

"I'm looking for a man who calls himself Jim Durand," he told his new fellows-at-arms. "He's a six-foot husky with big, bowed shoulders, a prize-fighter's arms and fists and a swarthy face that looks as if it had been sliced up with a knife some time or other. Anybody like that been around here recently?"

The two constables shook their heads. "Outside of these chaps and one or two bushmen we know," said Devon, "there hasn't been a living soul along this way in weeks."

"I lost his trail this morning," said Kit, "and so far haven't found it again. He's wearing a pair of square-webbed snowshoes that look as though they were woven over a waffle-iron. I hoped one of you might have seen his tracks."

"What's he wanted for?" asked Cross.

Kit had had a night and a day to think affairs out and to decide on his future course of action. He had made up his mind that in his dealings with Hell Bent he would play out the hand on his own responsibility, alone.

There were several reasons why he could not tell the constables the truth. If he let them know, for instance, that a murder had been committed in the old cabin at Great Owl Run they naturally would want to learn who the victim was, and their police-trained curiosity in that direction might lead to all kinds of embarrassing complications. They would search the river and perhaps find Jerry's body, and in his clothing or on his person there might be some identifying mark to label him as the real Sergeant Tearl. In which event Kit would have trouble explaining why he was wearing another man's uniform and perhaps even might be accused of his brother's murder.

It was too late now to abandon his imposture. Diane Durand knew him as Sergeant Tearl. If he had tried to change back to private citizenship she would discover the falsity of his previous claim: and having every reason to wish him out of the way, she would not hesitate to denounce him. He had to go on being a policeman.

As long as he was not found out there were advantages in playing out the rôle. He was the boss in this part of the woods, and every human being in the neighborhood had to step to his authority. By wearing the insignia of the police he held the moral prestige at any future meeting with Hell Bent. He could arrest his man or shoot him down, and there could be nobody to interfere or to question his act. Meanwhile, if he could learn anything of the old tragedy at Great Owl Run, he could keep the information to himself or use it as he saw fit. Circumstances would decide him. But for the present there would be no outside blundering to hamper him. It was safest to work alone.

So Kit did not allow the constables to think that he was much concerned over the fugitive's whereabouts. He said nothing about the man's being the ex-convict, Sim Bent, and was particular to use the alternative name of Durand.

"There's no charge against him," he said. "I'm looking for him on account of his niece, Miss Diane Durand. She followed him into the woods and somehow missed connections, and I picked her up farther down country. She's waiting at the old cabin down by Great Owl Run."

"You had his trail?" asked Constable Cross.

"Yes. He had two teams of dogs, one of which he drove ahead, the other running at his heels. I wasn't two hours behind him last night at midnight. There was no trouble following his tracks with a flashlight. But early this morning he suddenly turned east and entered that Yellow-Knife village by the long lake. That's where I lost him."

The two constables looked interested, but asked no questions. Apparently they hesitated to say anything that might reflect upon their superior officer's woodcraft.

Kit shook his head ruefully. "There are a thousand tracks around that camp, of course. Snowshoes and sledges and huskies' pads. The waffle-meshes entered on one side, and didn't come out again. Well, when I got there I searched the camp, looked in every teepee, talked to all the Indians. No good. The trail went into the camp, but the man wasn't there."

"What did the Yellow Knives say?" ventured Sergeant Devon.

"Hadn't seen him, that was all. It may have been true. He could have crossed through their camp while they were all parked in for the night. They sleep like a lot of mud-turtles. Maybe for a fact they didn't know a thing about him.

"I circled the village several times," Kit pursued, "but no waffle marks passing out."

"What do you think?" asked Devon.

"There's only one thing that could have happened. He must have had another pair of snowshoes with him, or else he stole a pair, and changed 'em after he got among the cluttered trails of the village. After that there wasn't any way of knowing which tracks were his.

"Well, I crawled into a teepee and caught a few hours of badly needed sleep," Kit finished. "Then I thought I might as well come on here and report."

He turned unexpectedly to the two trappers. "When did you two get here?" he asked.

Giffard's little eyes shifted uncomfortably before the sergeant's scrutiny. "This evenin'—early," he answered. "A little before dark."

"Either of you run across a stranger to-day?"

"No, sir," said Giffard.

"P'r'aps," insinuated the bearded Bruyas, "if we meet dis fellow we say de sergeant he seek for him. Eh, w'at?"

"Tell him if he wishes to find his niece to get in touch with the police post."

"It is a fonny t'ing to arrive in dis col' country when winter she come," Bruyas ventured to remark. "What is it he wish?"

"I understand he expects to trap a bit," Kitchener replied.

The two natives exchanged a fleeting glance, and Bruyas scowled and showed the ugly line of his broken teeth. "If he expect to use his trap on Great Owl Run we have somethin' to say about dat."

"Bruyas," explained the wizened Giffard, "runs his lines on the north side of that creek, and I on the south. There's no room for any others."

"What do you have—leases or something?" inquired Kit ironically.

"We have been on dose groun' for ten year," put in Bruyas darkly. "Dat's plenty long time so we can say odders keep out."

"Tell him anything you like as long as you don't make a police case of it," said Kit indifferently. He measured the pair with appraising eyes, and grinned at them. "After you've had a look at him you may not go quite so heavy on conversation."

Constable Cross had gone over to investigate the pot on the stove. He tasted and wrinkled his nose with a fine appreciation. "It's done," he announced.

Devon brought out a stack of crockery bowls and began dipping out the contents of the stew-pot. Places for three policemen were set at the one table boasted by the barracks. Giffard and Bruyas were served on the top of a packing box. The Yellow Knives were handed out their Christmas Eve dinner, catch-as-catch-can, crouched on the floor in the stifling hot corner behind the stove.

"We just received a radio message for you, sergeant," remarked Devon when Kitchener, as was the commanding officer's right, took his seat at the head of the table, facing the door.

Kit lifted his head quickly. "Where from?"

"Edmonton—from Inspector Bowman. He wants us to look into a murder among the Yellow Knives. I don't know just what it amounts to, if anything."

Kitchener nodded. This, he was thinking, was a fortunate excuse to return to the Indian village, which was not far from Great Owl Run. He could prowl about that neighborhood as much as he pleased, attending to his own affairs, and working ostensibly under the orders of Inspector Bowman. "They didn't say anything about it when I was in the village," he remarked.

"They wouldn't," said Constable Cross. "You can't cork-screw information out of those dull-blades."

"All right," announced Kitchener. "I'll go back down there in the morning."

Devon chuckled under his breath as he darted a triumphant glance at his fellow constable. He had predicted that Sergeant Tearl would turn out to be an agreeable chap. Here indeed was an officer after his own heart—a man who tackled a mean job himself instead of commanding an underling to do it.

"You tried to pump any of these three anacondas?" inquired Kit, glancing over his shoulder at the Indians, who were drinking their stew noisily out of tin pans.

"Sure," said Cross. "They don't know anything. But if you really want me to find out what they know, just say the word."

"Never mind," said Kit. "I'll make somebody talk when I get down below."

If the Indians knew they were the subject of conversation they gave no sign. The three continued to eat until the well-scoured bottom of the big cooking vessel came into view. This evidently was the sole purpose of their visit. When the pot was empty they wrapped themselves in their furs, stalked solemnly to the door and went out into the night without a word of thanks for the provender which the police had supplied them.

Giffard and Bruyas lingered after their meal for a couple of pipefuls of kinnikinnick mixed with tobacco. At length, however, Bruyas hoisted his bulk from the stool, upon which it might have been feared that he had become a permanent fixture.

"De leedle fox and mink will be lonesome waitin' in traps," he remarked. "I make my way back down. *Bon soir.* I see you again mebby. *Merci.*"

"I'll go with you," announced Giffard. He buttoned his cadaverous body into a bulky mackinaw coat. "Good-by, everybody." His piggy eyes shifted Kitchener's direction for a last squinting look, as though to make sure of remembering the sergeant if they met again.

He picked up his rifle and snowshoes, bowed his head to the blast that came through the open doorway, and followed Bruyas into the storm.

Devon, who was standing by the door, banged it shut. "If our nearest neighbors don't drop in again before next Christmas Eve," he remarked, "that'll make it once too often. If I had my choice between the two trappers and those Yellow Knives, I'd take a musk-ox."

Kitchener went to the window, scratched the thick frost with his nail, and looked out into the darkness. After a moment he turned back and started to gather up his duffle.

The constables observed him wonderingly. "What are you planning to do?" demanded Cross.

"I'm going back," announced Kit—"down towards Great Owl Run."

"To-night?"

"I don't know whether you two noticed, but this Giffard had a queer look in his eyes when I mentioned a girl left alone in that cabin." Kit scowled. "I don't know. Maybe he's all right. But I thought I might as well follow him back. He lives down that direction, doesn't he?"

"Yes, he does. The end of his trapping loop reaches that cabin on this side of the brook. Giffard! A measly animal. I wouldn't trust him anywhere on the outside of a jail cell."

"I thought not," said Kit. "Give me a fresh battery for my flashlight, will you?"

"Listen, sergeant," suggested Devon. "Let Cross go, or I will if you say so. There's no sense in your bucking this nor'-easter again to-night."

"Thanks," said Kit. "But I had plenty of sleep this afternoon. I'll go myself."

"We can give you dogs and a sledge," offered Cross.

"Don't need 'em. I left a team down at Great Owl Run." Kitchener slipped his arms into the parka that had been drying over the stove, and hitched his pack onto his shoulders.

"Don't know how long I'll be gone," he remarked. "If I happen to need either of you boys I can send word. You go on with your usual routine until you hear from me again."

Kitchener opened the front door and looked out into the blustering night. The trappers and the three Indians had vanished without a sound. But the line of their footprints turned westward, and presumably they were on their way home.

After a moment Kit stepped outside and kicked his toes into his snowshoe lashings. "If you see this Durand," he said in parting, "don't try to hold him, but keep in touch with him and let me know as soon as you can." He glanced back into the lighted, warm barracks room, and then resolutely faced the clouds of flying snow.

"So long," he called over his shoulder, and set forth on his return trip to Great Owl run.

CHAPTER XIII
LAST-STAND OUTPOST

In the great North the lands of "big-sticks" and "little-sticks" and the treeless arctic prairies are not divided evenly by the lines of latitude. There are no definitely marked borders of forestation. For long stretches the timber country dwindles through graduations of stunted, failing growth across the frontiers of the open barrens. But there are other places where the forests send out the massed array of their mightiest giants, like shock-forces, to wage the endless, bitter fight with the polar winds.

Great Owl Run stood at the head of one of these last-stand outposts of the great forests. A broad, sheltered valley and an unusual fertility of soil gave the trees a chance to root and grow tall and thrust their dense ranks northward in a hundred-mile fringe. Huge spruces and firs and wild, dark underwoods crowded each other in a jungle-like wilderness that reached to the southern edge of the deep-cut creek.

On the opposite bank of the stream the ground rose abruptly into a high plateau that was exposed to the furious assaults of the arctic gales. Here the forest stopped as suddenly as though the line had been cut level with axes. For a mile or so farther on a few dwarfed, wind-tortured trees struggled to hold their own, and after that there was nothing but the bare, frozen tundras reaching in a vast, appalling emptiness to the polar seas.

Kitchener Tearl came westward along the thickly wooded side of Great Owl Run as the smoky dawn was beginning to break. He had traveled all night down the creek, skirting the Indian village on the tributary lake towards the southwest, hurrying on his way because of the fear that Hell Bent might return to the cabin and leave again before Kit could intercept him. Kit was hoping at any time to cross the trail of the waffle-web snowshoes.

It had stopped snowing during the night and the wind was dying. Before the darkness paled Kit had seen patches of starlight through the scattering clouds. The storm was blowing itself out, and there was a promise of clear, below-zero weather for the holidays.

He was walking through the alders that skirted the high embankment of the ice-bound creek, scanning the ground before him, watching the shadows changing from purple to misty, twilight grays. The clearing and the cabin and the owl-infested woods, he knew, could not be far beyond.

As he peered ahead, expecting at any minute to see the break among the trees, he heard a sudden snapping sound behind him, and as he whirled to look he saw a man's muffled figure come out from behind a neighboring windfall.

Kitchener planted his feet apart and shifted his rifle for eventualities, and then his second glance reassured him. The newcomer was short and slight in build, in no wise resembling Bent. He shuffled forward into the open, and Kit recognized Giffard, the Runt.

The little trapper looked haggard in the early morning light, and as he drew nearer Kit noticed that he was limping slightly and that there was a streak of fresh blood across his left cheekbone.

"Hello!" remarked Kit. "What happened to you?"

"Who, me?" Giffard rubbed the back of his hand across his face, and then looked tentatively at his fingers. "Why, nothin' much, if you ask me. I just got torn a little in a bramble thicket."

To Kit the wound did not have the appearance of a thorn scratch, but he let the statement pass. "You live around here?" he inquired.

"My shack's down that way, about two mile in from the creek."

Kit eyed the man curiously. His back pack was thickly encrusted with snow, and it was apparent that he had not been home since he left *Saut Sauvage* the night before.

"Where does Bruyas live?" asked Kit.

Giffard pointed with his mittened thumb. "North side of the creek. He hangs out mostly along the barrens."

The little man moved closer, looked about him in a full circle, and lowered his voice confidentially. "Last night you wanted to know about an Indian murder, and I found out about one this morning. The Yellow Knives is more apt to talk to me than to a policeman. I run into a couple of 'em this A.M. and I asked 'em and they told me."

"Yes?"

"One of their bucks was shoved into an ice-hole on Long Lake by an Esquimau."

"I thought the Esquimaux had all gone back north by now," said Kit.

"Yeah. That's right. The bands come down in the summer to get wood for sleds and snowshoe frames, and they go back to the coast in the Winter for the seal hunting. But this man was taken sick an' left behind. He's been moochin' around here ever since."

"He murdered a Yellow Knife?"

"That's the story. Picked him up by the heels and chucked him through a hole in the ice."

"What's his name?" asked Kit.

"Oogly," said Giffard.

"Ugly?"

"Yeah. Only you spell it with an 'O.'"

"Where is he now?"

"That'd be hard to tell. The Indians have been hunting him for a month and ain't found him yet. He's too good a hider."

"Thanks, anyhow," said Kit. "I'll look into it."

He started on his way again, and after a momentary hesitation Giffard decided that he might as well follow along. The trapper did not actually accompany Kit, but hovered aimlessly a few paces behind.

They reached the clearing in the nebulous light of daybreak. Kit halted at the edge of the alders to reconnoiter. Before him lay half an acre of stumpy ground, hemmed in on three sides by the deep forest, and flanked on the fourth side by the steep-banked creek. The cabin faced the west, and stood on the sheer brink beside the stream.

Kit had seen the place only in a pitch-black hour of horror two nights ago when he and Diane Durand had stumbled out of the woods into the blood-spattered room. His eyes had grown hard and grim as he paused under the alders, inspecting the lonely dwelling.

The cabin probably had been standing there, weathering and rotting these many seasons. The place was more forlorn and tumble-down even than he had supposed. Yet somebody had been making a few pathetic repairs. Since his visit a square of old tarpaulin had been tacked over the hole in the roof, the door was properly squared in its frame, and the broken window-panes had been replaced with rabbit pelts. A wisp of blue smoke issued from the crumbling chimney. Apparently there was somebody inside.

From the cabin Kit's glance shifted across the dismal clearing. The snow was trampled every direction by a confusion of snowshoe prints. Perhaps they had been left there by Diane Durand, perhaps by others. He saw only that there were no waffle-web tracks. But this meant nothing. He knew now that Hell Bent was equipped with an extra, unidentified pair of raquettes. For all Kit could tell the man at this moment might be watching from one of the cabin windows.

There was nothing to do but accept the chance. Kit ventured into the open, but a hand reached after him to pluck at his sleeve.

"There's somebody in there," Giffard informed him in a husky whisper.

"Yes, I know. No doubt it's the young woman I was telling the constables about."

"There's somebody else," the trapper insisted. "A man. I saw his face at one of the window chinks."

Kit looked around with a sobering expression. "Which window?"

"He ain't there now," said Giffard.

Kitchener faced the man with a narrowing scrutiny. "You mean you saw him a while ago? You've been here before?"

Giffard's eyes dropped and he relapsed into a sullen silence.

"If you'll take the advice of the police," said Kit evenly, "you'll keep away from this place in the future." He turned on his heel and started across the clearing.

He advanced without a sound, a wary eye on the door and the window openings. So far he had passed unchallenged, but as he drew opposite the cabin the breathless quiet was assailed by a savage, barking chorus, and a pack of dogs came tearing around the corner of the building to fling themselves at the intruder.

They were Kit's dogs. Buzz-saw, the big Chinook, charged in the fore and behind him came the tatterdemalions that Kit had purchased in the Chippewyan encampment. The four beasts caught the familiar scent at the same instant, recognized their man, and they sat down in a half circle to yowl beseechingly for breakfast.

It was too late to arrive unobtrusively as Kit had hoped to do. He strode to the door and flattened himself against the frame, to be out of range of the flanking windows. The latchstring had been pulled through its hole, and he found that the bar was down. He rapped heavily with his fist.

The answer was unexpectedly prompt. "If you don't get away from here I'll shoot you again, and this time you'll get the full charge!" The voice came from behind the barred door—a woman's voice, tingling with hostility. It was Diane Durand.

"I beg your pardon?" said Kitchener.

There was a short, uncertain interlude before the girl spoke again. "Who are you?" she asked.

"It's Tearl."

"Oh!" she said, and there was another pause.

"Who'd you think I was?"

"Another man," she told him through the barrier.

"Giffard?"

"I don't know his name. I don't want to. A little, horrid, rat-faced thing."

"That's Giffard."

"You tell him to keep away from here."

"What did he do?" asked Kit.

"Nothing. He didn't get a chance."

"And you say you shot him?" demanded Kit incredulously.

"I certainly did."

"In Heaven's name—what for?"

"He came here and tried to give me a silver fox skin for a present. I told him I didn't want any presents, and for him to keep out. He tried to force his way in, and I slammed the door in his face. Then he went to get an ax, saying he was going to smash down the door."

Kit looked around at the furtive figure that still lurked at the edge of the clearing, and his left eyebrow slanted upward at an unpleasant angle. "I guessed right!" he muttered. "I thought so."

"What?" asked the girl.

"You mean you really shot him?" Kit asked again.

"When he started back with his ax from the other side of the clearing I let him have it."

"What with?"

"A shotgun. The one that was on your sledge."

"Oh!" exclaimed Kit, realizing for the first time that the girl was telling the truth. There had been a double-barreled twelve-gauge among the effects that Jerry had traded him, and also a box of shells. He recalled Giffard's limp and the furrowed streak over his cheekbone. Diane actually fired at the trapper, and a couple of the little missiles had found flesh.

"Well," demanded the defiant voice from behind the door, "I suppose I'm not allowed to defend myself."

Kit grinned maliciously at Giffard who, this time, was staying at a discreet distance. *Noondea*, the weasel, probably in the future would sell his silver fox pelts and not try to give them away to helpless-looking maidens in lonely cabins.

"Who's in there with you?" Kit asked the girl.

There was a dead silence on the other side of the door.

"Hello!" he persisted. "Did you hear me? Are you alone?"

Again there was no answer. Kitchener's half-smiling lips suddenly drew together in a set and rigid line. "Open that door!" he commanded.

"I'm not going to," returned Diane. "This for the moment is my home, and I'm not going to let anybody in."

Kitchener unslung his ax and leaned the handle against the door-frame. Then he shoved his pistol holster around to the front of his belt, and unfastened the flap. There was a stealthy movement behind the door crack and he thought he heard two people whispering.

The genial-featured Kit magically was gone, and in his place stood a hard-jawed, stern-eyed man, cool and nerveless and dangerous. There was somebody in that room with the girl, and his implacable instincts told him that that somebody must be Jerry Tearl's murderer.

He caught up his ax, swung the blade, and drove the bit deep into the quivering door. A second crashing blow slashed a six inch chip out of the wood above the latch-hole. A gasping protest sounded from within, and as he lifted his ax a third time the bar rattled suddenly in its socket and the door was flung open.

Diane Durand confronted him in the dim opening, her head up, her eyes aflame, a shotgun gripped against her taut body.

"You keep out of here!" she warned the intruder.

Kit scarcely noticed her. Intuition told him that she would be too squeamish to fire at such close range. A more imminent peril awaited him in the gloom behind her.

He tried to peer into the thick, smoky atmosphere of the cabin, and was aware of a gliding movement on the farther side of the room. The girl was attempting recklessly to bar his way. He strode across the threshold and grabbed the barrel of the gun. A tug and a twist, and the gun was wrenched from her hands. He flung the weapon through the door, into the snow outside.

"You—" she tried to say, and stopped with a choking sound as his elbow jammed itself into her ribs. He shouldered her aside ruthlessly and strode past her.

In the dingy light he made out two upright figures standing stolid and motionless before him. Both were short and squat in build. Neither was Hell Bent. He needed only a glance to assure himself of that. With his pistol clenched for business his glance darted around the murky interior, and then checked in blinking wonderment as a squalling little human cry suddenly greeted him from the bunk.

"There!" broke in Diane Durand in a tense and furious voice. "You've done it! I knew it! You've gone and wakened him!"

Kit was staring weakly at a tiny, squirming bundle, tucked up in a blanket on the lower bunk. He was too flabbergasted to speak or to think. At that moment an enemy could have shot him dead without a flicker of resistance on his part.

Diane had rushed at him in an outburst of indignation. "You bully!" she exploded. "You brute! I told you to stay out. Oh, doggone it! After all the time we've had getting him asleep! You've waked the baby!"

CHAPTER XIV
SQUATTER'S RIGHTS

Kit stared goggle-eyed, first at the girl, at the strange, dumpy figures watching him from the half-light by the smoldering fireplace and again at the small, kicking, whimpering object in the swaddling blankets. His puzzled glance finished the circuit of the room, and he saw there was nobody else. Feeling flat and foolish, he slipped his pistol back into the holster, turning his back for the moment, trying to believe that nobody had seen him take it out in the first place.

After he had surreptitiously hitched his holster back behind his hip he looked around at the girl. "Where's your uncle?" he asked, and his manner became stiff and dignified, as it should be with a sergeant of police.

Her brilliant eyes suddenly grew stony and uncommunicative. "I don't know," she said.

"Has he been here?"

"No."

"When do you expect him?"

"I don't know."

"Have you heard anything from him?"

"No."

Kitchener's vision gradually was accustoming itself to the dingy light in the room. The fireplace seemed to draw badly and the smoke hung like a blanket from the ceiling. He scrutinized the two shapes in the haze before him, moving closer to see them better and arching one puzzled eyebrow as his gaze shifted from one to the other.

They were a singular looking pair, not much more than five feet tall, as sturdy and rotund and solidly put together as a couple of thirty-six gallon barrels. Kit grinned at the thought. A couple of perfect thirty-sixes!

In shape and in outward appearance they were exactly alike. Both wore thick-quilted pants, long, loose shirts of dressed skins, and clumsy fur boots. Both had slant, mongol eyes set deep behind plumped-out cheekbones, both wore their slick, black hair in the same square-bobbed manner, both smiled at him blandly and confidently as a pair of amiable children. How he guessed it Kit could not have said, but by some occult system of identification he discovered that one was a man and the other a woman. He had never seen any people from the Arctic seas, as far as he remembered, but he knew at once that these two were Esquimaux.

He spoke abruptly to the masculine part of the team. "What's your name?" he asked.

The man seemed to know something of English. "Oogly," he promptly answered.

"Oogly?" Kitchener's eyelids twitched slightly as he stared at the round, good-natured countenance. "You don't mean it?"

"Yup!" The man beamed upon the stranger, apparently much pleased by this opportunity for introductions. He pointed with a stumpy thumb. "This one, my wife. Her name, Mayauk."

The woman's lips parted and her teeth flashed in a smile as coquettishly feminine as the most beguiling dimples of any beauty anywhere. Her features were as broad and flat as Oogly's, yet at that moment she seemed almost pretty, while her husband, even at his best, remained always as unlovely as his name.

"The baby," condescended Miss Durand, "is called Uttaktuak."

Kit looked curiously at the girl. "Friends of yours?"

"Yes," she said simply.

"How long you known 'em?"

"Since yesterday morning." Her glance strayed gently towards the compact little bundle on the bunk. "They just happened to find their way here. The baby had the croup, and they were frightened. I steamed it out and greased it up, and it's better I think—I hope." Her eyes turned resentfully to the intruder. "She might get well if she weren't kept awake by axes and hob-nail boots and the big, loud voices of the Royal Canadian Mounted Police."

Kit flushed, and then grinned deprecatingly. "I couldn't very well know that you had a baby here—now could I?"

"While I am living here," she said, "this is my home, my demesne. It's my privilege to say who comes in and who stays out."

"By what right?" he inquired mildly.

"Squatter's rights," she flashed back at him.

"You move fast," he laughed. "It was my belief that it took more than a couple of days and nights to gain a squatter's title. However, we'll let it go at that. This is your castle and moat and grange. The police'll stay out, unless"—his brows contracted and he looked at her pointedly—"unless they find you harboring a criminal."

She drew a short breath and the span between her curving eyelashes lessened by a fraction. "What do you mean?" she asked.

Kitchener spoke low, so that only she could hear. "Oogly," he said, "is wanted for murder."

Diane's pretty mouth sagged open, and for the next few seconds she could not seem to think of any fitting thing to say.

"Inspector Bowman radioed the *Saut Sauvage* outpost to get busy on the case," he informed her. "Oogly, it seems, upended a Yellow-Knife brave over a hole in the ice and shoved him through."

"You don't know that it's true," returned the girl impetuously. "Nobody saw it. Even the Indians who are trying to kill him—" Diane stopped short and bit her lip, as though she had decided that she was saying too much.

"Oh, they are?" exclaimed Kit. "I didn't know that!" He wrinkled his brow thoughtfully. "So that's why they won't talk. Sort of private feud. Going to settle it themselves in the good old-fashioned way." His glance searched the girl's anxious face. "Who told you they were going to kill him?"

"Why, nobody—" she began uncertainly.

"Oogly himself, wasn't it?" Kit hazarded.

Reluctantly she nodded. There was no evading the shrewdly questioning eyes that watched her so intently. "They've been hunting him for nearly a month—Oogly and his wife and baby," she admitted. "They were well hidden, and they probably wouldn't have been found—only the baby got sick, and they came out looking for help."

Her manner and mood had changed mercurially. The cold defiance of her eyes gave way to a beseeching warmth and softness. "There is no proof," she said—"only the accusations of a lot of irresponsible savages. Nobody saw any crime committed. You can't arrest him, can you, on anything as flimsy as that?"

Kitchener was not thinking about Oogly's escapades just then. He was seeing Diane with a new vision, discovering an unexpected sweetness in her glance and her tenderly curving mouth.

"I suppose not. I don't know." He really hadn't much sense of what he was saying.

"I'll let you see the baby some time," the girl vouchsafed. "It's got the funniest, snappiest eyes, and it says things in Esquimau. Think of it! A little baby that can talk in Esquimau! And poor Oogly! If he were taken away down south and put on trial—he'd die. You know that. In a foul, stuffy courtroom! A hunter of the wide floes who has never breathed anything but the clean, cold arctic wind! And if he dies there's nobody to look after Mayauk and Uttaktuak, and they'd both die."

She paused with a gulp, and Kitchener was amazed to see the sparkle of tears on her lashes. "It would be unfair. It would be cruel!" Her hand went to him and for an instant touched his sleeve. "Please! Please—you won't, will you?"

"I can at least promise that I'll investigate thoroughly before I—"

Kit checked himself and looked out through the open door of the cabin. A harshly quavering noise came from somewhere across the clearing, and as he lifted his head sharply he saw a great, dark object soar off against the dusky, morning sky. The thing drifted above the open ground, with a hollow, querulous cry, and a moment later disappeared in the black woods towards the south. It was one of the great, slaty-white owls, evidently going home after a night of foraging.

Diane had turned to peer over Kit's shoulder, and he felt a tremor suddenly pass through her slender body. "I hate them," she said in a voice of low intensity. "They cross over to the barrens at night to eat things alive, and they come back in the morning glutted. There's not a single small creature left living in this part of the woods."

Kit was not listening. His attention had been arrested by a movement on the edge of the clearing at the eastern side. He had left Giffard in the alders, and the trapper still waited there among the shielding branches, a peeping, skulking shadow. But he was no longer alone. Two other furtive shadows had appeared beside him.

As he watched Kit's eyes began to bulge. Instead of two or three there were now five or six of them—stark, gray silhouettes that had emerged stealthy-footed from the underbrush.

Diane had seen his back stiffen as he edged towards the doorway. "What is it?" she asked.

"Don't know. Stay where you are."

Kit leaned his shoulder against the door-frame and tried to see through the pearly haze of the dawn. He counted eight now, silent, somber shapes, forming like a skirmish line along the dark edges of the thickets, and as he watched three or four others stole furtively from the woods.

As though a soundless command had been given, the group all at once began to advance towards the cabin. There were a dozen or more of them, moving forward in a ragged file that spread the full width of the clearing. They came on without haste, but with a purposeful stealth and deliberation, dodging and gliding from stump to stump, as though they expected to get close to the cabin before they were discovered.

Kit suddenly stepped into the open. "Stop!" he shouted.

The on-creeping figures froze to immobility like so many partridges in scanty cover.

"What do you want?" he demanded.

Two of the advance intruders met the challenge by standing boldly erect among the stumps. The foremost of the pair was near enough so Kit could see the man's lean, parchment-like countenance and almost feel the intensity of the wary, watchful eyes. He held a carbine aslant across his flat-belted stomach, and Kit's ranging glance discovered that all the others were armed. They were Indians—Yellow Knives.

Kitchener was certain that he had seen the leader somewhere before. He was a tall and skinny savage, all ribs and knobby bones, with a dirty and grotesquely sharp face, like the face of a gargoyle that had been left in the weather too long in a sooty city.

"You give Oogly to us." The leader made his demand without heat, and yet there was a stolid resoluteness in his manner that would not be easily cowed.

Kit remembered the man now. He was one of the Yellow Knives who had dined last night at *Saut Sauvage*. The cadaverous one, he recalled, was known as Tom Salmonfish.

"What do you want with Oogly?" he temporized.

"We come get 'um," said Salmonfish coolly. "A big lot of us come now. We take 'um along."

"What for?" insisted Kitchener.

There was an unpleasant mutter of voices along the line, and the men on the outskirts straightened from their crouching postures and stalked over to form a group around Salmonfish. They made it quite clear that all were ready to back up their leader's demands.

"I'm not saying Oogly is here," Kit parried after a trenchant pause. "But if he were, why do you want him? What's he done?"

"He killed our man!" one of the younger Indians blurted out truculently.

"How do you know he did?" asked Kit. "Did anybody see him do it?"

He was aware of a light footstep behind him, and without looking around he knew it was Diane Durand standing at his elbow, one small hand firmly touching his back. "Don't give him up!" she whispered. "You can count on me. We'll fight 'em if we must."

Kit's glance swept the pressing circle of dark, sullen faces, estimating their potentialities for trouble-making. They did not look like a crowd that would be amenable to argument or reasoning. But Kit could do no less than try to make them see the light.

"Who saw this man killed?" he asked suddenly. "You make a charge. You say your man was murdered. Who saw it done?"

There was a restless stirring of feet, a grunted word or two, but nobody answered. There was no sign of receptive intelligence in the lowering eyes that were watching him and the door behind him.

"You, Tom Salmonfish!" Kit stabbed at the man with his forefinger. "Did you see this murder done? Or you? Or you? Or you?"

The pointing finger singled out first one and then another of the Indians. "Tell me! I want to know. I'm a policeman. If Oogly is a killer I want to arrest him. I'll take him to trial. If any of you saw the murder you'll have to come with us. I'll arrest you as material witnesses. You'll be forced to stand up in open court and make your charges. If Oogly's proven guilty we'll hang him. Come on. I want to know. Who saw the murder?"

"We don't want 'um hung," said Salmonfish, his little coal eyes gleaming with maliciousness and stubbornness. "You give Oogly to us."

Kit advanced a pace, but the threatening line did not yield an inch. The men all held carbines or rifles tightly gripped, and most of them carried knives and pistols loose in their belts. Three or four were thumbing the hammers of their guns, without even pretending to disguise the fact that the muzzles were menacing the policeman. The gang of avengers were beginning to chafe at all this parleying, and anybody could have seen that mere words would not hold them much longer in check. If their man wasn't handed over to them very soon, they would go in and get him.

Although Kit realized that his persuasive efforts were foredoomed to failure, he was determined to stave off hostilities as long as he possibly could. He looked around the glowering circle with a bright, accusing scorn.

"If there has been a murder," he challenged, "where is the body? Have you brought it with you? The body of the dead man? In law we call it the *corpus dilecti*. If nobody saw the murder done and nobody has the body of the dead to show, then there can have been no murder!"

It was a nice legal point and Kit could not help bringing it up, even though he knew in advance that the niggling little technicalities of his chosen profession could not possibly bear any weight with these surly children of the wilderness. In any event his peroration was punctured flat by an unexpected, startling voice, speaking up behind him.

"The body drowning under much ice. Nobody find um now."

Kit turned on his heel to see the broad-beamed countenance of Oogly cheerfully grinning in the doorway.

He closed one eye meaningly, trying desperately to warn the Esquimau to keep quiet. But Oogly perhaps did not understand the white man's method of issuing a warning with a sly eyewinker.

He pushed forward to fill the doorway with his rolling bulk and looked with good-natured triumph at the men who had come to take him away.

"Nobody find the body anymore," he declared. "No difference. He is dead a long time sure. Oogly killed um."

CHAPTER XV
THE NIGHT HARRIERS

It was too late to stop the Esquimau's talking. Kit stood dumbfounded, staring at him. Oogly either had gone stark crazy, or else he was a man devoid of fear. He had forced himself into public notice, and judging by his wide, incorrigible grin he was enjoying his unique position immensely.

From the demeanor of the Yellow Knives, a person unfamiliar with the Indian temperament might have imagined that they either had failed to hear or understand. Not a man moved nor spoke, not a muscle quivered. They waited for the outlander to go on, watching him in a dead, flinty silence, like wolves watching a swimming caribou.

Oogly was more than willing to oblige. He not only admitted killing the Yellow-Knife brave, but he told all about it in picturesque detail. He seemed to think it was a piece of work that his modesty ought not to keep hidden.

"The man him praying against my fish," he explained genially. "So drowning him had to be."

Kit no longer tried to interfere. What was the use? The mischief was accomplished. Oogly could swear himself blue in the face with denials, but nothing that could be said after this could ever sway or stay the purpose of the savages who had come to get him.

"What do you mean," demanded Kitchener—"praying against your fish?"

"So nobody of the fish would eat at my fishing hook," declared Oogly.

The Esquimau had come a step beyond the open doorway, so everybody could look at him while he told his outrageous tale. In his queerly chosen words of English, helped out by vivid pantomime, he showed them exactly how and why the killing was done.

Oogly, it seemed, was fishing through a hole in the ice on Long Lake, which emptied its chilly waters into Great Owl Run. He had been catching plenty of fish—innumerable fish—if his hearers could believe the number of times he jerked his pretended line out of the imaginary hole in the ice. Then along came the Yellow-Knife fisherman.

The newcomer chopped himself a hole not far from Oogly's splendid spot for fish. He dropped a line of his own in the water and knelt down on the ice.

The kneeling posture was the man's undoing. The Esquimau could tell that he was praying. When the fish stopped biting on Oogly's hook he knew that the Indian was praying against his fish. When the fish started to come wriggling and flapping out of the water at the other hole then he knew that the Indian was praying the fish onto his own hook. Oogly now was catching none, and the other man was hauling them out as fast as he could pray.

This, to the Esquimau's simple method of thought, was a justifiable cause for homicide. He walked over to the other fisherman, upended him by the heels and pushed him down headfirst through the hole in the ice. By making little explosive sounds with his puffed-out lips, Oogly showed them how the bubbles came to the surface for a minute or two, and then stopped coming.

"Awright now," said the Esquimau, winding up his tale. "Finean' dandy! Oogly go back and fishing lucky once again."

That was the story, and after its cheerful recounting Oogly leaned his squat bulk against the doorframe as he waited placidly to find out what the dead man's friends were going to do about it.

Kitchener was aghast. He had never heard a tale so bloodthirsty and at the same time so naïve and childlike in its telling.

He looked obliquely at the Yellow Knives, and nudged Diane's arm. "Inside!" he said under his breath.

"You come along now," Tom Salmonfish said to Oogly.

The Indian did not raise his voice, but the glitter of his eyes was like a baneful flame. He said something to his companions, and with that soundless, gliding motion that is peculiar to all forest-born creatures, the bunched group of men spread out right and left in a line that flanked the front of the cabin.

Kitchener backed into the doorway, shoving Diane and Oogly into the cabin behind him. He reached around with the toe of his foot and pulled the door towards him, so he would be able to slam it shut with the least possible delay.

There could be no doubt about the intentions of the Yellow Knives. They had made up their minds to seize their man, drag him away, and somewhere in the dark woods mete out their own cruel, remorseless justice, which demanded an eye for an eye, a tooth for a tooth, a life for a life.

Kit was not deluding himself. These men wore store shirts and refused to labor on Sundays, but under the veneer of the missionary teachings they were still the same savages as their fierce and brutal forefathers. If he tried to save Oogly it meant a fight to the death. They were a sinister-looking crowd at this moment, and they had made it clear that they neither respected nor feared the police uniform. He could hear the click of rifle hammers up and down the line, and he knew they were all set to rush the cabin the instant their leader gave the word.

Off on the other side of the clearing Giffard, the Runt, was seated on a stump, like an ominous specter watching events. No help could be expected from him. He had met with a rebuff that morning that his shriveled and spiteful nature could never forget. So he sat tensely now and waited, and Kit knew by the look of him that anything that happened to the occupants of the cabin would be all right with Giffard. He even might have egged the Indians on, had there been any need for that.

In the middle of the clearing, moving in the heavy snow between two stumps, Kit caught sight of a tiny, gray-furred animal which was struggling through the drifts, apparently trying to gain the shelter of the nearer thickets. It was an old, whiskered house-rat. Kit recalled that there had been rats in the cabin roof, and apparently this one had been gassed out of his home by the smoking chimney.

The human mind is subject to the queerest aberrations. It was strange that at this moment when Kit should have been terribly concerned with his own troubles he could find time to think about a rat. But this little creature was in a bad plight. It would starve or freeze to death surely if it tried to live in the woods, and if it were caught in the open by the predatory monsters that dwelt in the neighborhood—

Even at that moment Kit was conscious of a shadowy flutter in the air above him, and he lifted his head in time to see one of the great, snowy owls floating across the murky sky. The sharp senses of the Indians also had caught the impalpable whisking of sound, and, without exception, they too forgot their own affairs long enough to look up into the morning dusk.

The huge, pallid night-bird flew softly above the roof of the cabin and hovered for a moment to peer downward with his stupid, golden-tinged eyes. Kit heard the Yellow Knives begin to mutter among themselves in their own, ancient speech, and he saw them stir uneasily and crowd closer towards the wall of the cabin. It was not a move of hostility, but of fear, the impulse to hunt shelter. The savage faces were suddenly stricken with awe and superstitious dread. This bird, as all Yellow Knives knew, belonged to *Wetikoo*, the Devil's regions, and they did not wish him to fly above them.

The great owl was a weird apparition in the ghostly morning light. A soft, downy body, poised graciously on soundless wings, at first glance he seemed gentle and dovelike in his white-plumaged innocence. And then, at closer range, might be seen his frightful head, the diabolically hooked beak, the beautiful snowy floss of his cheeks and throat dabbled in fresh blood. He had killed and dined gluttonously many times through the night, and on his way back to the dark pits of the forest he could pause in the quiet of dawn for one more killing.

The owl saw the gray rat wallowing in the snow, and by an imperceptible movement of his expanded pinions he changed his course, slackened his silent flight. Some clairvoyance of instinct at that instant warned the rat of the stealthy form that had just skimmed the tree-tops. His sharp, twitching nose twisted upward, he spotted the monstrous thing drifting like a fog-wraith above him, and he tried to run, shrieking in terror.

For those few seconds the men in the clearing, white and Indian, lost sight of their own grim business to watch tensely this lesser drama of the wilderness.

The rat was doomed. Its tiny feet and legs sank deep in the loose packed snow and it piled a drift in front of itself as it tried to drag its body forward. The nearest thicket was a dozen yards away, and there wasn't a chance of its gaining cover.

The feathered legs of the owl reached down stiffly and the terrible talons opened for their clutching stroke. Unhurried, unexcited the big bird swerved and dipped earthward as lightly as a wafted ball of fluff. Backed against a stump the rat turned at bay, squealing insanely.

The owl had turned his staring eyes towards the men for a moment, and then he went about his butcher's work, as indifferent to the human spectators as though he were the unearthly spirit that the Indians believed him to be. The men of the forest were mortally afraid of the devils that owned these birds, and never dared to molest them. There was no beast of the wilderness able to cope with the giant owls. So they grew up without the instinct of fear.

Like a fleshless, disembodied thing, as aloof from the world, as quiet as death, the great owl swooped.

What prompted Kitchener's act, he could not have said. But somehow he found his pistol butt set comfortably in the arch of his hand. His sights notched themselves in line, and his finger squeezed the trigger.

He fired—not at the swift-moving owl, which was mostly invulnerable feathers—but at the crouching rat. Nothing could have saved the little animal, and it is better to die instantaneously than to be plucked to bits alive. Kit might have missed the rushing bird, but the rat was standing still. As the report slammed across the clearing the small, gray body flopped headless in the snow, twitched once or twice, and settled quietly at rest.

The great owl, almost scooping the ground, braked his descent as his victim crumpled beneath him. The connoisseur of death recognized death at sight. He was no vulturous feeder. He took his meat alive. With a throaty, hissing sound that was not like any earthly sound, he lifted himself on his shadows of wings, and vanished between here and there like a smoke-puff dissipating in twilight.

Kitchener straightened his back and eased out a breath that was threatening to burst his lungs. He looked at the beheaded rat lying so still under its stump, he looked across the clearing at the gaping-mouthed Giffard, and then he turned to look at the Indians.

Something had happened to the Yellow Knives in that astonishing moment. Kit felt the change in their manner, he saw it in their gawking faces and in their awed, incredulous eyes. They were huddled in an irresolute group not far from the cabin door, watching him askance.

In an intuitive flash he realized that a miracle had intervened in his behalf. These were no longer the fierce, rash men who would have shot him down and burned the cabin above him. They knew nothing about the law, but they knew much about shooting. They had seen him snip off a rat's head with his short-barreled gun at twenty paces. That sight somehow had spoiled their stomachs for fighting. That same, quick-firing gun might as readily pop off a half-dozen Yellow-Knife heads before they could stop its spitting.

It might be impossible even to down a man who dared to cheat one of the devil-birds of its prey. Such a one, who stood unsmitten afterwards and mocked at fate with one high-cocked eyebrow—it was more than possible that he also might be under the diabolical protection.

Kit read all of this in the guileless, bewildered faces, and he made the most of his advantages. He moved nonchalantly outside the doorway, keeping his pistol in his hand.

"You, Tom Salmonfish!" he said so sharply that the Indian jumped. "What do you mean by bringing your friends here? It's a bad place. None of you may get out again."

Salmonfish raised his anxious, squinting eyes, moistened his lips and started to say something. Then he ducked his head with a spasmodic movement and almost seemed to shrink within himself as another huge, blood-smeared owl sailed in from the barrens to cross low over the cabin roof.

Before the great, lazy-drifting bird had passed across the clearing a second and a third and a fourth hove in sight above the whited line of trees. One of them wheeled for an instant in his course, peered around below him with solemn, glaring eyes. It might have seemed for those few seconds as though he were trying to stare the watching men out of countenance, twisting his gory head from side to side while he circled and singled out individuals for his somber scrutiny.

The Yellow Knives refused to face the evil eyes looking down upon them. Their shoulders hunched up, their heads bowed, and they huddled together, looking absurdly like people who had been caught out unprotected in bad weather. Kit, who was watching them narrowly, suddenly raised his voice in a wild, singing shout:

"The owl and the pussycat went to sea in a beautiful pea-green boat.
They took some honey and plenty of money wrapped up in a five-pound note."

He howled the refrain after the owls and beat the time in the air with the muzzle of his pistol.

For a few seconds the Indians seemed to stop breathing, and they looked at Kit like so many petrified men. They could not have understood the words. It might have been an infernal chant for all they knew. In that hushed nook of the forest the profane outburst of noise was nerve-shattering. Two or three of the Indians on the outskirts began to edge away from the cabin, and those in front heard the uneasy shuffling behind them and were quick to catch the infection.

Before Tom Salmonfish could have realized what was happening he found himself alone, confronting the mad white man who dared to taunt the fearsome owls, who could shoot like a fiend, whether he really was one or not, and who was waving his deadly pistol with a crazy disregard for those in front of it.

Tom Salmonfish might have stuck, in spite of the owls and the loony policeman, if anybody had stood behind him. But his braves had thought of something to do somewhere else. Some of them were already half way across the clearing, peering furtively over their shoulders as the owls disappeared in the black timber below the creek. The remaining two or three lingered momentarily, and then they shambled in an aimless fashion behind their comrades.

"I'd beat it," said Kit.

Tom Salmonfish scowled after his departing friends, and then his morbid glance came back for an instant to the doorway. "We comin' back an' get um soon," he threatened. "Plenty time to-morrow. Plenty more of us."

He stalked away with dignity to overtake the last man of the file, who felt himself being crowded from behind, and stepped on the heels of the man in front of him. It was like a push given to a line of ten-pins. Those up ahead moved faster to keep out of the way of those in the rear, who moved faster to keep up. By the time the retreat began to lose itself in the underbrush on the farther side of the clearing it had begun to look like a contest to see who could go at the best walking clip, without running.

Kit closed the door and dropped the heavy draw-bar. He looked around the smoky interior, and laughed. Mrs. Mayauk Oogly stood beside him, smiling up at him, a friendly, cheerful smile. With a sudden surging of good spirits he leaned forward and kissed the Esquimau woman first on one roly-poly cheek, and then on the other.

This done, he thought there ought to be no partiality, so he turned and caught Diane Durand in his arms and firmly kissed her startled, open mouth. As the girl gasped and lithely struggled free he looked around at the man who had caused all the trouble.

"We've got a reprieve for you, Oogly," he said. "You lucky stiff! Now you can be hanged decently, as you should be, by the police."

CHAPTER XVI
THE HONORABLE MURDERER

The promise of future punishment did not bother Oogly in the least. He lived happily in his immediate moments, and anything that happened to him at a later date was something not to be worried about until that time came. Any day after to-day was too remote even to be thought about.

He gazed up in rapt admiration at the man who had chased off the Yellow Knives and laughed at their departing backs. Oogly was a humorist himself, and loved to laugh as well as anybody. His grin of appreciation included his chin, the top of his forehead and both frost-bitten ears.

Suddenly he thought of something that had been overlooked on this joyful occasion. He ran to the bunk and came back with the baby in his arms. "Uttaktuak want kissum too," he said.

"Being female," remarked Kit, "she would." He bent lightly and touched his lips to the funny little sleeping face that Oogly held up to him. Then he looked around at Diane with mocking eyes.

The girl was rubbing her mouth with the back of her hand. She flushed with annoyance for an instant, and then her mood changed and she smiled caustically. "You've certainly given us three women a glorious Christmas," she remarked in biting irony.

As she observed Kit from under her thick, hazel eyelashes her face suddenly grew sober. "Did you mean that?" she demanded.

"I always mean it," said Kitchener lightly. "Just ask any of the girls—"

She shook her head impatiently. "You know what I'm asking you. What you said about Oogly?"

"What did I say about him?"

"That you're going to arrest him, and—"

"Hang him?" Kit supplied as the girl delicately hesitated. "I would if I could. That's part of my job. He deserves it, but I don't just really see how it can be done. Not right away, anyhow."

Diane's features brightened. "You really meant what you told the Yellow Knives?"

"I'm afraid I did. You can't prove that a murder has been committed by the murderer's unsupported testimony. Odd as it sounds, that's the law. Oogly's confession isn't worth a darn without a substantiating witness and a dead body for an inquest. A man accused of a capital crime isn't allowed to convict himself. A nice situation, isn't it?"

"I think it's fine," said Diane.

"You think it's fine to let an admitted murderer go scot-free?" Kit scowled at her. "Maybe that's your idea of the way a world should be run, but it's not mine. I've got to try and find the dead man's body. Then maybe I can do something about it."

"I hope you never find it," said Diane.

"I go 'long when you go show you best places for looking," put in the irrepressible Oogly.

Kitchener eyed the Esquimau in perplexity. While he wore the scarlet of the police and called himself by his dead brother's name he was conscientiously determined to acquit himself in his borrowed rôle as sincerely and honestly as though he himself had taken the oath of service. The responsibilities that once had been Jerry's had shifted to his own shoulders. And now his first police case left him in a decided quandary. He hadn't the faintest notion what he ought to do.

In spite of himself he secretly felt the same sympathy and liking for Oogly that Diane Durand frankly expressed. By his own lights the little Esquimau was a good man. He loved his wife and baby. He would freeze for them and starve for them and die for them calmly if need be. Men who lived always so close to death as the people of the frozen seas, naturally would put the lightest valuation on human life. The loss of a few Yellow Knives to the world could not seem a very important matter to Oogly.

But if his own life were forfeit for a simple killing, that wouldn't be so dreadful either. He had showed clearly how he felt about it. If he had done wrong, he wasn't afraid to pay the penalty.

Kit would have arrested the man if he had had any evidence on which to found a charge. But there was none. There can be no murder trial without a coroner's inquest, and there can be no inquest unless the coroner's jury has a victim's body to sit upon. Legally he couldn't do a thing about it.

On the other hand, it was out of the question to allow an unrepentant murderer to wander at large in the forest. Oogly might take it into his queer head some day that others of the Indians were praying against him.

As Kit studied the Esquimau with a baffled frown, an idea struck him. If Oogly could be impressed with the enormity of his offense he might try to be a better man. There was nothing criminal or wicked in his flat, round face. He was looking at Kit now with an eager, dog-like friendliness in his uptilted eyes. There could be no doubt of his anxiety to please the man who had saved him. Perhaps he might be shamed into future good-behavior.

Kit stared uncertainly around the foggy room, and his glance lit on a row of shelves in the corner. During his recent absence Diane had unpacked the provisions he had left for her on his sledge and stored them neatly away in their original bags and boxes and tins.

After a brief inspection of the shelves Kit picked out a small can which was labeled "baking powder." He took off the tin top and laid it on the table. Using his heavy-bladed knife for a cutting edge and a billet of wood as a hammer, he cut around the rim, and broke out from the center a bright disc of metal.

The others grouped themselves behind him and watched with curiosity, but nobody asked any questions.

With the point of his knife Kit began tracing printed letters across the shiny surface of tin. He worked painstakingly with his tongue in his cheek, and when he finished he had engraved the word "murderer" across the smooth-faced disc. He punched a slot in the rim of metal, removed the strap from his wrist-watch and threaded it through the hole. Then he stood up at soldierly attention and faced Oogly sternly.

"Do you know who I am?" he demanded.

The Esquimau nodded. "Yup. You oneguy shoot-like-hell."

"I'm the police," said Kitchener severely. He tapped his chest, and then swept out his arms in a gesture that was meant to take in a hundred thousand miles of territory. "When I say anything it is the law everywhere. It goes! You get that?"

Again Oogly nodded. He accepted the statement. He could readily believe all of that.

"Look at me!" thundered Kit. "Straight! This is awful! This is a terrible thing! I'm looking into the eyes of a murderer—a common murderer who ought to be hanged!"

The Esquimau seemed to understand this too. He was watching Kit with grave intensity, and by the pained screwing-up of his face he showed how sorry and remorseful he was beginning to feel. His underlip hung out tremulously, as though he were a little, penitent child who was suddenly overcome by its own fearful wickedness.

Kitchener hastened on with the arraignment. "I hate to do this to you, Oogly," he said sadly. "But I've got to do it. You're a pariah, an outcast, a no-good man. People must know you for what you are. When they meet you in the forest or on the barrens they'll shrink from you, they'll shun you, they'll hurry the other direction. They'll be afraid to speak to you, because they'll know they're looking at a scoundrel."

"Come here!" Kit crooked a relentless forefinger.

After an instant's hesitation Oogly advanced a pace and waited uneasily.

Kitchener reached forward suddenly, and with the point of his knife cut two narrow slits in the Esquimau's skin shirt. He thrust the wrist-watch strap through the opening and fastened the buckle. Then he stepped back and regarded the man with judicial severity.

"If you can read," he said, "you will see that the word 'murderer' is written upon it. It is my order that you wear this all the time, whatever you are doing, wherever you go. So that all men may be warned and recognize you for what you are. It is the mark of crime, it is your badge of shame."

Oogly bent his head to look. Gingerly he raised his hand to finger the dangling, mirror-like bit of tin. After a moment he looked up with shy, anxious eyes. "Fo' me?" he asked in a hushed voice.

"For you, Oogly."

"This make people umfraid?"

"It'll make them afraid. They'll be filled with horror at the very sight of you."

"I keep um all time?"

"You're never to take it off."

106

Oogly turned to gaze at his wife, he glanced around towards the little bundle that he had just put back in the bunk, and then he revolved slowly to face Kit again. The look of respectful admiration that Kit had read in the man's eyes a moment ago had mellowed into rapt, slavish devotion. Oogly's head went up, the chest that wore the murderer's medal expanded by inches, an expression of pride and sheer happiness overspread his wrinkled face.

"Thanks you!" he said fervidly.

"What?" Kitchener stared at the man with wilting features. "What do you mean?"

He heard a snickering sound behind him and turned sharply to see Diane Durand standing with a hand pressing against her ribs, almost doubled up by the effort to keep her laughter to herself.

"Keep quiet!" he snapped.

"Your psychology is great," said the girl, and stopped for an instant to choke. "You had the right idea," she finished, "only something went awfully wrong with the psychology."

"Will you kindly keep out of this?" he commanded, and gave her an ugly look.

Instead of being dismayed Diane moved suddenly towards him, and before he could move his head aside she put up an audacious forefinger to touch his fiercely crooked eyebrow. "Hello, Cocky-bird!" she said demurely. "Honestly—I think it's cute."

Kit tried to erase the scowl, and found himself scowling worse than before. He was on the point of saying something disagreeable, but at that instant he caught sight of Oogly's strutting figure and honest, beaming face. The ludicrousness of the affair struck him, and he was forced to clutch suddenly at his own ribs and turn his back on the Esquimau. Somehow his eyes encountered Diane's elfish eyes, and before he quite knew what had happened he was grinning at her.

"My gosh!" he gasped. "What have I done?"

"You've given out a decoration," she said—"'*pour valeur*'."

"The poor idiot couldn't be any more pleased if the King had come from Windsor to pin him with the V.C.," Kit groaned.

"You'd better do something about it," said the girl seriously.

"Yes. I know." Kitchener whirled abruptly to tower stiff and erect above the Esquimau.

"Listen to me, Oogly!" he said crisply. "I don't want to have any misunderstanding. That medal is for only one murder. No more."

The little Esquimau blinked and waited with flattering attentiveness.

"Do you get me?" demanded Kit. "If I hear of anybody else being killed—good-by medal. I'll take it away from you!"

Oogly was startled and worried. "Noum else?" he faltered.

"No. No one else. It's only good for one. So please be careful. I wouldn't want to tell you that you can't wear it any more. But that's what I'll have to do if I hear of your killing another man. If you kill another person I'll take the medal and throw it in the creek and I'll never give you another one."

Oogly's mouth was twitching and for a moment it seemed almost as though he were on the verge of tears. He was slow to think things out, but as Kit waited uneasily he saw the bland, contented smile gradually reassert itself. "Oright," Oogly suddenly agreed. He touched his badge with renewed satisfaction. "People see um an' find out Oogly a good-murderer. Get umfraid an' no more come aroun' for bothering. Nobody hav' be killed no more."

"That's exactly the idea," agreed Kit, and breathed his relief. "But don't forget—if you ever lay a hand on a Yellow Knife, or anybody else—you lose the medal."

With a feeling that he had muddled through somehow, Kitchener dismissed Oogly from his immediate worries. He went to the door, opened it a crack, and peered out through the clearing. The silvery reflection of the cold, wintry sun was beginning to lighten the sky above the gloom of the forest. There were no Indians in sight, no sign of Giffard; the owls had gone to roost.

Diane came to the door to observe the melancholy Christmas morning. "I wasn't laughing at *you*," she said.

"Laugh all you like." Kit closed and barred the door, and smiled wearily. "If you can find anything funny in this heart-breaking hole, in Heaven's name laugh!"

"I was laughing," she told him, "just at the dum-foolness of things. I could have cried just as easily.

"If you want to know what I think," she went on gravely, "I think you're doggone clever. You pulled a couple of fast ones this morning."

"Laugh or cry, and think what you please," he said ungraciously. "We're just where we started in the first place."

"Mrs. Oogly and I," said the girl, "wish to invite you to Christmas dinner." She made him a mocking little bow. "We hope you accept."

"Sure. Thanks. I've got to stay until dark, anyhow. If Oogly or I step out of here in the daylight, there's an excellent chance of our being popped off. I suspect those Yellow Knives have only taken a little recess."

The Esquimau family had arrived at the cabin well supplied with provisions, the fruits of Oogly's prowess with his fishing hooks and iron-headed spear. They had brought with them a haunch of tender young caribou, a dozen brace of ptarmigan, lots of frozen salmon and whitefish, caught presumably during a lull in the Yellow-Knife praying, and quantities of blueberries, which Mayauk had dried and compressed into hard, black bricks.

By some necromancy of her own Mayauk persuaded the fireplace to stop smoking, and, with the white girl acting as cook's assistant, she achieved a Christmas dinner which was palatable, although somewhat greasy, and plentiful enough for famishing men. Diane's personal contribution was a great, soggy plum-pudding, made of white flour and sugar and raisins and blueberries and caribou suet.

When Kitchener was invited to take his place at the table he could not help wondering if anybody else in the world might be eating such an outlandish Christmas dinner to-day with such strangely found companions. He rather imagined that the championship for oddness went to this table.

He and Diane Durand called a truce for the afternoon. Kit tried to forget that his sole object in life at present was to hunt the girl's criminal uncle, and she did her pathetic best to be amiable and cheerful and to hide the harried look of anxiety that always came back to haunt her restless eyes. Of the four Oogly and Mayauk alone joined with honest good-will and untroubled laughter in a festive occasion which, to these two pagans, was not really an occasion at all, but just another bounteous meal to eat and another day of contentment to live.

Several times during the course of the dinner Kit excused himself to saunter to the door and peek out across the sun-glistening clearing.

"As soon as it's dark," he remarked, "Oogly and I are going to make camp down woods in the owlery. I don't think it likely that any Yellow Knife will go in there to look for us."

"What about Mayauk and Uttaktuak?" asked Diane.

"Let 'em stay here with you. The Indians won't bother them. They're after Oogly, and nobody else. And he'll be as safe living with the owls as he would be in jail." Kit turned to the Esquimau. "You afraid to sleep where the night birds roost?" he asked.

Oogly shook his head scornfully. "Hellno!" he declared.

"You expecting to stay around here?" the girl asked in a tone that was almost too careless.

"Sure," said Kit. "I've got to try to find the body of Oogly's victim."

Diane looked at him somberly. She knew perfectly well that his staying had nothing to do with the dead Yellow Knife. Her eyes measured him with a challenging hardness.

"I may not see you again," she informed him. "If a chance comes along to get out of this country, I'm going. This place is getting on my nerves frightfully."

Kitchener regarded her skeptically. She wasn't likely to leave until she could get into touch with her uncle, and the two of them had recovered the hidden gold-sledge. That's what she was here for. And Kit had seen enough of her inflexible will to feel certain that she would not run away and leave her errand unaccomplished. He would meet her again, undoubtedly, and their next encounter was not apt to be so agreeable for either of them.

He shrugged his shoulders. "If you need me for anything in the meantime you'll know where to find me."

"If I ever want anything from you," she told him stiffly, "it'll be on account of Mayauk or the baby."

"Send if you want me," he repeated.

The short-lived December day reached its noontide and waned as the pallid, heatless sun crossed the short arc and set beneath the white-topped forest. There followed the brief, breathless moments of the gloaming; then the stars broke with electric brilliancy through the frozen night, a thin, wan moon sailed into the sky, and savage, prowling life began to awaken among the dark coverts and underwoods.

Kit and Oogly made back packs of the few belongings that necessity advised them to take, they said good-by to the women, and quietly left the cabin.

The forest was full of noises, ice-stiff branches cracking of their own weight, the babble of the brook between the rifts of ice, the groan and strain of floes piling up under pressure, the long-drawn howl of a distant wolf, the horribly plaintive cries of owls arousing themselves after heavy sleep. There were other sounds, small, furtive stirrings, not so easily identified, that might have meant anything. For all Kit knew there might be twenty Yellow Knives hidden around the clearing.

He kept close to the brook, and Oogly followed in the silence of his fur boots. In a few seconds the two men reached the woods. No hostile shadows rose up to intercept them. They plunged into the nearest thicket and worked their way into the deepest tangles of the Great Owl woods.

Along the creek and at the edges of the clearing the glimmering of the moon touched the great columns of the firs, but in the denser woods not a ray of light penetrated the interlacing of snow-sheeted branches. But they did not need the power of sight to know when they stood under the roosting places of the owls. The dead, rank air about them pulsated with soft, feathery movements, and without seeing they knew that seeing eyes were looking down at them.

In a hollow of ground between two enormous tree stubs they dropped their meager equipment and made preparations for the night. It promised to turn extremely cold before morning, and they would need a fire. Kit didn't think there was a chance in the world that any Indian would venture into this owl-haunted pit in the darkness, or even in the daytime for that matter. Oogly gathered a few sticks of down-wood and some dry twigs for kindling. Kitchener struck a match and applied the light.

He was on his knees as the fire ignited and leaped into flame. Shadows and shapes emerged in the gloom and wavered drunkenly around the dancing firelight. One of the owls scooped past his head so close that he felt the rustle of pinions, and was gone again as mysteriously as though it had dissolved in the air. Kit was about to stand up and stretch his tired muscles to the warmth, and then he changed his mind.

There was a sound behind him like a hatchet driven into a block of wood. He looked around slowly, and then tumbled and rolled away on all fours in his haste to get outside the range of the firelight. A two-pronged fishing-head spear was sticking in the tree behind the fire, quivering there in arrested flight.

Kitchener bumped into Oogly and carried the Esquimau with him, tumbling through the brush and into a hole where an uprooted tree had once stood. It was a good crater to hide in, and they crouched together and peered back towards the mounting fire.

Somebody had hurled the fishing spear at Kit. He could see the double prongs buried almost to the haft in the trunk of the old fir. The shaft was pointed towards the brook. It must have come from that direction. Thrown with greater strength and ill-will than accuracy. A few inches lower and Kit would have been pinned to the tree like a beetle to a cork.

The intended assassin had moved as quietly as the owls. Kit had had no inkling of another presence in the jungle of trees. And now, if he hadn't seen the spear, he never would have dreamed that anybody was hidden near by.

He reacted with anger. "You go that way, Oogly," he whispered and pointed towards the brook. "I'll circle around. We'll get him."

Oogly had said himself that he was a good man in an affray. Kit could have asked none better. The Esquimau was not flurried, and he was not afraid. He owned a trade gun, but for close-in work he preferred his short, heavy hunting spear. He reached the weapon and drifted away as unobtrusively as the smoke from the fire.

Kit slipped behind the nearest tree and stole around from the opposite direction. He moved with utmost stealth, down through the alders that lined the edge of the brook. And then he stopped. The snow had been shaken off the branches near his head and a furrow was piled up underfoot. Somebody had crept through the underwood at this point. For a moment he waited. There was nobody in sight now, no alarming sound.

He pulled off his mitten and blew his breath on his chilly fingers. Then he screwed up his courage and snapped the button of his flash lamp. There was a snowshoe trail in the fresh snow. Instantly he doused the light. He had seen enough to drop him crouching, with every nerve at quivering tension. The raquette prints were waffle-webbed.

CHAPTER XVII
VANISHING FOOTPRINTS

Kitchener recognized the snowshoe tracks with a shock of surprise. A spear is not a white man's weapon, and he had supposed of course that one of the disgruntled Yellow Knives had thrown it. It hadn't occurred to him that his attacker might be Hell Bent.

For the first time Kit was brought to a full appreciation of his own danger. This Bent was a subtle and crafty man. He had outwitted the wily Jerry, and he had just missed his present attack by inches. It was an artful scheme. He must have been hanging on the outskirts of the clearing when Kit drove off the Indians. When Kit and Oogly left the cabin he probably trailed along close at their heels. He had obtained a native fishing spear somewhere, and he used it instead of a rifle. If he had spiked his victim to the tree the police would have hunted for a Yellow Knife, never suspecting that the killer might be a white man. Kit had escaped this time only by the merest good luck.

He realized that if he hoped to go on living he would have to move in the future with the utmost caution. Death might be lurking in ambush almost anywhere in the dark wilderness, at any moment.

The man had faded away into the gloom, but he could not escape from the betraying line of snowshoe tracks. Kit did not dare to use his lamp again, but by feeling the snow with his bare fingers it was easy enough to follow the departing prints. Patiently he groped his way along the trail, which curved out of the denser forest through clumps of snow-sheeted alders and willows, and ended finally at the top of the steep creek embankment.

The moon cast a cold, sickly radiance along the wooded shore opposite, but on this side a deep shadow hid the ice-bound stream. Bent must have dropped over the edge of the sheer embankment, but whether he had followed the ledges upstream or downstream, or was hiding below at the bottom of the slope, Kit had no means of knowing. This might be a trap.

As he hesitated he saw something rise up on the bank to blot out the face of the low-riding moon. A short, stumpy figure silhouetted boldly against the sky—Kit's reflex towards his gun checked as he scrutinized the apparition. Nobody but Oogly could be shaped like that.

Watching, he saw the figure suddenly start up in an erect posture. Two hands grasping a spear flung themselves above the man's head, and for twenty seconds he stood thus, stark and motionless, like the statue of some mythological figure posed in a battle scene. His glance was fixed rigidly on something in the brook course below him. Kit's lips were gripped in his teeth. He expected any instant to see the spear go. But for some reason it never left the warrior's hands.

Slowly the tense figure relaxed, the upraised arms dropped and lowered the weapon. Oogly turned his head and saw Kit. He looked hard for a moment, and then tucked the spear under his arm and sauntered back along the embankment to meet his companion.

"Did'n' kill um," he announced as Kit moved towards him.

"What?"

Oogly's wrinkled smile was visible in the moonlight. "Man he come along down by me," he explained. "No goin' murderum anybody." He inflated his chest on which proudly glinted the tin "murder medal." "Let um going on past along the water."

Kit regarded the Esquimau quizzically for a space, and then he returned Oogly's grin. Evidently Bent had passed up the creek within spearing range of the Esquimau hunter, who for just that moment was tempted to let fly. Then he remembered his promise and restrained himself. He hadn't wanted to lose his badge. So Hell Bent was still a living menace instead of a dead man with a spear in his ribs.

On the night of Jerry's killing Kit would have shot Bent down at sight. But that hour of madness had passed. He wanted his man alive. Later he might exact the full measure for his brother's death, but first he wanted the truth about that bloody day years ago. Bent probably was the only one left who could tell the story. If Kit got his hands on the man he would have it out of him. He'd wring him out like a sponge.

"You've done well," he told Oogly. "No more murders."

The Esquimau swelled visibly. He had been a good boy.

"Did he see you?" asked Kit.

Oogly shook his head and pointed upstream. Bent had hurried on his way without knowing how closely death had brushed him by.

The old cabin stood on the creek bank up that direction. The white man and the Esquimau went forward, hugging the line of alders. Not far ahead they struck a place along the embankment where the new snow had been disturbed. Man tracks ascending from the creek bottom. Waffle-webs had climbed out.

The trail turned through the creek brakes directly towards the clearing. They followed as carefully as cats in a burr patch. Across the clearing, among the stumps, straight to the cabin—the waffle-meshes had left their ominous marks before the closed door. The frozen moon gave just enough light to see by. Kit's breathing had grown painfully sharp. It looked as though he had his man if he were able to take him.

It was dark inside, quiet. Kit spoke to Oogly. "Knock. Tell 'em you want to see Mayauk." His voice was just audible.

The obedient Oogly thumped with his fur-mittened fist.

At first nobody answered, and then a voice in high-pitched alarm. "Who's there?"

"Nobody, just Oogly. Coming see Mayauk please."

"You, Oogly?" It was Diane Durand. She sounded somehow relieved. "It's a funny time to want to see Mayauk. Wait a minute." A soft footstep came to the entrance and the door was unwarily opened. "Come in if you must."

Kit had flatted himself against the log wall. For that moment he was unseen. Diane showed herself for an instant in the moonlight, her slimness hidden under the dragging folds of a huge, crimson Hudson's Bay blanket. "Come in, Oogly."

Her voice sounded very sleepy. Kit saw her face in the softening moonlight, the eloquent dark eyes, the shadow of the drooping eyelashes. Queer that her beauty should affect him in those seconds with a pang of sadness. The seigniors of France who won this country had such women for their wives—the Durantayes, the Demonvilles, the Frontenacs—lovely, dauntless, gently bred women who went where their men went. What it must have meant to come home out of the night and the storm to find love and loyalty and sweetness waiting in the doorway! Diane might have been fit to be a pioneer's wife. It was a pity. She might have been so fine.

The girl drew her crimson robe closer at her throat. It was Grandfather Tearl's old four pointer. She was sensible not to have scruples. To-night was bitterly cold, and she had no other blanket. Yet Kit could not help wondering if it had been laundered since the other night. He thought of Jerry and Bill Tearl and Hell Bent and his heart was hardened.

Diane admitted Oogly, and then she disappeared after him, neglecting to bar the door. Kit pushed the door softly and slipped into the room. He heard voices talking by the still-smoldering fireplace—Diane and Oogly, and then Mayauk's drowsy greeting. Somebody threw a pine log on the fire, and almost at once the bright, resinous flame blazed up.

Nobody had seen Kit come in. He shoved the door shut with his foot and edged along the wall. The firelight danced around three figures, the Esquimau man and wife, and Diane. But he saw nobody else.

Kitchener's quick glance went around the room. There were no angles or ingle nooks where any one could hide. Only the bunk, and he knew the baby was sleeping there. He blotted himself in the shadow as he stole along the wall, ready at any instant for anything to happen.

The bunk was barely visible in the darkness. Kit approached breathlessly. Hell Bent was contemptible enough to ambush himself in bed with a baby and fight from behind an infant body. Kit reached the bunk and groped back into the gloom. He found only a wee shape under the fur robe. Cautiously he felt into the upper section, and then along the floor underneath. Nobody was there.

He stood up, realizing that he had made another false move. Bent was not in the cabin. He must have eluded his tracker by the same trick he

115

had employed at the Yellow Knife encampment, switching snowshoes and mixing up his trail with a confusion of other prints. He had come only as far as the outer doorway, where the Indians had trampled the snow, and now he probably had followed them off into the woods, carrying the waffle-mesh raquettes on his back.

Unluckily Kit had disturbed the baby and the little thing began to whimper in the darkness. Diane turned and saw the shape by the bunk. She advanced a pace and stared.

"You!" she exclaimed. "How'd you get here?"

"Came in with Oogly. Didn't you see me?" From previous experience Kit knew how useless it would be to question her. Bent may have spoken to her, or he may have hurried on without her knowing. It didn't matter.

"What do you want?" Diane demanded.

Kitchener coolly circled the room and came back to the door. "Oogly forgot his toothbrush," he told her without a smile. "Found it, Oogly? Well, let's get on."

The Esquimau lingered only to bid a second good-by to the baby, and then he followed Kit out of the cabin.

There was no use trying to unravel Bent's trail. He had taken off his identifying snowshoes, and the tracks he left now would be indistinguishable from the dozen other sets of tracks that turned away from the cabin. Kit had begun to suspect that the man had reached some sort of understanding with the local Yellow Knives. If not he would be clever enough to win them over. They naturally would have only the bitterest feelings towards the policeman who had refused to give up Oogly to them. This was their own country. They knew the secret paths and byways of the wilderness, and they would have eyes and ears everywhere. With a shrewd and unscrupulous white man to stir them up their capacity for devilment had no limit.

Kit and Oogly went back to the Great Owl woods and re-built their night fire. Then they lugged their robes a hundred yards deeper into the timber, bedded-down under an uprooted hemlock, and slept fireless and shivering through the night.

CHAPTER XVIII
THE MAN HUNTERS

That evening was to begin the harrowing days and weeks of peril and hardship through which Kitchener lived in an incredulous daze, like a sleeper in the throes of a bad dream.

Kit and Oogly slept "cold" every night, and they never slept in the same place twice. The Great Owl woods was their refuge from the Indians, but there was a chance at any moment of Hell Bent's creeping up and sticking a spear or knife into their fur bags. Asleep or awake the menace lurked behind them. Like a pair of homeless rabbits they dug-in under windfalls and brush piles, wriggled into hollow logs, or spent the frigid night huddled against some shaggy tree-trunk, where unseemly eyes glared down and giant wings fluttered in the eerie stillness.

Daytimes they skulked and dodged through the woods and paid the price of life with a vigilance that never gave them a second's surcease. They were hunters, and at the same time they were ceaselessly hunted. Kit's every waking hour was given over to a single, undeviating purpose—to find Hell Bent and take him alive. But the man was gifted with an uncanny elusiveness.

The ex-convict seemed to take an infernal delight in tantalizing his enemy. Kit often crossed the trail of the waffle-meshed snowshoes. He would follow with extreme caution, casting back and forth in half-circles to avoid the dangers of a deliberately planted ambush. But he never once caught a glimpse of the trail-maker. The waffle-webs always ended blindly in some well-traveled pathway, where the wearer shifted to his spare snowshoes and mingled his footprints with those of other passers-by.

So far the ex-convict apparently had made no attempt to recover the hidden sledge-load of loot. Presumably he was afraid to make any definite move while a policeman was on patrol in the neighborhood. Unhampered, he was able to evade his Nemesis. It would be another matter to attempt the long trip southward, dragging a heavily laden sledge through the deep snow. Before he could safely go ahead with his original errand he would have to dispose of Kit as he had dealt with Jerry.

Kitchener seldom left the Great Owl woods in the daylight, and he never showed himself in the open. Yet he was shot at mysteriously on several occasions. He would hear a bullet tearing through the thicket that he had thought was screening him, and an instant later the dry report of a rifle echoed somewhere through the rift in the trees. He would duck and scramble for a deeper cover, and later would maneuver around from the rear to find a departing trail at a place where a man had stood and a gun had rested for a moment in the snowy crotch of a sapling.

These wanton snipings he was inclined to lay at the door of Oogly's enemies. He had seen their tracks criss-crossing the forest along the outskirts of the owl pits, and knew that some of them were always prowling in the neighborhood, waiting with a deadly patience for the Esquimau to come out. And their hostility towards Oogly naturally included Kit.

The Yellow Knives were good stalkers, but notoriously bad shots. The snipers so far had missed their mark, and that was one reason why he had blamed the Indians for these furtive attacks. He had a feeling that if Hell Bent ever glimpsed him over rifle sights it would be the end.

At least once every day Kitchener made it a duty to creep to the edge of the clearing and assure himself that the cabin door was shut and that smoke was still curling out of the chimney. Diane and Mayauk had not been molested.

So Kitchener was justified in his first belief that the occupants of the cabin would be ignored. The Yellow Knives would know that two armed and resolute women at loop holes might wreak havoc among an attacking party. They would know further that Mayauk would never let herself be taken alive. To kill her would be worse than futile. Mayauk and the baby were the anchors that held Oogly in this section of the wilderness. Let them die, and he would pack up his scanty belongings and vanish northward over night into the trackless barrens, where the Yellow-Knife vengeance could never find him. It was to the interest of Oogly's enemies to allow his wife and baby to dwell unharmed in the cabin on Great Owl Run.

The January moon waned and black nights of storm and sleet and frightful cold set in, and the wilderness lay in death under the white scourge of winter. By craft and by stealth Oogly and Kit contrived somehow to eat and to sleep and to evade their enemies. And Kit hunted his man, and failed, so far, to get him.

The sun all but disappeared over the southern bulge of the world, and then gradually began to come north again, a hazy, pallid ball, lacking warmth and the power of giving life. Sometimes Kitchener encountered the two local trappers in the woods. He would gossip with them briefly, and then go his way, liking neither the sneaky-eyed Giffard nor the sullen, black-bearded Bruyas.

On one occasion Constable Devon made a patrol downstream to find out if all was well with the sergeant. Kit did not want police interference in an affair that was decidedly his own. He told Devon that he was still investigating the Yellow-Knife murder, assured the constable that he was in no need of help, and sent him back about his business.

Kitchener had not talked with Diane Durand in weeks, but one night, after the return of a full moon, he met the girl while roving the banks of the creek.

He was working his way downstream, hidden by the shadows of the willows, when there appeared above a snowy knoll a slender graceful figure in a hooded mackinaw and calf-length breeches.

The girl of necessity had become a huntswoman. A brace of partridges and two or three rabbits hung at her belt, and she carried a shotgun in the crook of her arm.

Kit held his position in the thicket, waiting for her to come opposite him. The moon-rays touched the curves of her cheeks and lips and her small, firm chin, giving her face an expression of childlike wistfulness. She looked thin and tired and most unhappy.

As Kit observed her calm and pensive features it struck him that nobody but a monstrous cynic could ever believe that she was actively involved in her uncle's murderous schemes. Bent might have told her anything about the gold-sledge, but Kit would not let himself think that she knew the whole truth. If she were as bad as that, then nothing in the world ever could be right, and he would be glad to pass out of it. If, like her uncle, she looked on Kit as an obstacle that had to be put out of the way, here was her opportunity. She had her shotgun. He stepped suddenly before her with his hands in his pockets.

The girl halted as the tall, gaunt shape loomed in her path. She peered fearfully for a moment, and then her tense shoulders relaxed and she drew a long breath.

"Oh," she said, "it's you. Hello."

She moved a pace nearer and her glance swept to his face. He had shaved that morning with ice water, but nevertheless he felt that he was not a very presentable object. His clothing had grown a bit seedy and he knew that his face must have taken on a few haggard and care-worn lines since he saw her last.

Diane seemed kindlier than he remembered her and just for a moment he thought he caught a trace of pity in her lovely eyes. "How are you and Oogly?" she asked.

"All right. We're getting along." He did not think it worth while telling her that they had spent every hour and minute of the last few weeks in the shadow of imminent death.

"Mayauk and Uttaktuak are well," she informed him. "Particularly the baby. It does you good to see what a little husky he's getting to be."

"How's Diane?" asked Kit.

The girl lifted one shoulder in a curt and reckless movement. "Well enough," she said.

She pulled off her mittens and put her cupped hands to her mouth. Then she wriggled her fingers and beat them together, trying to restore the circulation. They were strongly shaped, competent little hands, chapped and rather grimy, more like a boy's hands than a girl's.

Without thought or actual intention Kit took one of them into his, and doubled her fingers under his warm palm. "I guess you're not used to this sort of business," he remarked.

"No." For a moment or two she allowed her fist to lie quiet, as though she gathered comfort from the touch. "You can get used to anything, though," she added sturdily.

Then she raised her eyes level with his. "Have you seen my uncle?" she asked with a directness that startled him. She released her hand and put it back in its mitten.

"No," he said.

She looked around the thicket that sparkled in the moonlight in white, lacy designs. Her straight eyebrows met in a troubled pucker. "If he's anywhere in this part of the world he should have heard that I'm here. And then he should come and find me. I don't know why he doesn't come."

Kitchener faced her with a smile that had grown a bit acrid these days. She didn't fool him. He not only believed that she had seen and talked with her uncle, but he rather imagined that she would know about where to find him at this minute. What was she trying to put over, he wondered? Probably fishing to find out how much he knew. His face had grown stony. She wouldn't learn anything from him.

"Maybe he's gone back south," he suggested.

"I don't know what's happened." Diane shook her head. "It's funny I haven't heard anything from him. It's darned funny!"

Kit sat down on the edge of a snow terrace and brooded grimly upon the icy world. "I thought you were going back yourself," he said after a moment.

"It's easier to come in," she told him, "than it is to get out."

"I offered to help you out," he reminded her. "But it isn't too late. I'll order one of the constables to escort you down to the rail head."

"Don't bother," she said. "I'm in no hurry to leave."

She moved to the snow-bank, hesitated for an instant, and then sat down beside him, crossing one booted ankle over her knee and clasping her leg between her hands. "This is a wonderful place!" she sighed.

"Wonderful for what?"

"For me." She pushed off her hood, shook her ruddy hair in the moonlight, and gave him a full, close-up view of her darkly shimmering eyes. "Do you know, I've always had somebody to cook things for me and bring 'em in on a tray and clean up afterwards. I don't believe I've ever washed a dish before in my life. And now—" Her mouth crooked ironically. "I shoot my own rabbits and clean 'em myself and scorch 'em without anybody else to blame, and eat 'em to the last scrap, and scour up the pans afterwards."

"Is that supposed to be wonderful?"

"Isn't it? I thought it taught you to be self-reliant and unselfish and a little humble. Everybody says so. If I ever get back, I thought I might be a better girl." She turned to him appealingly. "Do you think maybe I might?"

Kit didn't know whether she was laughing at herself or at him, or was really half in earnest. She was the most enigmatical woman he had ever met. There was no way of guessing the thoughts that kindled those deep eyes, with their singular trick of being serious and humorous at the same time.

"You're a pretty good girl now, aren't you?" he said, and stirred uneasily. He wished she wouldn't sit so close and look at him so intimately. And then he began to despise himself for a fool, because he realized with a sudden shock that he wanted fearfully to feel her tangled hair under his fingers, to bring her face even closer and to find out the meaning of her disturbing eyes. In that moment he knew that if he ever lost his grip on himself, he was gone.

But he was watching himself to-night. He didn't want any recollection of a foolish weakness and a softly moonlit evening to make life cruder by contrast and more unbearable. He stood up abruptly and looked away somberly into the thickets. Hell Bent might be creeping up even at this instant. "If shooting and cooking rabbits makes people good," he said, "Oogly is a saint on earth."

Diane half stretched her hand towards him, as though to invite him to come back, and then dropped it listlessly. "Well, I'm not," she declared with a sudden harshness of voice. "If anybody wanted to know, I'm bad."

Kit measured her quizzically. She sounded as though she were passionately ashamed of something, and yet she watched him with a queer glow of defiance.

"Not in any way you'd ever think," she added morosely. "It's not so much badness as—as just being idiotic."

"We're all of us a bit of that," he said, and faced her wryly. "Just what form does yours take?"

"Think I'd tell you?" she flashed at him.

Kit started to open his mouth, and then shut it. Through the silvery night there ranged a queer, unearthly sound—something between a sigh and a croak and a hiss—a voice that was horrible because it lacked reality.

The girl started up to her feet and then sank down in the bank of snow. Kit saw her shiver, and he himself felt an electric chill running down his spine.

"It's only one of the owls," he told her, wondering why he never could get used to these ghostly disturbances in the upper air. This one in particular startled him every time he heard it. He had never seen the bird, but he knew it by its voice, which was hoarser and croakier than any of the others. Oogly told him once that this one was a spirit that had caught a cold on its way out of hell.

"I know it's an owl," said Diane. "And I know who he is. It's Shedim. And I hate him worse than all the rest of them."

Kit contemplated her face gravely. It was strange that she too knew this bird and had given him a name.

The voice crossed invisible above them, passed over the brook, and faded away somewhere in the north.

"They're my bad thoughts," said the girl at the end of long silence.

Kit peered down at her. She never had seemed more in earnest.

"Whenever I think something bad," she pursued, "one of the owls comes. It always happens. As though they were something that had just been released out of my head." She was not looking at Kit and he had a feeling that she had forgotten he could hear her.

"It's the oddest thing," she mused. "My bad thoughts are owls. And the night I thought the very worst thing I could think of, this one came for the first time. His name was Shedim. And I've heard him every night since, croaking in the sky."

She raised her head and found Kit staring at her. "Honestly," she said, "I almost half believe such truck." She smiled somewhat grimly. "Maybe I'm going a little goofy from lonesomeness."

"I'd kill him," Kit advised.

"I can't," she said mournfully.

"You've got a shotgun. I'd wait up until daylight, and when Shedim comes back from the red hunting I'd let him have both barrels."

"You can't kill a bad thought with a shotgun," Diane said.

"I can," Kit told her soberly. "You lend me that gun and there won't be any Shedim around here after to-morrow morning."

She shook her head. "Suppose I don't want him killed?"

"Why wouldn't you? If I had a bad thought flying around in the air I'd knock him for a row of feathers."

"No! The thing's born and alive, and all the killing in the world won't kill it. And what's worse I wouldn't want it killed—I couldn't bear it—"

"Diane!" Kit sat down again and tried to see into her eyes. She was no longer the girl he had known—the competent, self-possessed Diane. She was beginning to sound hysterical.

"What's this awfully bad thought about?" he demanded.

"Do you think I'd want you to know?"

"I do know!" he shot at her.

"You don't. You couldn't!"

"It's about me," said Kit.

Her lips parted and wild alarm showed itself in her eyes.

"I guess you can't help hating me like that," he said drearily.

"Hate you!" She turned to him and he heard her choking breath and felt the potency of her eyes, brought close and recklessly seeking his. "If I did—" She laughed crazily. "Oh, my God!"

Suddenly she was on her feet, standing over him. "What's the use of our talking?" she said measuredly. "You and I have nothing to say to one another—ever." Her high tone changed to something suspiciously like a sob. "If you ever meet me again, don't stop me. Let me alone!"

She picked up the shotgun, pulled her hood down over her head, and before Kit had recovered from his astonishment she was gone.

He stumbled erect and stood with his left eyebrow perched at its highest attainable angle, gazing after her. He started forward as though to follow, and then he changed his mind and his feet anchored themselves in the snow. For an interval he waited, irresolute and dejected. He sighed and shook his head sadly. Then he turned decisively and strode back to camp.

During these recent moonlight nights Kit and his Esquimau companion had borrowed the habits of the owls that lived about them. They slept days and did their hunting under the cover of night. But this night Kit turned in early. He tossed and twisted in his sleeping bag and was unable to close his eyes until dawn. And then, just as he finally dropped off into a doze, Oogly came back from his night's fishing.

The Esquimau brought four or five fish and a coiled line, which he dropped under Kit's windbreak, while he yawned and sat down to pull off his frozen boots.

Kit opened one eye, started to shut it again, and then opened both. Fastened to the fishing line, a few inches above the hook, he noticed a battered slug of metal that glinted yellow in the early morning light. He suddenly sat up in his bag and snatched up the coil of line.

"What's this?" he demanded.

Oogly looked around. "A sinking," he explained.

Kit hefted the slug and turned it in his fingers. Oogly had split the hunk of metal with his knife and pinched it around his line for a sinker. It was soft, and heavier than lead, and there was no mistaking its glinting color. To weight his line the Esquimau had used a chunk of pure, raw gold.

"Where'd you find it?" exclaimed Kit. In one movement he was out of his bag and on his feet.

Oogly winked his slits of eyes. He saw no reason for excitement, and remained his placid self. "Fishing along fast bottom, hook 'em up. Plenty lots more."

"Where?" cried Kit.

"You want to see 'um?"

"You're darned tootin'. Come along and show me."

Oogly was perfectly willing. He conducted his comrade through the thick timber to the bank of Great Owl Run. The two men made their way upstream through the thickets, and the Esquimau halted presently on the overhanging brink, not far from the cabin where the two women lived.

This was the place. In the snow lay a moss-covered pouch, from which spilled forth a double handful of blackish, corroded lumps like pebbles, but which, under Kit's tremulous knife-blade, changed magically to the color of virgin gold.

Oogly pointed towards the stream, which, at this point, ran too swift to freeze. "I catch um fishing an' hook um up," he said.

Kitchener stared breathlessly at the boiling water. The Esquimau must have snagged the bag by accident, and after helping himself to one of the "sinkers," which he needed for his line, he dumped the rest on the bank and unconcernedly went his way.

With shaking hands Kit crouched to lift the pouch. It was made of some sort of rawhide. But instead of rotting, some chemical action of the water had hardened and stiffened the bloated skin until it was like a sheet of stone.

For a space Kit squatted on his heels, dribbling nuggets through his fingers. All at once he stood up and looked down over the brook embankment. The racing water had cut its way under a shelf of the rock. The deep, black channel was farther out, but here it looked to be rather shallow. For just an instant he hesitated, and then began stripping off his clothing.

Oogly looked on wonderingly, but had nothing to say. Anything his friend did was correct in his eyes.

Kit stood in his underwoolens, and reached for the Esquimau's hand. "Hang on and don't let the current pull me out."

He slipped over the curve of the shelf, held his breath, and then heroically dropped into the water.

The cold was like sharp blades cutting his flesh. But it was something that had to be borne, and he gritted his teeth with the desperate resolution of a martyr undergoing torture. The stream level did not quite reach his arm pits. By clinging to Oogly's hand he moored himself against the gurgling current.

He trampled the bottom below the shelf, and found a heaped-up slimy mass, which he knew by the feel to be a pile of full, heavily-weighted bags. His toe groped along a mossy, waterlogged framework—the guard-rail, "gee" pole and upcurving runners of a long submerged dog-sledge.

CHAPTER XIX
LOST LOOT

In that tremendous moment Kit lost all sense of the cold that chilled and numbed him to the marrow of his bones. A tingling pulsebeat rang in his temples and throbbed in his fevered blood. He forgot that dawn was at hand. He forgot his lurking enemies. He took no account of his stiffening muscles and chattering teeth. He had found the lost treasure sledge. It had taken its final plunge over the embankment to be engulfed for the years in Great Owl Run. This was the place. A brave woman had died here, and men had fought and killed and vanished. Here the valiant Bill Tearl had taken leave of the remembering world.

Scarcely realizing what he was doing, Kit ducked under the water and came up with a bulging, slimy sack in his hand. He deposited his burden on the shelf, and went under again for another, and for another. There was no need to look into the swollen bullhide sacks to know what they contained. No metal excepting raw gold could have the heft of these bags.

He brought them up, one after another, until warning cramps forced him out of the water. For a few minutes he ran up and down the bank, beating himself with his arms, while Oogly trotted behind, slapping him with stinging and resounding slaps. As soon as his blood felt the resurgence of life Kit went back into the brook. Five times he climbed in and out of the water and at his fifth shivering emergence he lugged with him the last bag of gold.

That appalling job was done. He looked from the heap of sodden bags towards the sky which, as usual after an overly bright moon, had turned threateningly black. There was a promise of more snow to-night. If it snowed hard enough the evidences of this morning's work would be buried before to-morrow.

Kit had decided what to do next. He would transport the treasure to another pool, and he alone would know the secret of the new hiding place. So to thwart Hell Bent. While Bent was trying to re-locate his loot, Kit would be given the leisure for his own grim hunting. And if in the end Bent should kill him, then at least he had struck back at the killer with a last sardonic jest.

He told Oogly as much as was needed to enlist that amiable savage's assistance. A half mile farther upstream they found a spot under a sheer bank where black ripples ran deep under a sagging ice-bridge. They were able to carry only two of the plethoric bags apiece. These they lugged to the marked spot and dumped them overboard.

They made a dozen trips that morning, back and forth, burdened with bags of gold, which they jettisoned in the swift current of Great Owl Run. Luck favored them to-day. Their enemies presumably took it for granted that they were sleeping out the daylight, as usual, in some well-hidden nook of the Great Owl woods. There were no snipers dogging them this morning, no curious intruders crossing their trail. And before their task was finished it had begun to snow.

The dreary downfall began with a misty sleet, which changed presently to white-drifting flakes. Kit had grown sick of the snow as a man wearies of an unremitting disease. But now he looked with satisfaction at the fluff that had begun to fill his tracks. By this time to-morrow nobody could know that he and Oogly had been tramping up and down the creek bank.

He watched the dark ring of ripples as the last bag hit the water and sank out of sight. The Great Owl treasure had found a new resting place, where it might lie untouched for twelve or fifty or a thousand years. Who knew?

Although Kit was soaked to the skin under his outer clothing, he felt overheated after his heavy labor. Unless he dried out immediately he risked pneumonia or worse. He and his companion were starting back for the shelter of the Great Owl timber, when Oogly broke away through the alders. Kitchener followed, to find the Esquimau scowling above a fresh snowshoe trail that came down almost to the edge of the creek.

The two men peered into the thicket. The tracks were not half an hour old. Their maker obviously had been standing in concealment, looking down at the creek. With sinking heart Kit realized that some one had watched him while he toiled up and down the stream.

There was no sound save the whisper of snow in the frost-hard branches of the alders and willows. The intruder must have fled at his approach. He examined the tracks again. They were not the narrow, skiing prints of the Yellow Knives, nor Hell Bent's waffle-webs. But he knew whose they were. A pair of rounded Chippewyan squaw raquettes, too light in build for a man's weight. He had seen these same tracks too often to be mistaken. The trail maker was Diane Durand.

So the morning's work was wasted: unless he gave the quietus to Diane. The watchful Oogly may have noticed the sudden dour molding of his face and jaw, that sinister Tearl look which meant that one of the tribe had solved a knotty problem to some one's else disadvantage. He turned curtly.

"You go to the cabin," he said, "and stay there to-day with Mayauk. If the white girl leaves or anybody comes to see her, you come to me at our camp, right away."

Oogly's squinty eyes held the same look that a malamute's eyes hold for the man he trusts. Kit took his leave without any misgivings, confident that the Esquimau would never fail him.

He retraced his steps to the Great Owl woods, chanced a small fire to dry his underwear, and later turned into his bag and slept the day through. When he awakened in the early evening he found himself in a welter of snow-filled darkness.

All of Oogly's worldly belongings, combined with his own, formed such a meager kit that he was able to bundle everything into one pack, which he toted through the woods and across the clearing to the cabin door.

Diane admitted him without protest when he knocked. "Hello!" said the girl, and there was nothing in her voice or manner to betray any guilty consciousness of her morning's activities.

Kit looked at the ground before tramping into the doorway. The afternoon's snowfall had covered the old trails, and there were no fresher tracks arriving or departing. He shut the door and thumped down his pack.

"Get ready to pull out," he commanded. "All of us are traveling to the police outpost to-night."

The calm announcement produced a silence, which Diane broke into at last with a brittle laugh. "Anybody may go who wishes," she said. "Which leaves me out, because I don't wish to."

Kit did not raise his voice. "We want to start at once. Please hurry."

He saw the girl's silhouette grow taut in the reflecting firelight. "Are you by any chance," she asked carefully—"in earnest?"

Kit didn't think it necessary to answer. "Oogly," he suggested, "will you call the dogs and hitch 'em in? Everything we've got we can carry on the one sledge."

"Because if you are," put in Diane, "you'll have to get over it. I'm not going!"

Kitchener faced her unsmiling, maddeningly supercilious. "Mayauk will help you to pack. If not, I will. Only hurry. And this time we leave off the 'please.'"

"Why, you—" She stopped and glared at him. The Diane of the moonlight was gone. This one was resentful and bitter and untouchable, yet he never felt an allure more poignant than the beauty of her sultry and stormy eyes.

He was utterly cold at this moment, because it would have been so easy to be otherwise. "Oh, very well," he cut in. "If you force me—I arrest you."

"What?" she shrieked.

"If you want the whole formula: I warn you. In the name of the king—"

"What for?" she cried. "By what right?"

"Vagrancy!" he said.

Diane's mouth opened and closed and opened again. She was so outraged that for those seconds she was unable to speak or even breathe. "Why—why—you—what do you mean?" she finally managed to gasp.

"The word has only one meaning. A vagrant is a sort of a hobo without visible means of support."

"You're calling *me*—" It was too humiliating to say. She ripped open the throat of her shirt with a gesture so violent that one of the buttons flew across the room. From beneath the open collar she jerked a string and a chamois bag. The bag was torn wide and she pulled out a roll of yellow-backed currency so thick that her fist was barely able to close around it.

"And you say I have no means of support!" she taunted him furiously.

"What's that?" he asked mildly.

"It's money! I haven't counted it: but I guess there's a couple of thousand or more!"

"What's it for?" inquired Kit.

"What's what for? Money?" Her pretty mouth attempted to sneer. "Why, my dear sir. Money is to spend. To buy things with."

"What things?"

"Anything! Anything you want!"

"Where?"

She blinked and looked at him a trifle uncertainly. "At the stores," she finally said.

"What stores? I haven't seen you buying anything. The flour you eat, the salt, sugar, bacon, beans—I gave you. You're using my matches and my shotgun. You don't even own the blankets you sleep in. Yet you say I have no right to arrest you for vagrancy. Well, you're under arrest."

The girl's face changed from red to white, and then went red again. "I'll pay you for anything of yours I ever had," she informed him. "What's the price?"

"I'm not in business," he told her. "You'll find the nearest store-keeper at Edmonton, or maybe McPherson. When you get down there you can buy anything you fancy. Here we don't recognize money, because there's nothing for it to buy. That's why I'm transporting you to Edmonton. You won't be a vagrant there."

"You're not—" Diane was almost crying with mortification and rage. "I won't go!"

"Remember the first morning I met you?" inquired Kit. "You were trussed up with a pair of handcuffs, riding on a policeman's sledge. I've got those same handcuffs, and I've got a sledge."

"Oh you—you rotter!" she said with a vitriolic intensity.

"So was the other bird. And you had to travel with him. Ready?"

Diane stood stock-still, her great eyes searching his face with a helpless, hunted look. Her impassioned resolution seemed to waver. Two tears trickled from her lashes and glistened on her cheeks. "What can I do," she moaned, "when a bully and a brute—so much bigger and stronger—and I'm just a girl—"

"Certainly you are," said Kit.

He turned away to spare her his smile. He should have done this before, he was thinking. She had worried and hampered him more than he would have admitted. But now he soon would have her off his hands, out of his sight and, he hoped, out of his mind. She knew where he had sunk the gold. But that no longer mattered. It would be months before she could see her uncle again. Long before that time Kit should have settled up his score with Hell Bent.

With Diane sitting by in sullen hostility, the other three soon gathered up their belongings and loaded up the dog sledge. They closed the cabin and started eastward in a swirling storm, Oogly breaking trail, the baby riding in a nest behind the dogs, Mayauk handling the "gee" pole, and Kit and Diane trudging speechless in the rear.

Through the long, blustering night they held their steady pace, and shortly after the crack of dawn they arrived at the police outpost of *Saut Sauvage*.

Constables Devon and Cross were at home. The two officers tried valiantly to hide their astonishment and welcomed their unexpected visitors with a hospitality that was warmer than the bleak quarters in which they lived.

Kit explained affairs in a few words. "This is the girl I told you about. Looking for her uncle and hasn't found him yet. And this wilderness is no place for a child."

He was short and brusque in his speech—a commanding officer telling a subordinate what to do. "I want you, Constable Cross, to make a patrol south and take her with you. She says she doesn't want to go, but that's just too bad. Technical charge of vagrancy. You can let the inspector decide what to do about it."

Cross looked furtively at the girl, and blushed. His simple face reflected the pride he felt in being chosen for a responsibility, the joyous anticipation of a visit to civilization, and also a painful, gawking shyness at the thought of the company he would have on his way out.

"It isn't really right for a young girl to be roamin' about alone in this country," he stammered. "You'll find it's better, miss, to be away from here."

Diane studied the constable coolly, and then, for just an instant, a gleam of malicious amusement tinged her eyes. Kit intercepted that glance, with its sly and tantalizing humor for mischief-making, and somehow he did not envy the doughty constable his journey out of the forests.

After their night's trip the wayfarers were glad to accept the comforts of the police shack. The rear storeroom, with its cots for guests, was turned over to Diane and Mayauk. Kit and Oogly stayed awake only long enough for breakfast. Then they crawled into the constables' bunks and throughout the snowy daylight slept the sleep of the righteously weary.

Subdued voices, the scuffle of feet, a poker rattling in the fire-box of the stove, the faint rasp of snow falling aslant on the log walls and tar-paper roof, the savor of meat cooking—Kit awakened amid lazy sounds and pleasant smells. The frosted window square opposite him loomed opaque against the outer blackness of the night.

Constable Cross was bending over the bake oven on the stove. Devon sat in low-voiced conversation with a man whom Kit had not seen before, a broad-backed man with a bullet head, hatrack ears and a round-necked hair-cut. Diane, Mayauk and Oogly were nowhere visible.

Kit hitched himself into his clothes while lying in the bunk, and then opened the skin curtains and slid out onto the floor.

In a far corner of the room, beyond the angle of the bunk, he discovered Diane. The girl was seated on a camp stool, a lock of auburn hair tipped over one straight eyebrow, her pert nose in the pages of a big book which she held balanced on one crossed knee. She evidently had spent the snowy afternoon ransacking the outpost's supply of literature. Old books and lop-eared magazines and tattered newspapers littered the table and the floor about her chair. She appeared as aloof from the rest of the company as if she had retired to a private apartment with a "no admittance" sign on the door.

As Kit stretched himself and sauntered across the room the stranger turned to stare at him. The man's face, which was close shaven and unwholesomely pale, had the battered, hard-used appearance of a third-rate prize-fighter's mug. His eyes were as protuberant and held the same metallic coldness as a frog's eyes.

"Oh, good-evening, sergeant," said Devon, standing up. "This man came in on us out of the storm this afternoon. His name is—*um*—"

"Pettijohn," supplied the stranger. "How-da-do, sergeant."

"Where're you from?" inquired Kit without much interest.

"The States."

"Yeah? You must enjoy chilly weather to be coming up here now."

"Oh, any time's good enough for my business," said the man. "I'm a missioner. Our people sent me to look after the welfare of the Indians."

Kit surveyed the stranger ironically. He wondered what sort of welfare the Yellow Knives might acquire from this ornery-looking plug-ugly. Then he turned away indifferently. What the intruder did to the Yellow Knives, or what they did to him, didn't really seem to matter.

The kettle was humming on the stove, and Kit poured out a basinful of the first hot water he had reveled in for weeks. He scrubbed his face and neck and hands, and then paused before a wall mirror with its chained comb. He was plastering back his wet, sleek-black hair, when he heard a chair scrape on the floor. Feet stumbled across the room. A voice cried out:

"I knew it. I knew it!"

The comb dropped to swing on its chain. Kit looked around. He saw Diane under the lamp. In her hands she clutched an open book—a volume bound brightly in scarlet and gold. There was not a vestige of color left in her face. She breathed fitfully and heavily. A ruddy light glinted in her wide spaced eyes.

Every man in the room gaped at her.

"Look at this!" she said to Constable Devon. "Your police year book. The *Scarlet and Gold*!"

"Yes," said Devon, puzzling his eyebrows. "Yes, it is!"

Diane's laugh was harsh and cramped, utterly different from her real laughter. "He says he is Sergeant Buck Tearl." For a moment her glance fixed Kit rigidly, and then she softly laid the book on the table. She tapped the open page with her finger, and stepped back.

"Here," she said, "is a photograph of Sergeant Buck Tearl."

CHAPTER XX
SCARLET AND GOLD

In the moment of his betrayal Kit had the ghastly sensation of a man whose lungs had been suddenly pumped empty. His heart stopped, his brain went numb, the sense of living stopped for those few shocking seconds. He felt as though he had been stripped bare and pilloried in a public place. Faces surrounded him and eyes looked at him, and the silence grew almost too acute to be endured.

The page of the open book was glossy in the lamplight. He saw the half-tone photo in the upper corner, the strong-jawed, bold-eyed likeness of his brother Jerry. Sergeant Buck Tearl, stalwart in any such crisis as this. But Jerry was gone, out of it. Kitchener and his brother looked nothing alike. Anybody could see the photo and know with certainty that Kit was not the man whose name and the record of whose deeds was printed here in the blackest of ink. And he was alone now, with no Jerry to turn to, standing at bay in the sacred scarlet.

Devon and Cross were hanging over the table looking at the book. Then both raised their heads to look at Kit. All trace of expression was wiped from their faces. The ruthless police visage—their faces might have been chopped out of the same slab of marble.

"Well?" said Devon.

Kit said nothing. What could he say? They had him. Impersonating an officer! A black crime in the police books. These men were terribly jealous of their own. Looming, hard years—a long stretch—the least punishment he could expect. Well—

There was nothing to do but face it out. His back stiffened as though he were to meet an assault. One eyebrow cocked upward. He had known that this might happen. Only it was strange the way it had been brought about. He would have gotten away with the masquerade if Jerry's funny old picture hadn't bobbed up to ruin him—

"What about it?" demanded Devon.

As though a command had been given, the pair of constables circled the table, one from one side, one the other. A hard, round muzzle jammed itself into Kit's ribs. Somebody ripped open the flap of his holster, and his gun was gone. Searching hands passed skillfully up and down his person. A chain clinked, something glinted in the lamplight, steel cuffs bent themselves around his wrists and snapped fast.

Sergeant Cross pulled up a chair. "Sit down!"

Kit sat. He hadn't tried to resist. They would have had every excuse to kill him. His self-control had come back to him. He was thinking clearly and rapidly.

"Why'd you do it?" asked Devon.

"Warn you!" put in Cross.

Kit's head turned instinctively, seeking Diane. But the girl had withdrawn into the background, keeping out of his sight. Oogly had climbed down from the upper bunk, fully clad, and was standing with Mayauk, looking on. From the dismayed expression of his face it might have seemed that the Esquimau's whole world had fallen apart.

Oogly's gaze reached Kit. For just an instant his narrow eyes held a gleam that might have been mistaken for intelligence, and then his dull and stolid look returned.

"Too much hot here," he announced abruptly. "Me an' Uttaktuak. Going for walking." He took the baby from Mayauk's arms and moved across the cabin. "Nobody cares?"

Nobody did, apparently. The constables didn't look around. Oogly opened the door and went out into the snowy night.

"You don't have to talk—if you don't want to," Cross said to his handcuffed prisoner.

Kit acknowledged that remark with a rasping smile, and held his tongue. He had decided what he had to do. There had been enough scandal in the Tearl family. The ugly talk about his father; Jerry leaving home under a cloud. And now Kit. He'd be the first Tearl jail-bird.

Well, nobody had to know it. He'd keep the name out of this. Spare little Jane that shame anyhow. Nobody could make him tell who he was. It wouldn't do a particle of good to identify himself. Even if he proved to them he was the sergeant's brother, what of it? His offense was not lessened. If he could make them believe that he had donned the uniform at Jerry's suggestion, it wouldn't help him. And Jerry's memory would be blackened....

"Where is the sergeant?" Devon suddenly shot at him.

Kit saw no reason to withhold all of the facts. "He's dead."

"Huh?" The muscles around the corners of Devon's mouth stiffened visibly. "Where? How?"

"In the old cabin down at Great Owl Run. Six or seven weeks ago. You lose track of time. He was killed and dumped out of the window into the creek."

The constable's lips formed a soundless exclamation. "Who the hell killed him?" he snarled.

"This girl's uncle," said Kit quietly.

A hurried step across the room, and Diane confronted them. "It's a lie!" she said.

"Wait a minute now. Hold on!" Devon's steely glance shifted from Diane to settle upon Kit. He sat significantly silent for a moment, his features limned austerely in the shadow of the lamp.

"Where'd you get the uniform?" he asked abruptly.

Kit's lips set tighter. He was in danger of entangling himself if he said too much. As Cross had said, he didn't have to make any admissions. He'd have to think out his story and be very sure that all the parts fitted together. There'd be plenty of time for that. He wasn't on trial now.

"Where'd you first meet this man?" Cross asked Diane.

"Down around Port-o'-Prayer."

"Was he alone?"

"No. There was another man with him."

"Who?"

"He was—I didn't know at the time. But since I've seen this picture I think—I'm sure—he was Sergeant Tearl."

"Yes?" said Cross sharply.

"Yes!" echoed Devon, and swung around menacingly to Kit. "Killed him yourself, didn't you? Killed him for his uniform!"

"No," Kit replied, meeting Devon's gaze, steel to steel.

"Do you know if he did?" the constable jerked over his shoulder at the girl.

"No. I—I don't know."

"Was he wearing the uniform when you first saw him?" Diane hesitated. Kit saw her blanched face beyond the table. "I—I can't say. If he had the scarlet tunic then it didn't show under his outer garments. I only noticed it—after we had reached the cabin!"

"Where the murder happened?"

The girl shuddered. "There—yes."

Kit smiled a twisted, acid smile. The girl was doing her best to convict him of murder. She wanted him taken down country out of her uncle's way. Innuendoes and half-truths, told with a show of reluctance—she had made a grave case against him. And he would let it go at that for the present. He wasn't sure how much of his own side of the story he wanted to tell. Anyhow, it would be useless to say anything now in his own defense. Nobody'd believe him. He had been caught in a uniform that didn't belong to him. Almost as heinous a matter as being a spy in wartime. They'd take him to the inspector's headquarters no matter what he said—or tried to prove—they'd hang him if they could.

Devon and Cross were already formulating plans.

"I'll take him down," said Devon, whose seniority gave him a slight advantage. "Starting at daybreak. He'll talk when the inspector puts on the clam-squeezers."

"What the deuce do you suppose his lay was?" asked Cross indignantly, discussing the prisoner as though he were not present. "Bumping off a policeman, and then coming around in sergeant's chevrons, giving orders to you and me?"

"You leave it to the inspector," said Devon.

"When you take me down, you'd better take this girl too," interrupted Kit. "Whatever I've done she's as bad or worse than I. Ask her to explain why she's hanging around the Great Owl woods. Make her tell you her uncle's right name, and then find out what he wants here."

"When we want any more orders from you," said Devon, "we'll post you for a commission."

"While I'm gone," Devon suggested to Cross, and turned his back on Kit, "you'd better see if you can find Buck Tearl's body. If he went into the creek he'll be there still, or down along the Vermilion River."

"I'm going to look," said Cross.

"This last storm is busting up the ice. You'll find plenty of open water and big jams all the way down. You look well. We've gotta have the body—"

"Ask her about the sledge-load of gold," interrupted Kit, and shot a malicious glance at Diane. "Ask her how it came to be where it is now. Get her to tell you all about it."

Devon faced about, winking. "What do you mean—sledge-load of gold?" His curiosity rebounded to Diane. "What does he mean?"

"Why—I—" The girl hesitated and her glance wandered uneasily towards the stranger, Pettijohn. The man was sitting with his arms hugging the back of his chair, his jutting ears as avid as a pair of funnels.

"Oh, ye-ah!" drawled Devon. "Just wait a minute." He spoke almost too politely to the visitor. "You said you were going on down to the Yellow-Knife camp to-night."

"Well, yes, I thought I might—"

"All right!" agreed Devon pointedly.

Pettijohn stood up, disconcerted. He didn't want to go. That was clear. But the invitation was too plain to be missed. "Well," he decided, "I guess I might as well be going along."

Devon picked up the man's steaming mackinaw and held it for him. He gave him his snowshoes and rifle and helped him to buckle on his back pack. "Sorry you gotta be going," said Devon. "Well, so-long anyhow. Come and see us again sometime."

"Thanks awfully!" said Pettijohn wryly. "Thanks for the dinner and everything. Well, so-long, everybody."

A moment later he had tramped out into the night.

Devon crossed to the front window and scratched into the frost rime with his thumbnail. He applied his eye to the gouged place and then bent his ear to listen. For a minute or two he waited thus to make sure there was no eavesdropping. Then he turned back to Diane.

"All right now. What's all this about a sledge-load—"

He never finished. The heavy door banged open, admitting a gust of snow and a white-furred figure that looked more like a shaggy, stampeding musk-ox than a man. Then the door was closed, the wavering light steadied, and they saw it was Oogly.

Kit never before had seen the Esquimau aroused from his transcendental calm. Now he was fairly exploding with excitement, horror. "*Uttaktuak!*" he yelled.

Everybody turned, petrified, to stare. Mayauk's eyes had grown into dark circles of alarm. A sharp incoherency of speech was wrung from Diane's parting lips. Kit stumbled up from his stool. The two constables stood with sagging jaws.

"What?" exclaimed Devon.

"The baby!" gasped Diane. "Uttaktuak! Something's happened—"

"Down between ice—falling in creek!" Oogly's voice broke through above his labored breathing. "Can't reach 'um—drowning—"

"Where?" demanded Cross.

"In creek—ice— Oh, my gosh awful!" wailed Oogly.

Mayauk screamed and darted for the door.

"Come on! Show me!" Devon put on one mitten, and didn't wait to grab the other. He seized Oogly's elbow and thrust the Esquimau ahead of him out of the doorway.

Constable Cross snatched blindly at the wall pegs, got a blanket and a cap, and then he was gone after the others, banging the door behind him.

In their dash to the rescue it might have seemed that they had forgotten their prisoner. But there really was nothing for them to worry about. A handcuffed man would never get far in the wintry forests.

Kit started to follow, and then ruefully clinked his manacled wrists, and sat down again. Diane was left alone with him.

The girl had checked her first impulse to rush out into the storm. As the running footsteps faded away in the blustering darkness she turned wildly to look around the cabin. The tea-kettle. She filled the vessel afresh at the water-butt and put it on the stove to boil. If the rescuers were lucky enough to come back with a frozen morsel of human flesh in their arms, there'd be no waiting for "first-aid" treatment. Somebody had to stay behind.

She poked up the fire and crowded three fresh logs into the fire-box. Blankets were brought from the bunk and draped over chairs by the stove. She found an old door brick and put it into the oven to heat. Then she went to the back window, scraped off the pane, and tried to see out of doors.

Kit had followed her movements about the room, watching with dreamy, half closed eyes. Then, fervently, after a long silence: "I do hope they get her!"

"Yes," agreed Diane, her nose still pressing the glass.

There was another endless lapse after that: two beings in one room, listening for the same sounds, thinking kindred thoughts, acutely conscious of one another, separated nevertheless by a barrier as heartbreakingly wide as the polar ice-pack. The clock ticked quietly on its shelf, the kettle began to hum its homely refrain, the draft whipped and lashed up the red-hot chimney; outside they heard the snow slatting across the roof, the hurry of the wind, the crack and groan of the broken ice-floes in the creek, crawling, sliding—

Diane faced about suddenly. "What a frightful night!" she said.

Kit saw her eyes, pitiful somehow, haunted with a tragic lonesomeness. He knew she was not thinking of the weather.

"You and I have done frightful things to each other," he said.

"You forced me," she answered dully. "You forced me to do it."

In the flash of his smile there was a melancholy sweetness, without resentment or reproach. "We ran afoul of things that had us licked before we started. It might have been so different."

"I know. You think I don't?" Tears gathered and glistened for an instant on her eyelashes, and then she winked hard and flung back her head. "I'm sorry—"

Her hand gripped towards Kit, to be arrested half-lifted, half-open. "What's that?"

A tumult of heavy sound welled out of the night: a slow rumble gaining force and momentum; a splintering and grinding; the crack and crash of small field-pieces cutting loose in furious volleys; the ground, the cabin walls trembled against a sudden violence breaking out of the darkness.

Kit and Diane were standing at the rear window, without remembering how they got there. The black head and the ruddy head were touching as they tried to see through the same window-pane. Smothering darkness without. They caught the surge and rush of big water let loose.

"*Saut Sauvage!*" muttered Kit. "The rapids! The ice-dam has gone out."

"My God!" she whispered.

The battering crunch of great ice cakes, hitting and breaking up. A man shouted somewhere shrilly. A sudden swelling and mingling of all sounds in one thundering outburst. Then, as abruptly, the roar ceased. A jar and a jolt now and then, slacking to quiet. Only the wash and splash of rapid water running free.

Kit did not hear the shack door open. An indraft of snowy air hit the back of his neck. He turned his face from the window. Oogly was standing in the doorway.

Diane whirled. "The baby? Where's the baby?"

Oogly ignored her. He came into the room and forgot to shut the door. His slyly puckered eyes brought their message for Kit alone. This, he seemed to think, was no time to bother with children or women.

"Finean'dandy!" he announced. "You an' me go up along barren land. Sea no frozing later. Big whaling ship come along inside pack-ice. You go away on whaling ship—nobody arresting you anytime then."

Oogly was trying to be nonchalant, but obviously he was pleased with himself. It was beginning to dawn upon Kit that the Esquimau in some mysterious manner had had a hand in the breaking-up of the creek floes. He had lured Devon and Cross out of the shack with a wild yarn about the baby. Kit studied the man's unemotional countenance in suddenly growing alarm.

"Oogly! Where are the constables?"

For the first time the Esquimau allowed his self-appreciation to appear in a widening grin.

"Constables riding on middle water. Noum coming along back a long while now."

CHAPTER XXI
HEADING NORTH

Kitchener felt a sickness and emptiness under his ribs. His comrade, one time a murderer, again had taken direful measures. He peered in consternation at the swarthy, round face that looked forth so genially from its ice-encrusted hood.

"Cross—Devon!" he accused furiously. "Drowned—you've killed them!"

A hurt, almost tearful look clouded Oogly's soft, seal-brown eyes. "Noum!" he protested vehemently. "Sitting on ground along water middle. Can' get off now."

"What? They're out there, and still alive?"

"You betchum!"

By stumbling speech and vivid gesture the Esquimau tried to explain just what had happened. In the center of the stream stood a long, narrow island, a pointed ridge of rock, like a backbone, humped up above the surface of the rapids. Ice cakes, broken from the tunnels upstream had piled up on the nose of this island, forming a big jam that reached from bank to bank.

The observant Oogly had noticed this place when they arrived at the police shack that morning. When he saw the handcuffs snapped on his friend's wrists his fertile mind had immediately devised a plan to outwit the police.

He used poor little Uttaktuak for a bait. The constables responded humanely to his cry for help, followed at his heels across the ice to the island. While they were poking in the crevices, listening for wailing sounds of human distress, Oogly had crept under the head of the hanging floe.

As an experienced timber-driver is able by a sort of sixth sense to stick his peavy into the key-log of a log-jam, so the expert ice-man knew which block of ice it was that held back the crowding, straining mass behind it. Oogly simply and unerringly had found the critical wedge upon which the backed-up tons of ice were precariously suspended. He had chopped and pried for a minute with his spear head, and had jumped clear as the floe suddenly toppled and split apart, to go thundering and foaming downstream on both sides of the island.

So much he told in casual words, helped out by his lucid pantomime. That part of the story meant nothing to Oogly. He had made his way to the bank, leaping from one submerging ice-chunk to the next. The policemen had not been quick enough or sure-footed enough to escape as their shoreward bridge fell to pieces about them. Oogly gurgled with amusement at the huge joke he had played.

"Constables have a seat on middle rock," he said.

Kit only wanted to be certain that this was true. He did not wish to have any drowned policemen on his conscience. Without waiting to hear more he ran out of the door and picked his way down to the embankment of the rapids.

In the welter of the falling snow he made out a smudgy shape that was just a little blacker than the darkness itself. It was the island—the tongue of rock, jutting high and dry in midstream. He heard the big cakes of ice washing by at his feet.

He raised his head and hailed the middle of the stream. "Hello! Devon? Cross?"

Yes, there was somebody. Voices—one of them shouted with rage. "Who the hell did that?"

Kitchener laughed and turned away. It was all right. The constables were unharmed, marooned in the middle of the creek. In his haste to the rescue Cross had grabbed a blanket instead of a rope. They could huddle up for warmth and there was no danger of their being swept away. In a day or so a new ice-bridge was sure to form, and then they could walk back to shore again.

Meanwhile Kit had no intention of waiting for the next freeze-up. While he didn't precisely approve of Oogly's methods, he at least saw no reason to be stupidly quixotic over fortune's sending. The alternative was unthinkable. It meant a long prison term, or worse, if they took him south. The cards would all be stacked against him.

Oogly's plan was to dash across the barrens for the Arctic Sea. The idea was inspired. The trails would be swept away by the time the constables got off their island. It was a ten to one shot that they would cast southward after their quarry. And Kit would be heading due north.

Queen Maud Sea! The chance to carry out Jerry's unfulfilled mission. He could seek for the white man who wore a police badge under his artikis. That business could be settled, that ghost laid one way or another. Then, as Oogly suggested, the whale ship—around the point of Alaska, Frisco—New York! Nobody in this country knew who he was or where he came from. He'd be safe in New York.

Someday he could send a trusted agent to recover the sunken gold bags. He wouldn't touch the stuff himself. But a pension fund for the R.C.M.P.—that was the idea. A memorial to Jerry. The Tearl memorial fund, sent by an anonymous donor. His heart was thumping, a thrill of excitement was in his blood, imagination ran riot. He was pulling up stakes, taking a new deal all round. He'd be on the march soon, heading north.

At the shack doorway Kitchener bumped into Oogly and his wife. Mayauk was scolding about something. As Kit came up the Esquimau turned aside to a deep snow embankment, plunged into the drift to his shoulders. Then he came up with a squirming, fur-clad bundle in his arms. It was Uttaktuak, making cheerful sounds and kicking her feet. Oogly must have dropped her there before he went out to the floe. Mayauk snatched the baby from her husband's hands, and peace was restored.

Oogly followed Kitchener into the cabin.

"Finean'dandy!" grinned Kit, and shoved up his manacled wrists. "Can you get these things off?"

The Esquimau found an ax and indicated that his companion was to lay his hands on the doorsill. Kit complied dubiously. Unfortunately the key was on the island with the constables. To use a file was apt to prove an endless job. Kit held his right wristlet against the hammering block. Then he set his teeth and gave the word.

Oogly swung with his full strength. The butt of the ax crashed down squarely upon the arch of steel, cracking the brittle, highly-tempered metal as though it were glass. The band fell apart and Kit's wrist was free.

He winced and looked at his hand, and then grinned up weakly at Oogly. The astonishing Esquimau had struck off the shackle without crushing the bone underneath, or even bruising the skin. More confidently this time Kit offered his other wrist, and a second blow rid him of his humiliating bonds.

He kicked the broken links aside. Diane Durand stood under the lamp, looking on uneasily.

Kit's jawline reasserted itself as their eyes encountered. He didn't propose to leave her behind to carry the tale of the sunken gold to her uncle. If he were unable to settle the long accounting with Hell Bent, at least he'd make sure that the man was done out of the loot.

"We're going out by way of the Arctic Sea," he informed the girl. "You too."

He had expected fierce resistance. But Diane was too clever a girl to squander her courage and strength in a futile struggle. She was shaken and dazed by the turn of events, and she knew she was beaten. "After all that has happened," she said wearily, "it doesn't matter much where I go, or with whom, or what happens next."

Kit and Oogly hurried their preparations for departure. The constables had Kit's service revolver, but his rifle and Diane's shotgun were on the sledge, and the Esquimau had kept his musket and hunting spear. They took a couple of blankets from the police store and helped themselves to such provisions as were needed to replace their own diminished supplies.

As they must travel fast, they cut their equipment down to the last possible ounce. And it was decided that Mayauk and Uttaktuak should remain behind under the protection of the police. Oogly promised to send for them when the tribes drifted south again with the coming of summer.

The three strangely-met *voyageurs* set forth in the night and the storm, beginning a journey that appalled the imagination. They would bridge the creek at the first opportunity, and then strike due north across the vast stretch of the wind-swept barrens. Some day, by fortune's leave, they might reach one of the isolated whaling settlements on the ice-bound sea. For the present Kit preferred not to let his thoughts dwell upon the uncertainties of the coming weeks.

They drove their dogs down the shadowy line of the creek, Oogly running ahead, on the look-out for a favorable crossing place. The night was half gone before he finally shouted and turned the team leader. Instead of hummocks and crevices and crawling floes, he at last had come to a naturally formed bridge that was solid enough and level enough for crossing by sledge. He turned and haled the trotting dog-team on behind him. And then he stopped and crouched and peered forward under his hood.

Buzz-saw, the team leader, checked himself at the Esquimau's heels. He threw up his head, tested the air once with his nose, and let out a warning growl. An ugly chorus, snarling and barking, answered the challenge from across the frozen stream; then, an instant later, men's voices hailing the darkness in alien gutturals.

Without a word Kit swung the "gee" pole, while Oogly turned at a lumbering trot to break trail downstream. No need to stop for questions. The party across the way had to be Yellow Knives—a hunting band, no doubt, coming back from the barrens.

The Esquimau's enemies, of course, had long since familiarized themselves with the peculiarities of his only pair of snowshoes; also Kit's. They'd pick up the trail as soon as they crossed the creek and identify the tracks. Then they'd come on like wolves running a caribou herd.

Oogly's eyes had learned to see in the great Midnights, and he led the way now, picking the best ground unerringly, cruising as fast as an ordinary woodsman cares to travel in the full sunlight. He would know that his one slender chance was to stretch out his trail so far ahead of the Indians that the friendly snowstorm would have time to bury it.

The huskies caught the infection of alarm. Danger for men means danger for dogs. They jumped after Oogly, half-galloping, with the lightly laden sledge singing over the downy new snow. And in the rear, whooping yells broke out in a significant babel to reëcho down the hidden valley of the creek.

The Yellow-Knife village was pitched on the south bank of the stream, about midway between *Saut Sauvage* and Great Owl Run. In the darkness the fugitives failed to make out the huddle of skin teepees and shanties until they suddenly found themselves in the midst of the sleeping encampment.

It was too late to detour. Two score of grave-like mounds in the snow exploded suddenly like bombs as buried huskies sprang to life and action. Bounding, yapping forms circled in from all directions, trying to get at Buzz-saw and his team-mates, raising a din that must arouse every comatose Indian for two miles around.

Kit closed up on the flanks of his team and beat off the charging beasts with a clubbed rifle barrel. For just a moment Oogly slackened pace. His snaky dog-whip licked out, right and left and behind him, popping like fire-crackers. The savage outcry changed suddenly to anguished yelping. Again the Esquimau plunged into his stride and went through the main street of the Yellow Knives, with Buzz-saw a jump behind him, and Kit and Diane racing for the "gee" pole.

In a moment they were out of the village, hugging the line of willows as they fled down the banks of the creek.

Bedlam had broken loose in their rear. Women shrieking, men yelling to one another and bedamning their frenzied dogs, rifles wantonly firing at nothing: the town had gone mad. It wouldn't take the bucks long to find out who their passing visitors were, and then to hitch sledges and take the trail. Instead of a single hunting party, the fugitives in a few minutes would have half a village in pursuit.

Many weeks of snow-tramping had hardened both Kit and Diane for the physical ordeal they must face to-night. Oogly had trained with sledges on the wide Arctic tundras since the days of babyhood. In a long race he could outlast the best of the dogs. Any of the three probably was as trail-fit as the average starveling Yellow Knife. If the dogs only stood up for the night in the traces there was a chance of their wearing their way through.

Kit had kept a watchful eye on Diane, but apparently at this moment she had no desire to leave him. There was a blood-chilling savagery in the sounds behind them. For the present she had as much incentive to run as Oogly and Kit.

The events of the remaining night went by like the spinning of hazy dreams. Shadows fleeting along half-seen trails; snow and darkness and cold; the straining snap of harness thongs, the humming of sledge runners and the steady crunching of snowshoes, the *pat, pat, pat* of furry feet digging along: they gained the Great Owl cabin clearing, and Kit shouted to Oogly to turn.

Away to the left swung the dogs, with their forerunner a stride ahead, among the stumps and headlong into the blackness of the "haunted" forest. The sounds of pursuit had dwindled to silence. But out of hearing did not necessarily mean out of striking range. There were teams and men running the plainly marked trail. The fleeing dogs knew it, and Kit and Oogly and Diane never lost the occult feeling of being pushed hard by danger behind them.

The owls were away from home, out foraging over the frozen prairies far to the north. It was deathly quiet under the trees. Oogly was familiar with every inch of the ground here, and he cut through the owl woods, dodging low, avoiding the great trunks by some uncanny method of perception. They struck the creek again several miles farther down, near the point where Kit and Diane had first come into this country from the south. Here they found an ice-bridge crossing. They worked over to the north bank, groped their way through the stunted, wind-torn thickets on the opposite shore, and turned their faces at last towards the Arctic Sea.

There was hope now that their pursuers had been shaken off, or at least held up for a while in front of the Great Owl woods. No Yellow Knife would venture into that unhallowed pit of darkness, unless the lust of the chase had keyed him up to a fine, high point of frenzy. Then he might go anywhere, dare anything. In any event the savages might circle the forest and strike the trail where it crossed farther downstream. But this would mean a clear gain for the fugitives of an hour or two or three.

Unfortunately the wind had whipped around into the southwest some time in the night, and the promise of heavy snow had failed. It had grown colder and calmer, and the great, soft flakes had turned to a misty sleet. Oogly, the weather-wise, had announced that they might see blue sky in the morning.

There was nothing to do but to keep going, to make all the distance they could while the dogs stood up. It is astonishing how much reserve vitality the ordinary human being holds on tap if the emergency call is great enough. Earlier in the night—hours and hours ago, it seemed to them now—the three fugitives had known the torture of overtaxed hearts and lungs, an unquenchable thirst, the dry taste of blood. Then they had caught their "second wind." A pleasant numbness seemed to drug their physical sensibilities. Legs and bodies moved automatically, without effort. Breathing became easier. Indeed it seemed almost unnecessary to breathe. It was as though they had been running and could keep on running always.

Daylight caught them far out on the frozen prairies. As a mariner loses his landfall in the night, so they had lost sight of the peopled world. A dead-level sea of snow and ice surrounded them. There was not a tree nor shrub, not a speck of color within range of straining eyes. The clouds had blown clear, and the early gray of the sky changed gradually to the flawlessness of hard, blued-steel. The sun came up, and the white monotony of the barrens became an aching, dazzling glare.

Diane was drooping again, staggering now and then as she tried to hold the killing pace. Oogly's face looked as drawn and bloodless as smoked moosemeat. Kit was beginning to suspect that in time he might reach the end of his "second wind." The breathing of the dogs sounded like the rattle of broken skid-chains. They stopped by mutual consent, because nobody could go much farther.

Behind them the horizon line was a scintillating glaze. Landmarks all had vanished. The Great Owl forest had been left so far in the rear that not even a smudge of color showed against the field of snow. There were no specks or dots anywhere to betray the existence of beasts or men.

At the left the Vermilion River pursued its endless course northward, held between treeless snow banks so low that the dykes of the waterway, even at a short distance, could not be distinguished from the rest of the flat, sweeping landscape.

The travelers camped on the river ice, because at least there was some slight protection behind the low embankments.

Kit unpacked their alcohol stove and started coffee boiling. "Ready for breakfast?" he asked Diane.

"No, thanks. Not hungry. Sleep. I want to go to sleep."

He unstrapped a fur bag and spread it in the lee of an ice hummock. The girl stayed awake only long enough to pull off her boots. Then she crawled into the warm pocket, and ten seconds later was asleep, with the sun beaming into her face.

Kit and Oogly dined on chunks of cold pemmican, washed down with scalding swigs of coffee. Then the Esquimau stumbled off behind the parked sledge, rolled up in his robes and started snoring. The dogs had dropped in their tracks the instant after they were fed. Kit alone stayed awake.

He turned, squinting, to gaze back over the glistening reaches of the open tundra. No sign as yet of pursuit. But his own trail, the ruthless thread of fatality, linked him with the horizon. At any moment he might see little, evil shapes moving in the shimmer of the sun.

Sighing, he picked up a blanket and tucked his rifle beneath his arm. He seemed to have been elected unanimously to the post of responsibility. Oogly was dead to the world, with his head wrapped in a robe. Diane lay on her side, a glinting, silky wing of hair tumbled over her eye, her mouth relaxed in a faint, unwitting smile.

For just a moment Kit's gaunt features were robbed of their guarded sternness. His glance hovered wistfully as he half leaned over her, and then, with an inexorable shrug, he turned on his heel and trudged back to the southward.

For two or three miles he walked the down trail. Then he picked a defensible spot behind the river bank, where he spread his blanket and stretched out on his stomach to watch over the line of northbound footprints.

If his enemies came out on the barrens the trail would lead them past the ambush point. He could take them on the flank, and by surprise. They wouldn't get him for a long while. He was loaded down with cartridges, and he was covered on three sides. Oogly and Diane would hear the shots. They'd have time to run for it again. Kit was confident that he could hold the Yellow Knives long enough to give his companions a safe start. Better one than three.

All of that morning Kit lay on his blanket, keeping vigil.

The sun had come up in the southeast, and it was from that direction that his pursuers must come. He lay on his diaphragm and stared into the sun.

An endless morning. He had nothing to do but to gaze across the flat wastes and try to keep his eyelids open. It was a wearying, painful prospect, snow and ice stretching everywhere, shadowless, colorless, a vast mirror reflecting the sunlight.

A merciless sun. A silvery, frigid incandescence pouring balefully upon the world. The snow remained as hard as crystal, and flashed and sparkled like the dancing of flame.

An appalling silence. Even the wind is without noise when there is nothing to interfere with its blowing. The tick of Kit's wrist watch, the thud of his pulse, were mighty sounds in ears attuned to an absolute vacancy. He could hear the friction of his toes when he wiggled them for warmth in his ribbed-wool socks.

A forlorn panorama. Sometimes he saw with an astonishing clarity, seemingly for miles and miles, but there was nothing to look at. The boundaries of earth and sky were so much alike that he could not tell surely where one left off and the other began.

The waves of cold on the snow-fields sometimes waver visibly like heat waves on the desert. In the flickering daylight he later began to see things. Men and dogs and sledges and shifting herds of musk-ox moved distantly before his widening gaze; then a black, bumping object, like a locomotive laboring over a rough road-bed. By that time he knew something was wrong. He studied his finger tip for a minute to bring his pupils back in focus, and when his glance ranged the far tundras again there was nothing whatever in sight.

If the Yellow Knives were coming he wished they'd come.

The queer mirages formed and faded for a while, and then a dullness stole over his vision. When he took off his mitten again to concentrate on his forefinger, the finger somehow looked bigger than it should and a trifle vague in outline. The heatless sun, strangely, felt as though it were beginning to burn his eyeballs. The muscles of his eyelids started to twitch, and he could not hold them still. And he began to notice a pinprick of pain in the nerves behind the bridge of his nose.

For relief he allowed his eyes to close against the glaring sunlight. And he went to sleep, to awaken suddenly in a sweat of terror. He had dozed off. He had failed his companions, when he was supposed to be on watch. Nothing had happened. The silence was as intense as ever, and there were no shadows beneath the coldly blazing sun. That was nothing to his credit. He had slept.

He looked at his watch, and had no idea of the time of day. The watch dial and the hands and numerals fluttered in a kaleidoscope of changing colors. He gazed across the tundra and the colors swam off ahead of him into the horizon.

His eyes felt as though something had blown into them. Sticks or cinders. He rubbed them with the back of his hand, and then stopped because of the smarting. If the Yellow Knives were coming, please let them come while he still could see them.

In the meantime he could not endure the agony of the snowlight and the sunlight. He let his eyes close again—for just a second. His chin was propped on his forearm and his face stared insensibly across the white barrens. And the second lengthened into minutes and the minutes into hours.

What aroused him he did not know. The movement behind him was so stealthy that a man in his full waking senses might not have noticed, nor had reason to look around. But Kit sprang to his feet as suddenly as though an alarm clock had banged off by his head.

A towering, muffled shape stood over him. Twilight and cold—the sharp, calm, bitter cold of the arctic evening. His eyes were all wrong. It was as though he were trying to look through fuzz. There really was something, though—an erect figure on two feet—a face and a body and a rigid arm, and a pistol muzzle pointing at his head.

CHAPTER XXII
OOGLY

Dazed as he was, half-blind, half-awake, Kit recognized his fate. Intuition was better than eyesight. This was no Indian. It was Hell Bent. He knew that. Everything was as good as ended. There'd be a flash, and then the obliterating shock, nothing worse than that. His mouth twisted sardonically.

"What are you waiting for? Go ahead and be damned!"

Funny the man didn't fire. All these weeks, gunning for Bent and Bent for him—

The man whirled with a snarling sound in his throat. Something had stumbled up from behind the river embankment. Kit was vaguely aware of a broad shape and heavy feet crunching the snow.

"Oogly!" he yelled. "Back! Get down!"

The stocky figure swayed on outspread legs, a heavy, two-handed spear poised above his head.

A streak of flame reached above the snow. The sound of that one shot, out of all the pistol shots Kit had ever heard, lingered in his head with a reëchoing of horror.

The spear-thrower lurched forward violently, and his spear was gone.

A second shot and a third, point-blank; the stench of gas and powder-burnt fur; a squat body on staggering legs, that still would not fall; writhing sinews and muscles in Kit's clutch and a fist trying to pound his face: everything was dreadfully mixed in his brain, events and their sequence of happening.

He remembered the feel of the hot steel in his hand, but how he got the gun he did not remember. Afterwards he found torn flesh under his nails; but at that moment he only knew that the butt had settled down in his fist and he was looking everywhere and softly crying because he could not see well enough to shoot.

Gliding snowshoes moved off hurriedly in the dusk. Everybody in the wilderness would have heard by this time that Kit was deadly with a six-shooter; nobody could have learned as yet that anything was wrong with his eyesight. The intruder had fled. To follow would be hopeless.

Kit groped behind him and his arms circled a stumbling, furry hulk—Oogly.

"He got you, didn't he?" said Kit, and lowered the sagging body to the snow.

The Esquimau said nothing. He was fumbling at the front of his shirt. The tufts of fur were matted together, warm and wet. But it was not that that bothered Oogly. He was pulling at the bit of tin on his chest—his medal—trying with failing fingers to unbuckle the wrist-watch strap.

"Murderem once more," muttered Oogly.

Kit felt something come into his throat to choke him. Oogly believed he had killed another man. He had flung his spear, and did not realize that the first pistol shot had spoiled his aim and stolen the force from his stroke. By breaking a promise he had forfeited his medal.

"No, Oogly." Kit slipped off his mitten and stilled the uneasy hands. He saw no reason to disillusionize the man. Let him think that his last spear-thrust had been magnificently delivered. "It's a good murder this time. You saved my life. The medal's still yours to keep. You've won it twice over. This time it's something for pride. It's yours now forever."

"Keep um?" whispered the Esquimau.

"Nobody can ever take it away from you."

"Thanks—thanks you—" Oogly tried to sit up, tried to laugh. But the sound died choking, and the broad body grew slack and heavy, and slipped down from Kit's arms to lie in the snow.

Kit touched the man's pulse and his temple, and then he stood over the quiet, baggy shape in the snow. "White men!" It was a short and savage ejaculation. "I knew a better, Oogly. The best man I ever knew was not a white man!"

His voice broke and a sudden wetness soothed the dry stinging of his eyes. Oogly had no other funeral oration.

Kit stooped and scooped handfuls of snow over the motionless body. He patted the surface down and shaped out a clean, smooth grave-mound. Oogly's destiny always had marked him for nothing less and nothing greater than a mound in the clean, cold snow.

The sun was gone and it was growing darker. How good the darkness felt in Kit's swollen eyes! He picked up the captured six-shooter. Yes—this was it—carved ivory butt, engraving on a silver name-plate. It was the gun he had seen Hell Bent wearing, Inspector Bill Tearl's old service revolver. Kit shoved the weapon into his empty holster. Well, it was back in the family now. The last Tearl had three more shots on his hip.

He left Oogly and went back to camp—trudged wearily up the frozen river until he came to the place where a sledge was parked and dogs bounded forward to greet him.

"Diane?" he said.

There was no reply.

"Queer!" Then louder: "Hello—Diane?"

The dogs leaped up, pawing at him, and he trod on their back toes to keep them down. There was nobody in camp. The sleeping bag was empty. And the red Hudson's Bay blanket seemed to be missing. Further search discovered a sheet of paper pinned to the topmost duffle-bag on the sledge.

Evidently it was a note from Diane. She was gone. Probably she had escaped as soon as darkness fell. Kit's jaw hardened. He might have expected it. Diane would be on her way back to Great Owl Run, looking for her uncle. He shrugged unpleasantly. Well, what of it? He couldn't stop her now. Let her go.

Kit struck a match and frowned at the sheet of paper. There was writing, but the lines wabbled and ran together when he tried to read them. He flipped out the match and gave up the effort. It didn't matter what she wrote. What did he care? He crumpled up the paper and threw it away.

As soon as the dogs were fed, Kit went to bed. He was worn to utter exhaustion. His two or three hours sleep that afternoon meant nothing at all. If he expected to get on he could do with no less than eight or ten hours of solid, unbroken rest. Maybe his eyes would feel better by morning. If anybody came in the night it couldn't be helped. He simply had to sleep.

But strangely he didn't drop off in a delicious sense of forgetfulness. In fact, he couldn't lie still. His bag didn't fit him. One minute he felt too hot, and the next, too cold. Finally he went to the trouble of unlacing himself and crawling out of the flea-bag, a mean and undignified undertaking. He staggered around in his stocking feet, and finally found the wad of paper that he had thrown away. Then, with Diane's note buttoned in his shirt pocket, he crept back into his fur pouch and went to sleep.

The pitiless morning sun appeared in a frosty-blue sky. For miles and miles around, the snow fields flashed and glinted and threw back the sun-rays with a blinding brilliancy. Far to the southward black figurines, no bigger than pencil strokes, moved in the undulations of light.

Kit had discovered the approaching specks the moment he awakened. He studied them briefly, and then made leisurely preparations for their reception.

In the first place he decided to stay where he was. His dogs were footsore, and, with the possible exception of Buzz-saw, none of them was fit for work. There'd be some fresh, first-rate teams in the gang that was coming across the tundra. They'd run him down in no time. And he might not find such a favorable place to dig-in farther along.

The river bank here bent at a sharp angle and rose up from the ice sheer as a breastwork. He hauled the sledge to the brink and banked up a shelf of snow on which he could stand shoulder-high and peer over the packed duffle. The niche in the river bank protected him in front and on two sides. They could circle and get him from behind. But the river was wide here and it was a long-range shot from the prairie on the other side. They'd have to burn up a lot of cartridges, perhaps.

He arranged his own shells in a neat row along the runner of the sledge—ninety-two for the Winchester and fourteen for the shotgun, which, for some reason, Diane had neglected to take with her. These were more than enough. If he lived to use half of them he wouldn't complain.

A quart pot of strong coffee and the most extravagant breakfast his larder afforded: he fried his bacon just so and carefully browned his corn-cakes and used half the can of egg-powder and his last tin of ham to crisp a beautiful omelette. Into his coffee he dumped the entire jar of preserved cream that he had been saving for some purpose or another, he hadn't quite known what until now. It was the best meal he had eaten in two months.

His eyes didn't hurt much this morning. They looked inflamed in his pocket mirror and the lids were a bit puffy, but he could see what was going on. He threw a blanket over his head to shut out the light as long as he could.

But he could not long ignore the approaching figures. They were coming in a sweeping line, running up yesterday's trail—Kit's trail and Diane's and Oogly's. He didn't bother to count. There were six dog teams and twenty or thirty men. All Yellow Knives, excepting, perhaps, the tall one who strode in the rear.

This last one was unrecognizable at such a distance. But he stood a full head above the others and he did not walk like an Indian. A white man—who else but Hell Bent? In all probability the savages had been of two minds about venturing out on the bleak barrens, until Bent returned last night and stirred them up again. Now he was showing his good generalship by letting the Indians rush into range ahead of him.

The foremost of the party caught sight of the sledge on the embankment. Kit heard the yells as the advance dozen fired a spattering volley and charged. Two or three bullets dusted the embankment, but the rest plopped short.

He slammed his rifle bolt. A .30-'06 soft nose. No caliber of bullet ever brought more woe into the world. Four-hundred and fifty yards, thereabouts. Allow for refraction. Allow for wind-drift. Two and a half from three, plus one—

This long range rifle practice was too much like surveying or dressmaking for his taste. Give him a six-inch pistol barrel and an offhand mark.

He felt the savage buck of the gunstock. One of the distant figures went down on its hands and knees, and tried to crawl, and couldn't.

Somehow he didn't hate these men because they were trying to kill him, but because they were forcing him to deal with such beastly arithmetic. He gritted his teeth with annoyance. Fortunately the others had stopped. No more for the present.

The devilish sun was mirrored into his face by the shining miles of snow. It was as though a billion white-burning lenses were turned full into his eyes. He tried to see across the blazing levels with his eyewinkers almost shut.

The advance squad had scattered and scrambled back for the sledges, leaving the fallen one, a blot upon the snow. Kit could see them talking, using their hands vehemently. The tall man came forward and seemed to have much to say.

For a half hour or more they held their council-of-war. Kit watched them as a basking seal watches at the edge of his diving hole, opening his eyes for five seconds and closing them for thirty. But the sun-rays seemed to bore through his naked eyelids.

The Indians at last decided what was to be done. The six sledges separated and were driven out in skirmish order, right and left from the center and fronting the river course. The dogs were unhitched and chased off into the background. Then a couple of Yellow Knives dropped prone behind each of the loaded sledges.

A nerve in Kit's left eyeball had begun to jump and quiver, and he couldn't control it. Yet he still was able to make out what was happening. A party of a half dozen braves detached themselves from the line and started off in a wide circle across the sun. These obviously intended to strike the river farther south and to swing back along the opposite shore to attack Kit's ambuscade from the rear. It would take this bunch an hour or so to work into position, and for the present he dismissed them from his worries.

The real menace now was the sledges in front. He stared at them for a moment, and was under the impression that they were moving towards him. He blinked and passed his hand before his face, and looked again. Surely! Each sledge was gliding forward, propelled by the unseen men who wriggled flat in the snow behind it.

Kit now understood his enemies' strategy, but it had been a costly business finding out. The Yellow Knives could approach with their backs to the sun that streamed like molten silver into Kit's squinting, tortured face. The snow field was beginning to dance before him in garish colors. He dared not even think the word, but he knew what was happening to him. Trying to make out things in a quicksilver flood, with his eyes boggling in his head—

Rifle firing! Sullen thuds of sound at his left and in front of him—he listened for bullets in the air. Some of them plunged into the snow, not very close. One went above him, turning end over end, buzzing like a June-bug. Rotten rifling that wouldn't spin a bullet properly. Something hit the sledge resoundingly a dozen inches from his nose, and one of the deck supports was sheared in two, neatly as the slicing stroke of a sharp ax.

They weren't all using trade guns. Somebody else was doing a problem in long-distance arithmetic.

Kit tried to locate the sharp-shooter. That crisp, whip-like report meant high-power and meticulous rifling. Puffs of black powder smoke drifted above the sledges—all but one. That one stood farthest back and in the center of the line. By an exertion of will Kit forced his eyes to stay wide open long enough to concentrate his pupils on the midmost sledge. No smoke there. Anyhow, maybe not. His vision had cleared for a few seconds, and now the red and gold clouds were beginning to roll back in front of him. The middle sledge had seemed to be farther away than the others. Probably Hell Bent was sprawled behind that one. He'd be the one to have smokeless powder cartridges.

A bullet tore through the six fat duffle-bags lashed in a row on Kit's sledge. He picked up the distant object again—a vague smudge in a spectrum of fiery colors that wouldn't stay still. No trajectory tables or micrometer calculations were possible; just shove the butt to the shoulder, and guess, and pull the trigger. He couldn't even see the sights.

What was the use? Damn his eyes! And the sun and the frightful, glaring snow! A trickle of syrup was running out of a punctured can over his bare right hand. He wiped his hand in disgust on the back of his shirt.

His four dogs were crouching at his feet, and he absently scratched a rough, uplifted head.

"That you, Buzz-saw?" He laughed crazily. "What you sticking around here for? Why'nt you beat it?"

The firing seemed to be getting in closer. Banging explosions not only in front and to the left, but off on the right now. The bullets were dropping around him. They sounded like skate-blades cutting into crusty ice. Buzz-saw's hot tongue was licking the rest of the sticky mess off his fingers.

He started to fire at the echo of the guns, and then changed his mind. If he missed a few times running they'd guess what was wrong with him, and jump up and come on headlong. Let 'em crawl up, thinking he was deliberately holding his fire. It would take them longer to get here, anyhow.

Not that it mattered when they came.

There was a spot in back of his nose that seemed to be the core of his troubles, a swirling and flashing, as nerve-racking as fireworks in his head. The eyesight—what a sensitive, perishable gift! Maltreat it for a few minutes, and it is gone. He couldn't see a thing. There were nothing but shrinking nerves and agonizing colors swimming around in the places where his eyes ought to be. He was blind. He was snow-blind.

The rifle was of no more use to him than a dictionary. He chucked it away and groped for the shotgun. This was the tool for a blind man. Fourteen shells. Some held bird-shot and some buck-shot. It said which was which on the wads, if he could read them. No difference. He'd try to get them all in at the last minutes when everybody was jammed around him so close he couldn't miss.

He tried the safety and broke the breech and snapped it shut again. A slug hit the ground by his face and spattered with the noise of an ice-pick chipping ice. Another knocked a welt of fur off his hood and ricocheted across the frozen river in two clanging jumps. He must have stuck his head up too far without knowing it. Blind and blundering!

Buzz-saw let out a terrific growl. Kit dropped his hand to feel the dog crouching with every muscle tense and his back ridge abristle. The keen, snarling muzzle was pointing north, down the river-course.

"What? What it is, boy?"

Kit suddenly flung up his gun and turned in sightless staring. Something—crunching, gliding in the hard snow below the river bank—coming towards him. He thumbed off the catch, finger crooked, sighting for the sound.

"Hello!" said a voice. "Hold it! What do you think you're doing?"

The blood seemed to drain out of Kit's brain. A swaying weakness overmastered him. The gun barrels wavered and sagged in his hands—too heavy to hold. He couldn't move, or think, or speak.

Somebody strode up to him, and a big, strong, rough-sleeved arm suddenly wrapped itself about his head and squeezed his ears.

"Hello, Kit," said the astounding voice. "Hello, Cocky-bird!"

CHAPTER XXIII
BROTHERS-IN-ARMS

Kitchener lost his shotgun as a wave of giddiness swept over him. His hands went up, incredulous, feebly groping, to cling to a pair of big, fleshly shoulders, to feel the warmth and vitality of solid human strength holding him on his feet.

"Jerry," he said. "Jerry! My God! Jerry!"

"Who the hell did you think it was?" asked the bright, mocking voice that Kit would have known anywhere, anytime, in any world or state of existence. Jerry Tearl!

"I thought— They killed you. I thought you were killed—Jerry!"

"Who killed me? Have you gone nuts or something? What's the shootin'— Hey—you damn fool—keep your head down!"

"Back in that cabin. The bloody old red blanket! And all over the floor and window sill. I thought they got you."

"What cabin? What *are* you talking about?"

"Back at Great Owl Run. Grandfather Tearl's old Hudson's Bay blanket with a bullet hole in it. I thought you'd been murdered—"

"Who, me?" Jerry broke in with his scornful laugh. "I wasn't at Great Owl Run. I went down the Vermilion, straight to the sea coast. The blanket. Oho! I'm beginning to get you. I had the blanket strapped on the back of my sledge, and some of the duffel you'd traded me. It must have come loose and fallen off. I discovered it was gone late one night when I went into camp, several miles farther down the Vermilion than the Great Owl fork. Somebody picked it up. That's all."

Kit was laughing while tears ran from the corners of his inflamed eyelids. "Jerry! I don't know what to *say*." His fingers contracted in his brother's bulging biceps with bruising force. "Why, you—you doggoned old scut!"

"Steady-on there, bird!" Kit felt a pair of fingers poking experimentally into his eye-sockets. "What's wrong with you, Crow-eye?"

"Nothing. Just a little blind—snow-blind. The cursed sun—and the snow—"

Jerry made a queer sound with his lips. "You mean to say—you been carrying-on here—and can't see?"

"Trying to."

"What's it all about—?"

A chunking hunk of lead slapped a metal brace of the sledge and burst into particles around their ears.

"Pardon me," said Jerry, "may I cut-in?"

He stirred, then steadied, and five rifle-shots rattled spitefully over the river embankment. The clip tinkled and he shoved in a fresh round. "Slaveys—Yellow Knives? What's the racket?"

"Yellow Knives," said Kit. "It's a long story."

"If I could shoot like you used to," remarked the sergeant, "I'd have got that baby with the red cap. But I'll bet his ear's burning. They're not pushing in quite so fast."

"It's the ones behind," said Kit. "Where are they now?"

Jerry was silent for a moment. "Yeh!" he observed at length. "Six of 'em—making way around to the west. The bunch in front are going to hold us until the others are in our rear. The second bunch are going to be the bananas. Well, we had lots of fun when we had it."

Kit heard a scratching sound, and a savor of strong pipe-tobacco drifted into his nostrils. Then Jerry moved off a few paces along the river, and said something in thick, rasping syllables of speech that Kit was unable to understand.

A second voice answered in heavy gutturals. Kit threw up his head with a start, his facial muscles contorted in a straining effort to see through multicolored mists. Jerry had brought a companion with him, an Esquimau, judging by the talk.

"Who's that?" Kit demanded.

"Just a friend," said Jerry lightly. "He came down with me from the Arctic Circle."

Kit sighed and shook his head. One more victim in the trap. On the other hand, if this newcomer was anything like Oogly, he'd be a stout comrade for a last-hour stand.

The sergeant was giving the man some sort of instruction in the Esquimau tongue. Feet moved down the slope, and then Jerry came back to Kit.

"I've got him planted on the river ice to guard our rear. He's a good man, a crack shot, but there are too many of 'em for us, and they'll get us all before sundown. Well-o, Cocky-bird, we'll go out of this heathenish country together!"

The rattle of rifle-fire in front of them had died away to only an occasional report. Jerry's recent burst of shots had taught caution to the crowd behind the sledges. They'd hold their real attack, of course, until the men in the rear were in position.

"Jerry! Who do you suppose was murdered in that cabin?"

"I don't know. How do I know? Say, how'd you get in this jam, Kit? Who started it, and why?"

"Oh, there was some trouble about a man that the Yellow Knives wanted to kill—who was shot down last night by Hell Bent. Bent's here now, keeping 'em ribbed-up. That business back at Great Owl Run—somebody was murdered there that night. Trail of the body dragged across the floor and dumped into the river."

"No!" ejaculated Jerry. "Oh—that's how! I *found* him."

"What?"

"Body in the river. About fifty miles north of here—on our way back. A tall, raw-boned chap with a bullet in his back. Drifted out from an ice hole and washed up on the bank. Poor devil! Must have floated all the way down under the ice—Great Owl Run into the Vermilion River. Funny thing about him—"

"Hell Bent killed him," interrupted Kitchener. "And I thought it was you!" He blinked and dug the back of his fist into his eyes. The pain came and went in waves. But if he forced his bare eyeballs to endure the daylight he could still see something of his blurred surroundings. Jerry sat on the snow-shelf with his knee locked in his fingers and a pipe in his teeth.

"Bent's square-meshed tracks went to the cabin," Kit ruminated. "Why did he shoot this chap? Who do you suppose he was?"

"Keep 'em shut, Kit," advised Jerry. "Not that it'll do any good now, but they won't hurt so much. The only thing that'll cure snow-blindness is a long stretch of total darkness." He laughed grimly. "Well, I guess we're going to have that soon—a long, long stretch."

"Who do you think he could be?" Kit persisted doggedly.

"The dead man? I went through him, and he didn't have an identifying mark on him. But I'll tell you something that he did have—in an old wallet, buttoned up with a big bunch of money. A stack of old express company and postal money order receipts for five thousand dollars each—dated in January for twelve consecutive years. In whose favor do you suppose they'd been made out, Kit?"

"I don't know. How'd I—" Kitchener's chin lifted sharply. "You don't—you don't mean—"

"Yes. The slips were all made out in the name of Mrs. William Tearl, New York City. The source of the mysterious annuity. That man, whoever he was, was the chap who has sent five thousand dollars to our family around the first of every year. He could have told us a lot of things, I guess, if we'd got to him in time. And now he's dead."

"But who—why?" Kit faced his brother blankly.

"Don't know. Any guess you'd make would be only a wild shot. Maybe Dad did something for him some time, or he did something to Dad, and he's been squaring accounts with his conscience ever since. And for some reason wanted to remain incognito. Funny he should be at the Great Owl place the night Hell Bent got there—and is murdered by him."

"Here it is!" said Kit tensely. "This chap must have been mixed up some way in Dad's disappearance. Maybe he felt responsible somehow for what happened. Tried to make it up to Mother the best way he could—by sending money. When Bent is released from prison this chap goes to the old cabin and waits, figuring Bent'll come some day. Sounds as though there was an old score between them that had to be reckoned up. And Bent came and settled it for keeps by killing this other chap when he was asleep."

"Maybe," agreed Jerry. "But anyway you fit it together it's guesswork." He touched his brother's sleeve. "By the way, I didn't introduce you to my friend."

"Who?"

"The man who came down with me from Queen Maud Sea."

"Your trip up there turned out to be a bust, didn't it? I never did pin any hope in that business."

"My friend didn't want to come," pursued Jerry. "But I made him believe that I wouldn't be able to make the return trip unless I had a good hunter with me, and I finally persuaded him to see me down as far as the police post."

Jerry spoke to the man on the river ice. "I want you to know my brother," he said. "I'm Jerry Tearl. This is Kit Tearl." He stressed the name with a peculiar emphasis.

There was a momentary silence. Jerry seemed to be waiting for something. Kit at length heard him fill his lungs deeply. "His name is Kablunak," said Jerry. "He belongs to the Ahiagmuit tribe."

"Yes?" said Kit, and stopped with a sudden, queer breathlessness. "Kablunak! Why—that was the name—wasn't it? You said— Kablunak! Why—why, that means 'white man,' doesn't it?"

"Yes." The fingers on Kitchener's sleeve gripped a little tighter. "This man only talks Esquimau, but he is not an Esquimau. His own language—he's forgotten it. He's lost his language, his identity—everything. Everything is completely gone."

"You—what do you mean?" gasped Kit. His blinded eyes were turned wildly towards the tall, straight-formed figure of the stranger, whom he saw as in a blurring fog.

"He was frightfully wounded a number of years ago," said Jerry in a slow, curiously strained voice. "A bullet in his head. You could see the scar if you were able to see. That bullet snapped something in his brain—what do they call it?—aphasia—forgetfulness. He doesn't remember a thing. He doesn't remember who he is or where he came from or what he had been."

Kit was breathing hard, staring tragically through the mists. "My God!" he whispered.

"A party of Esquimaux found him in the snow in the forest down yonder, apparently dying. Twelve years back. They bundled him on a sledge and took him north with them, and nursed his body back to health, but not—not his brain."

"Who is he?" whispered Kit in agonized suspense.

"He became one of the Ahiagmuit," stated Jerry. "In the years that he lived with them they came to accept him as their chief hunter, their leader—"

"Who?" Kit demanded hoarsely.

Jerry's hand was a vice, clutching his brother's arm. "He's a lean, tall man with a white mustache and a shock of snow-white hair, a hawk's face, and a pair of steel eyes that glow sometimes with a strange inward flame. And under his artikis he wears the badge of the royal police."

CHAPTER XXIV
THERE WERE THREE

Kitchener was on his feet with a stabbing breath, stumbling down the embankment. In his dim-sighted, watering eyes the erect figure on the ice loomed like a specter in an unbelievable dream. He reached awe-stricken towards the stiff, unresponsive silhouette.

"Dad!" he said in a stifled voice. And again, in sudden, breaking emotion: "*Dad!*"

With a quiet, gentle dignity the man drew away from the hands that had touched him. Jerry hastened forward and crooked his arm about his brother's shoulders.

"No, Kit! I've talked and talked with him, and he doesn't get me. It's no use. Save yourself the heartbreak. He knows us only as a couple of white men whom he's just happened to meet out here on the barrens. That's all."

The tears that drenched Kit's eyes were not wholly the weeping of tormented, aching nerves. His father! Inspector Tearl of the Royal Canadian Police—wearing the garb and living the life and thinking the thoughts of an Ahiagmuit Esquimau! The pathos of that stern and lonely figure—the man who had emerged out of the ghostly years, and did not even know he had come back to his own.

The old man said something in a strange tongue, and ended with a kindly laugh.

Jerry answered with an unusual gentleness of voice.

"What is it?" Kit asked with a sound that was like a sob.

"He sees what's wrong with you, and he says that snow-blindness sometimes makes men act queerly. But he likes your looks and is glad to have made your acquaintance."

"To make my—" Kit could not finish. He felt as though he were stifling.

"I found him on Queen Maud Sea, sitting by a seal hole with a spear in his hand," said Jerry. "His tribesmen told me that they have not known a starvation winter since he became one of them. A white man's brains to help them through the long midnights. They adored him."

Kit was too choked-up to speak. He had never heard of a more complete tragedy than this. Bill Tearl, lost to the world and to himself—not knowing who he was or where he came from—spending the years in an Esquimau igloo. Death in itself is not so terrible. But to die, and still go on living! It might not have been so bad if utter forgetfulness had blotted out everything of the past. But was it possible ever for the memory to go into a total eclipse?

Life for Bill Tearl must have been a fantastic nightmare. Wandering through lonesome, six-months-long nights. Bewilderment and yearning and discontent. There must have been times when the smoldering fires of the poor, estrayed brain, the vague, vain efforts to remember, would overwhelm him like a madness.

Kit found himself fumbling at the snap of his revolver holster. If there were only some way to touch the spark that surely still lived in the darkness, to set off the lost train of recollection! He pulled out the engraved, ivory-butted revolver and offered it to the man who called himself Kablunak.

"Inspector William Tearl!" He tried desperately to speak clearly and steadily. "This is your gun. Please take it back again. It's the old six shooter your men gave you when you left to take command of the outpost at *Saut Sauvage*."

He could almost see the grizzled face of the old sergeant who had made the presentation years ago, and he recalled the little speech that accompanied the gift.

"May it never fire first," he said; "may it never fire too late."

The old man took the gun from Kitchener's unsteady hand. He turned it over and examined it minutely, barrel, trigger-guard, the engraved silver name-plate, the beautifully carved butt. After a moment his hand cuddled the stock and he sighted at some imaginary target. Then he broke into a pleased, gentle laugh that snapped the awful tension like the parting of a chain.

He asked some question in the Ahiagmuit dialect, and Jerry let go a pent-up breath that was almost suffocating him. "He doesn't understand. He doesn't recognize it. He—he only wanted to know if you were loaning it to him."

"Tell him it's his—it's his very own," Kit said in a gulping voice.

"I thought—for just a minute, there was something in his eyes. As though something was trying to remind him. And then it faded—was gone."

"Tell him!" Kit pleaded. "Make him understand, Jerry!"

"I've told him—dozens of times. And it just doesn't register."

Jerry turned and exchanged a few sentences with the old man, and then he looked back somberly at his brother, and shook his head. "He thinks you're giving it to him—as a gift—between comrades who are willing to fight together. That's as much as I can make him understand." The sergeant's hardlimned features held a strange, boyish wistfulness. "He says it is a fine, handsome gun—to thank you very much—to tell you that if he were ever privileged to use it to protect your life, it would be a trifling return for such a splendid present."

Kit could not trust himself to speak.

"Where did you get it?" asked Jerry.

"The gun? Grabbed it from Hell Bent—last night. If it hadn't have been for my eyesight I'd have got Bent—"

Something screamed across the river terrace behind them and stopped with a tearing, meaty *curump*!

"Lookout! Down!" Jerry seized Kit and shouldered him back into a niche of the embankment.

Kit wrenched himself loose and squirmed about, impotently gripping his shotgun. "Jerry—who's hit?"

"One of your dogs! Stay there! Cut him nearly in two. Dum-dums—"

Jerry snatched up his rifle, and fired, and cursed with a lilting gayety. "How can you hit 'em when you can't see 'em?"

"The bunch in the rear?" asked Kit.

"And how! They've buried themselves under the snow, with nothing but peep-holes. Just a landscape to look at."

"You hate to have to kill 'em," said Kit. "The poor, misguided fools. If we could only get Bent, there'd be a chance."

"Yeh," mocked Jerry. "Hate to kill 'em! Where's this Bent?"

The first shot was followed by others, mean, vicious sounds whipping through the sunlight. Another dog went down, got up and tried to walk, dragging his hind quarters, and crumpled gasping in the snow.

Jerry was crouching at Kit's back, squinting into the snow-glare, trying to find a living mark. "Look!" he suddenly gasped. "Dad!"

"Huh?" exclaimed Kit, twisting around.

"He's trying to crawl up on them—across the river. With the revolver!" He raised his voice in sharp warning. "No! They're on this side too! Dad! Stay where you are!"

Instantly he recollected, and his English shifted into a lingo of harsh consonants, the meaning of which Kit could only surmise. But the old man paid no heed.

He was out on the river ice, sprawled flat, pushing a little breastwork of snow ahead of him, hitching his way across the stream as though he were stalking caribou. The Yellow Knives ambushed on the west side would make short shrift of the trapped defenders—unless they were quickly suppressed. So the one-time policeman had chosen that hazardous job for his own.

Heedless of the bullets that nipped the air about him, Jerry was on his feet, hurrying down the slope. The old man was more than half-way across the river, and now was shielded from the sight of his quarry by the rising embankment above him. But the opposite terrace no longer served as a buttress behind him. He had crept out into view of the men who were firing from the sledges on the eastern side.

Kit and Jerry had been partly sheltered in the rear by a break in the embankment. The old man kept himself covered with snow as he crawled ahead. Only the top of his head was showing. But the dogs were huddled out in the open. The first few rounds from the west bank were picking them off.

Evidently the attackers proposed to make certain of their victims by first destroying the means of flight. There was to be no last-minute dash for safety with the sledges. Kit's team was wiped out in two minutes. Buzz-saw was down, back-broken. Two of the Chippewyan huskies lay stone-dead, a third was trying to walk on two feet, with his muzzle plowing the snow. Jerry's leader was out, and numbers two and four had tumbled together in the traces, moaning and kicking feebly.

"Bent's in back of the middle sledge!" gasped Kit. "High power and a deadly shot! Jerry! Dad! Come back!"

The bright, windless morning was filled with hard, electric cracklings—ripping, snapping sounds breaking in from both sides of the river. Two dozen or more savages were at work now, combing over the defenders from both directions with a venomous cross-fire. The heavy explosions echoed back and forth with a sullen malignity. At bay between the embankments of the wide river-bed, the three trapped men were left the grim alternative of taking it either from one shore or the other.

The pain in Kit's eyes throbbed intermittently like a jumping toothache. Sometimes a fire spectrum wavered before him, or again the colors washed out in white blankness, as though a bucket of snow-white paint had been dumped over his head. At intervals his eyesight was restored briefly, so he could see things through a weaving film.

He made out a dull, dark shape on the river ice, crawling doggedly; and Jerry, stooping, moving down the embankment....

Through the snow glare there rushed a high-pitched wail of sound, faster, shriller, more hideous somehow, and overriding all other sounds.

It reached the river and stopped horribly with a soggy thump.

For a moment Kit was overcome by a ghastly sickness. He heard the clean report of a small-caliber rifle whip back above the line of sledges, and at the same instant he heard Jerry's anguished cry.

"Dad!"

Jerry was down in the middle of the stream, bending over a snow-shrouded shape that did not move. He went on his knees and stood up again with a limply dragging object in his arms. Up the embankment he staggered, clutching his burden, breathing thickly through his teeth. Unhurried by the bullets that cut the air about him he crossed the open ground to the eastward terrace and laid the fur-clad form at his brother's feet.

"Dad!" he said, and trailed off in a dull monotone. "They got him for keeps this time."

CHAPTER XXV
INSPECTOR TEARL

Kit gripped his eyes tightly shut, and then opened them again and tried to see. He dropped and buried his hands in the muffling, snow-crusted furs. "I heard it hit," he said.

"Right behind the ear," whispered Jerry. "Craziest thing I ever knew. Almost the same place where the other one hit him—years ago."

A chunk of lead threw a spurt of snow in Kit's face. He peered about wildly, and then sprang to his feet and hauled his parked sledge down from the top of the embankment. He swung the runners about and shoved the load of baggage alongside the prone body. Then, with his head down between hunched-up shoulders, as though he were plunging into a hail storm, he ran down the slope among the strewing of dogs.

He found a short ax, and with numbed sensibilities he struck twice. The whimpering ceased. He drew his knife and slashed the traces free. Then he bent his back to the tug and started up the embankment with the second laden sledge.

Jerry caught the idea, and hurried down to help. They rushed the sledge up the terrace, lifted it with its baggage, and stood it on top of Kit's sledge. Before the marksmen across the river had spotted their range both dodged into the protected alley between the piled-up sledges and the crest of the river bank.

For the moment they were barricaded against their enemies on either side of the stream. Jerry had dropped his rifle and was stooping low over the wounded man. At length he looked up gravely and shook his head. "He's breathing—that's all."

A while ago Kit had wept over the man who came back from the years of living death. Now he was strangely unaffected. It was as though the well-springs of emotion had suddenly dried within him. Actual, physical death was not so terrible.

He stared towards Jerry for a moment, and then groped for his rifle and drew himself flat on top of the embankment. Hell Bent was over there behind the middle sledge. Bent at last had finished his incomplete job of twelve years ago. It seemed to Kit that his own life had been shaped and consecrated to this one moment. Just give him his vision long enough to mark his man and align his rifle-sights, and he would ask nothing else of fortune, ever.

He was fumbling with his rifle, gray-faced and grim, trying to pin his sight on the sledge that sheltered Bent, when Jerry grabbed his ankle. "Come down, Jackass!"

Kit kicked back in an effort to loosen his brother's grip, and then his body went taut and a queer, shivering sensation ran up and down his spine. Somebody had shouted from under the embankment: not Jerry; a wild, unearthly voice that rang through him like a Jehovian trumpet.

Awed, shaken to the depths, he tumbled down from the bank of snow, to find Jerry locked with a struggling, bloodied figure that was trying to stand erect behind the sheltering sledges.

The miracle was not so much that the man still lived with a bullet in his brain, but that an unconquerable vitality flamed in the lean, gaunt body to endow him for those few moments with a will and lithe muscular strength to overmatch the brawny Jerry.

Bill Tearl, as he might have been a dozen years ago, his head high, his gun in his fist, a deathless valor sustaining him in his last embattled hour!

"Behind that stump!" he cried. "There's another under the windfall! I'll take him! Durand—over your shoulder—behind you—look out!"

Kit was staring in utter stupefaction. This was not the gentle, vaguely smiling man who had come down out of the Northland with Jerry. The lax shoulders had stiffened, indolence had kindled into a blazing resolution. He was no Esquimau, either in thought or in speech, but a determined white man at bay, fighting for his life.

167

"It's Bent!" he declared. "And Bruyas! And that other little weasel—what's his name—Giffard!" He had remembered his own tongue, and was calling to somebody in furious, hard-clipt words.

"Hold the dogs. I'll take care of this side. They want the gold sacks. Let 'em come and get 'em!"

"My God!" said Jerry. "He thinks he's back there that day—at Great Owl Run."

Kitchener had stumbled to Jerry's assistance and was trying to pinion his father's straining arms. "Dad!" he said. "Wake up! Come out of it! It's Kit! Listen to me!"

The old man did not seem to hear the soothing voice. He wrenched his arms free, whirled and stared at the ground behind him. "They've shot her from behind—murdered her!" His speech throbbed with pity and horror. "That lovely girl— Ah, the devils!"

The bullets were whining and snapping overhead, but if Bill Tearl heard them he thought they were the bullets of another bloody day, long ago. The missile that had hit him a few minutes before must have re-opened the lead-scarred brain-cells and let in remembrance. Recollection had come to him, and with it, delirium. His mind was back in the Great Owl forest, re-living the tragic scene of his last rational hour. A sleeper who had awakened at the place where his long sleep began.

"Hell Bent did that," he avowed. "If you don't kill him, Durand, I'm going to."

He turned and looked squarely at Kit with eyes that evidently saw another man. "Here! The chamber's full. Take this one!" He reversed the ivory-handled gun and shoved the butt into Kit's hand. "Listen, I'll keep 'em busy here by this poor girl. Leave your rifle. He's under the windfall. If you can work around behind you can nail him."

Kit thrust the revolver into his holster, and curved his arm about the old man's shoulders. The bullets were singing around them with the pertinacity of blood-thirsty mosquitoes. It might have seemed for just those few moments that a derisive fate was protecting them.

"Dad!" Kit beseeched. "Please! Let's get under cover."

Strangely, the old man yielded. The tense figure relaxed in his arms and he lowered the sagging weight behind the shelter of the sledges.

"Who—who's there?" asked the inspector in a wandering voice.

"It's I—it's Kitchener."

"Who? Little Kit?"

"Yes."

"Who's that with you?"

"Why, it's Gerald."

"Jerry?"

"Yes." Kit felt as though something had been stuffed in his throat to shut off his breathing. "It's—it's Kit and Jerry."

His father's hand groped upward to touch his face, and then strayed over his shoulder and down his arm to clutch at his hand. For an instant the sinewy fingers gripped him tightly, and then he felt them slipping, growing weaker.

"What are you two boys doing here?" Bill Tearl asked with a sudden severity.

"We—we came to find you."

"What do you want? Why did you leave home?"

Jerry was down beside them, his hand on his brother's knee. "He's gone all the way back now," he whispered. "He knows us now and he thinks we're a couple of little kids."

The hearing of the dying man was astonishingly alert. "What did you think you were," he demanded—"men? Now listen to me, you boys. I don't want you tagging after me. I've got a job to do, and this is no place for you.

"I want you to go back to your mother," the inspector commanded, while the brothers knelt over him with heads mutely bowed. "Tell her I've got some business to attend to, but I'll be back as soon as I can. I'll be home shortly."

"Yes, Dad," Kit assented in a breaking voice.

He thought it was the end, and was taken unawares when, with a sudden, uncanny resurging of vitality, the dying man twisted out of his arms and stumbled up in the red-spattered snow.

The old inspector yelled with a frightful incoherency. "The gold bags! The dogs—broken loose. Runaway! Hey—Durand—stay there. I'll stop 'em—"

He was on his feet, swaying, staring with excitement across the barrens. Before the brothers could interfere he stooped and snatched up a rifle.

"Look out there, you!" he shouted. "The fool dogs. They'll go over the creek bluff! Whoa! Haw, you fools! They've gone. The sledge. Drowning, the poor brutes. And the sledge!" He laughed with a grim mockery. "Snowing! Trail soon blotted. Murder for gold bags, and the bags are gone. Who'll find 'em? Funny world. Murder for nothing—"

He snapped off his speech to glower across the river embankment. "Hell Bent! You know where they went overboard, do you? Followed, eh?" The white mustache lifted in a ferocious smile. "All right! See if you live to salvage 'em!"

He broke away from Kit's detaining hand, and with a spasmodic strength that was not to be denied, he flung himself against the river bank and scrambled up over the mound of snow. Against the white, shadowless tundra he stood in stark outline, an erect, straight-poised figure, advancing towards the sledges with a rifle in his hands.

The guns were blazing away in a furious concentration, up and down the line in front, and from the other side of the river. Three or four powdery snow puffs spatted out of the old man's clothing like dust out of a beaten rug. Inspector Bill Tearl tried to advance on his weaving legs, and then toppled and went down slowly and solemnly as a crumbling tree-trunk, and lay still with his face towards the midmost sledge.

CHAPTER XXVI
ONE WHOLE MAN

The two brothers were both over the bank, crawling in the scuffled snow. Kit scarcely noticed the buzzing bullets. He shook his head in petty irritation, as though he were annoyed by a swarm of gnats. Jerry had reached the fallen man, and grasped one of the limp ankles. Kit caught hold of the other leg. They wriggled backwards and dragged the body with them over the terrace and down into the shallow trench behind the sledges.

Kit spoke with a curious, measured calmness. "It's a lot better to remember and die," he said, "than to forget and go on living."

Then his voice thrilled with a swelling emotion. "They had to kill him—not once—but three times!"

Jerry said nothing. He was giggling like a girl in a most amazing falsetto.

Kit turned to him blankly. "What's the matter with you?"

"Fun-ny bone," exclaimed Jerry, and tried to stop his spasmodic gasping. He moved half way around to exhibit his right forearm, which hung from his elbow like an old, fagged rope-end. "One of the dum-dums—smashed the bone. It—it's not so darned funny as—as it sounds."

Kitchener grasped his brother's hairy, dangling wrist and explored with his fingers up under the dripping sleeve. "Gee, that's rotten, Jerry." It gave him a pang to feel the magnificent muscles changed in a moment to numbed and useless flesh. "When was it?"

"Just as we came back over the bank." Jerry was in control of his fretted nerves again. He laughed ruefully in his own deep voice. "Doggone 'em, Cocky-bird. They've got us winging. You've got no eyes to speak of and they've turned me into a port-sider. Well, there's still one whole Tearl left if we combine our good points."

Kit had ripped the puckering string out of his hood. He pushed up the sleeve and wound a tourniquet above the broken elbow. This was as much as he could do for the present.

Jerry dug into his pocket for a pipe and tobacco pouch, and stuffed the bowl full with one hand. Then he struck a light and inhaled with a gusty sigh.

For the moment Kit was bending in gentle abstraction over the body stretched alongside the sledge. He took off his mitten and his warm fingers touched the upstaring face. With a caressing lightness he traced the line of the rugged features, the high, bulging brow, the keen, hawk-like nose, the straight-formed mouth compressed in death, and the square and dogged chin. Then he softly folded together the flaps of the rudely made Ahiagmuit hood.

"Did you hear what he said, Jerry?"

"Umph. He fought that old fight all over again."

"You can fill in the gaps without much trouble and know about what happened back there that day."

"He and the two musk-ox hunters, the brother and sister, were traveling south in a heavy snow storm with the gold sledge," suggested Jerry. "They were ambushed somewhere near Great Owl Run by Hell Bent and some chaps named Buya—what was it?"

"Bruyas. Bruyas and Giffard. Those two!" The muscles of Kitchener's mouth contracted. "I might have suspected before. As ornery a pair as you ever want to see. They're still living down there—trapping. They must have been a couple of the guides that came back from the musk-ox country, along with Hell Bent. It's certain now that they were in the bunch that attacked Dad's party. He evidently saw them at the time, and knew them."

"The girl in the party," mused Jerry—"she must have gone down at the first few shots. From then on it was a free-for-all. Dad and this other man—battling from behind the sledge of gold bags. And the dogs got scared in the midst of it all and bolted."

"And ran for a few miles," put in Kit—"with Dad after 'em. And Hell Bent after Dad."

"The other two," supplemented Jerry—"what's their names—stayed behind to fight it out with Dad's friend. That chap, standing over his dead sister's body! After seeing what he had seen I guess he wouldn't give much of a damn what happened to him. Probably just went shootin' crazy. My guess would be that he ran those two scuts clear out of the woods."

"Meantime," pursued Kit, "the frightened dogs must have reached the bluff that runs along with Great Owl Run. Swung in too close, lost their footing on the slippery incline, and went down into the creek, dragging the sledge with them."

"My gosh!" Jerry checked his pipe-stem as he was about to put it between his teeth. "Why, it must—maybe it's there still!"

"It is. I found the bags, and shifted them."

"You what?"

"Found 'em—at the place where the sledge dumped off the bluff, years ago. I dived for the gold bags, brought them up and jettisoned them farther up stream, where Bent won't easily locate them."

Jerry stared for a moment. "Smart boy!" he declared finally.

Kit wrinkled his forehead reflectively. "Here's what happened. Dad saw the dogs take their last plunge. Hell Bent was chasing close behind, and he also saw it. These two were the only ones who knew what had become of that sledge of gold."

"They faced each other in the snow storm on the brink of Great Owl Run," Kit ruminated. "They shot it out, and Bent fired first."

"That's it, of course," assented Jerry. "Left Dad there for dead, helped himself to one bag of nuggets, and went his way. Meant to come back after his pals had passed out of the picture and salvage the rest."

"Those other two," said Kit—"Bruyas and Giffard—they must have made a shrewd guess at the truth. Knew the treasure was still around here somewhere. Sticking in the neighborhood all these years. Living by their trapping, and hunting for the lost sledge."

"Yep. And waiting for Bent to come back. Probably they heard he was in the jug. But they'd know that as soon as he got out he'd come back here, and they were sitting tight waiting for him to betray himself to them."

Jerry knocked the ashes out of his pipe and lifted his head cautiously to peer over the top of the river embankment. The shooting had almost ceased in the last two or three minutes, and the continued quiet was beginning to grow ominous.

"The two middle sledges have pushed in close together," he remarked casually. "They're holding a pow-wow." He glanced across at the waning sun. "The daylight won't last much longer, and they're probably thinking they ought to do something about it pretty soon. I wouldn't be surprised if they rushed us anytime."

Kit was strangely unconcerned over the war councils of the Yellow Knives. When they decided to come on they'd do it, and worrying wouldn't stop them. For the moment he was much more disturbed by the revelation of past events.

"Jerry!" he broke in sharply. "The murdered man you found with money-order receipts—what did he look like?"

"Why, he'd been a pretty tall guy I'd say—six feet or more." Jerry faced his brother curiously. "Dark, keen-featured chap, black hair shot with gray, clean-shaven, couple of welts across his cheek like old knife or bullet scars. He had on a tannish mackinaw—"

"Jerry!" Kit sprang to his feet, forgetting that the top of his head offered an inviting target for any of the Indian marksmen who happened to be looking that direction. "Do you know who he was?"

The elder brother looked startled. "Why, yes," he said after a moment. "Sure! The man who was in the fight with Dad. The brother of the murdered woman."

"Of course!" he ejaculated after a briefest pause.

"Funny I never thought of that before! That would explain the money orders. He dragged Dad into that mess. After Dad disappeared he felt that he owed the family something, and started sending the annuity—"

"Wait!" interrupted Kit. "That isn't what I'm getting at. Do you know who he really was?"

"Huh?"

"You heard the name, didn't you? The man who stood fighting over his dead sister?"

"It was—" Jerry scowled in an effort of recollection.

"Durand," said Kit.

"That was it. I remember now—" Jerry stopped as he caught the expression of his brother's face.

"The man I met down at the Chippewyan village, weeks and weeks ago!" burst out Kit. "He tallies in every detail with your description of the body in the river. Unquestionably he's the man who was murdered in that cabin. Diane's uncle. She told us his name was Durand—Jim Durand. And we didn't believe her. You said he was Hell Bent!"

"I thought he was," Jerry started to say, but Kitchener stopped him.

"You put me on his trail, made me think he was a scoundrel. And he was Dad's friend, and ours! We might have gotten together, if we'd only known. And now he's dead, and we aren't much better off ourselves." Kit's voice rose in sharp accusation. "Jerry! How'd you ever make a dumb bull like that?"

"Now hold on!" protested the sergeant. "Take it easy. I supposed he was Bent. Gosh! He came into the wilderness at the time and place I was expecting Bent. I didn't get a close look at him, and when I saw him through the thickets he was wearing a hood. And remember—you told me yourself he was carrying the old ivory-butted .45 that had belonged to the inspector."

"Yes. And you saw a few minutes ago how he got it. Dad himself handed the gun to him in the thick of the scrap. And he carried it ever after, up until the day somebody killed him at the Great Owl cabin."

Kit scowled at his brother. "I thought it was you who had been killed that day, and that Bent did the job. But Durand was the victim. Who do you suppose the murderer was?"

"If you must be oratorical," said Jerry pleasantly, "don't bob your head around up there where a bullet can knock it off." He reached up with his useful hand and pulled his brother down behind the embankment. "How do I know who that particular gunman was? Maybe it was the real Bent himself, or maybe Bruyas or this other trapper."

"These two trappers probably had kept tabs on Bent," Jerry pursued. "They would have known that when he got out of the cooler he'd be coming up to recover the hidden sledge. They'd be laying for him, and for anybody else that butted into the proceedings."

"The man who disposed of Durand took the gun and his snowshoes," Kit ruminated. "A pair of waffle-webbed snowshoes that I'd followed down the Vermilion River to Great Owl Run. The murderer, whoever he was, put them on instead of his own when he fled from the cabin. That's what brought about the confusion of identities. Afterwards he used those same raquettes to mislead me. And all the time I took it for granted that he was the same man I'd trailed through the wilderness from Port-o'-Prayer.

"All this while I thought Jim Durand was Bent," Kit went on bitterly. "And Diane! Because he was Diane's uncle, I suspected her of the evilest things. Why, I treated her as though she were some criminal. And she hated me—"

174

Jerry had not forgotten to watch the Yellow Knives. Every minute or two he had hoisted himself to peer over the terrace. His warning grip suddenly closed over Kit's arm. "Now!" he interrupted coolly. "You save the shotgun until they're in close. I'll try to chime in with a left fistful of .45s." He laughed devil-may-care. "Well-o, Cocky-bird, we were a good family while we lasted."

A babel of yells breaking out suddenly along the east shore were flung back in a whooping chorus from the other side of the river. Pieces of lead clipped the air in a gust and knocked up the snow crust in flying chunks.

Kit crept against the rampart beside his brother. He pushed up his head warily, with no more than a hand's-span of his skull risking itself above the embankment.

"They saw Dad go down, and they've about figured out how wabbly we are," muttered Jerry. "They'll whoop it up a minute, and then one'll get reckless enough to start, and they'll all come."

Kitchener was trying to distinguish substance in the milky haze that seemed to have flooded the barrens. He felt as though inflated bags had been sewed into his eye-sockets. Wavering, uncertain things loomed vaguely and distantly—men or dogs or sledges—they were shapeless and unreal and wouldn't stay still.

"Half of 'em are up, testing us out," Jerry informed him. "And there's a white man, waving them on."

"What's he like?"

"Big lookin' zob with a black beard."

"Sounds as though he might be— He's the one who picked Dad off—and poor Oogly."

"He's crouching with his rifle now, trying for a crack at us. If I only had my right arm!" Jerry groaned impotently. "Nice, easy shot around four hundred. We could pay off the hands—"

"Jerry! You've got it!" Kit's voice was so fiercely exultant that his brother turned to stare. "Are they still where they were?"

"They are now. But they won't be long. Any second—"

"Where's my gun?" Kit cut in. "The sights are set at the correct range, windage and everything. All you need to do is to notch 'em point blank."

"Yeah! And then what?"

"I'll pull the trigger for you. I'll squeeze it so gently you won't even feel it."

"My gosh!" For an instant Jerry surveyed his brother with glowing approval. "Why—why, you blood-thirsty little gnat."

With his hand reaching behind him he stooped and came up with Kit's rifle. He chucked the butt to his shoulder and leaned his weight against the terrace.

Kitchener stepped behind and circled the sergeant's broad back with his arms. He pulled the firing-bolt pin, and dug his chin firmly into the hollow of his brother's neck. Then he crooked his forefinger under the trigger-guard.

"Look out!" grunted Jerry. "Here they come!"

Without actually seeing, Kit's instinct told him that the line of men had surged forward. The yelling swelled into an appalling savagery, he caught the distant crunch of oncoming feet. Bullets were plowing around his face.

Jerry's brawny bulk settled, stiffened. His breathing stopped. He became rock-like in his transcendental calm. Kitchener waited in readiness. Seconds passed—minutes, it seemed to him. He could hear the advancing snowshoes cutting through the snow. The suspense was growing unbearable.

"Jerry!" he whispered. "What's the matter? Can't you line 'em?"

"A second!" soothed the sergeant. "He's kneeling to fire. It's hard to hold a rifle with one hand. Easy now! I'll say 'go.'"

The back muscles hardened to steel—the physical rigidity of the cool marksman inexorably engrossed.

"Ready!" said Jerry crisply.

Kit's trigger-finger clenched to the steel—put on all but the final ounce of pressure.

"*Go!*"

CHAPTER XXVII
HELL BENT

The curt voice and the rifle report cracked out together as a unity. Kit felt his brother's shoulder yield with the kick-back of the heavy discharge. He grabbed the rifle and shoved another cartridge under the bolt. Jerry was straining forward, breathless, staring.

"Hit!" Jerry's cry rang jubilant, and then checked lamely. "No...."

Kitchener gawked at the snowy barrens. His throbbing, visionless eyes overtaxed themselves in feverish uncertainty. He desperately wanted to see, and he couldn't.

"Yes!" The grimness of Jerry's speech sent a shiver through Kit. "*Yes!*"

The racket along the river had choked off as abruptly as though unseen hands had gripped a score of wildly shrieking throats. The senseless outburst of firing dwindled, almost ceased. Kit was aware of a sudden lagging of footsteps up and down the line of advance.

"He stood against it for a few seconds," explained Jerry. "I thought we'd missed."

Jerry spoke in a casual, chatty tone. The tension had lifted. He was his carefree, natural self again. "But he buckled up finally, as though he had the gripes, and rooted his nose in the tundra. He's lying out there like something that the dog fetched. The brother act was the hit of the piece."

Kit at that moment was not sorry that his eyes were spared the need of seeing. He was not squeamish. But also he was without morbid curiosity. Jerry's description did not sound pretty.

A few minutes ago Kit would have given his eyesight permanently for a fair shot at the man who had killed Inspector Bill Tearl. But now that it was over his wrath had simmered down and left him cold. His conscience did not disturb him. He knew that he would never feel the slightest twinge of remorse. It was as though he had merely helped to execute the decree of a higher judgment. The dead man had been one of the world's ugly liabilities, and they had simply wiped him off the debit column. Kit was thankful only that Jerry shared the responsibility with him, fifty-fifty.

The quiet was a bit disconcerting after the recent hubbub. Evidently it was the white man who had incited the Yellow Knives to the pitch of daring that brought them out from their cover. But the white man was down, and Kit sensed the wavering in the line of attack. These Yellow Knives knew him. He had bluffed them once before....

With the Winchester at a menacing slant he planted his knee on the embankment and scrambled to the top. He stood boldly erect and faced the tribesmen. Two or three bullets, hastily fired, whanged past him.

"Come down, you idiot!" gasped Jerry.

Kit's blinded gaze moved slowly, unflinching, across the invisible arc of the prairie. "Stop!" he shouted, and threw up his hand.

"Are you fools?" He queried them cheerfully in a voice only loud enough to reach across that narrow area of snow. "You know me! And my brother shoots straighter than I do. You've seen what happens. We'll kill ten of you before you get here, and the few who live now will be hanged by the police later on."

"You tell 'em, Cocky-bird!" he heard Jerry chuckling behind him. "Gad! They're half wilting right now."

"Tom Salmonfish!" Kitchener called. "And you, Athu! You needn't hide behind the others. I see you're there. Come forward a little way. I want to talk to you. You needn't be afraid." He spoke with disarming friendliness. "The man who shot one of us and made fools of you is dead. There can now be peace among us."

No shots had been fired in the last minute or so. These men at least had accepted the truce long enough to hear what he had to say. He caught a creaking of snowshoes as somebody stirred restlessly off at his right. "We come get Oogly," one of them announced, dispassionate and stubborn.

"Oogly!" Kit echoed the name with apparent amazement. "He's not here. Didn't you know? Oogly's dead!"

There was quiet for a few seconds after that, a hushed and incredulous interval.

"I'm telling the truth!" Kit broke in sharply. He pointed southward with his finger. "Down the river, three or four miles from here—go look for a mound of snow and a spear sticking in it. Dig in that mound, and you'll find Oogly."

The silence of the next moment or two was nerve-racking. Kit was just able to distinguish a few blurred shapes confronting him in a gloomy, watchful immobility.

"Oogly's not here I tell you!" Kitchener insisted earnestly. "Salmonfish and Athu—come and see for yourselves." With a splendidly magnanimous gesture he tossed aside the rifle, which he was unable to aim anyhow, and exhibited his defenseless hands. "You two come on." He smiled benignly. "You needn't be afraid."

"Show yourself," he said over his shoulder. "Let 'em see you're unarmed."

"Right behind you!" said Jerry.

"You needn't worry about anything that happens afterwards," Kit reassured the Yellow Knives. "You can go your way and everything will be forgotten."

For a dozen seconds, perhaps, the issue hung in the balance. But from the hesitation of the tribesmen it was clear enough that Kit's talk had made an impression. He had long since taught them a wholesome respect for his marksmanship. Although he had dropped his rifle, anybody could see an ivory pistol butt sticking out of his holster. There was no foreseeing how many of the tribesmen might go down before that deadly gun if hostilities were suddenly renewed. And at Kit's back stood the hard-jowled Jerry, whose potentialities as a fighter still must be reckoned with. Probably also a few of the more reflective minds had begun to ponder dubiously about the white man's law, which, in its own manner, at its own leisure, was capable of reaching a merciless arm even into the remotest wilderness.

Besides, they just wanted Oogly. They had no real quarrel with anybody else.

Kit suddenly was aware that two of the men had stepped out ahead of the line and were coming towards him warily.

He waited with apparent indifference. The advancing Indians finally ventured to the river's edge, and he allowed them to look over the embankment.

"You see," he said, "there were only three of us. My brother and I and—the man who was shot."

There was an uncomfortable pause. "What you do after we go away?" one of the Indians finally blurted out.

"Nothing," said Kit. "The white man was to blame, not you. You killed our dogs, but we will forget that. If you leave now, nothing will ever be done to you. You have my promise."

"Oogly dead?" temporized the tribal spokesman.

"I said so. You search where I told you and you'll know that I'm telling the truth. Oogly is dead."

"Good!" said the man heartily.

He said something in his harsh jargon to the nearest group of his comrades, and then flung up his arm to signal to those across the river. It seemed to be a pacific gesture.

Jerry had been watching suspiciously, with his left hand tucked under his parka. He relaxed with a twisted smile. "You've got 'em on the run, Crow-eye. They're going to call it a day."

The two Indians had turned on their heels to stalk away, but Kit motioned them to halt. "Just a minute," he commanded. "Who was the man who told you you'd find Oogly here?"

"Bruyas," one of the men informed him.

"Is that Bruyas lying off there by the sledges?"

"Yup!" said the Yellow Knife carelessly.

"All right. You may go now."

Kitchener picked up his rifle and dropped down beside his brother. "Bruyas!" he mused. "I'm beginning to think that he was behind most of our troubles. Bruyas, and probably Giffard. I shouldn't doubt if one of them was Durand's assassin. And they guessed, of course, why I was hanging around the Great Owl forest. Figured I knew too much and thought they'd better put me out too. They wanted a clear field for Hell Bent when he arrived. The only thing I don't understand is why he bothered to follow me into the barrens."

"It's quite likely," Jerry suggested, "that they'd heard the same rumors we did about the mysterious white man at Queen Maud Sea, who might turn out to be the lost Inspector Tearl. You were posing around as Sergeant Tearl. When you suddenly struck north it would be natural for them to suppose that you were off to hunt for the old man. His return would be fatal to them. They grabbed the chance to stop you before you started by sicking a crowd of irresponsible smokies on you."

Jerry was leaning against the terrace, eyeing the Indians. "It looks as though they're leaving us," he remarked. "They're hitching in the dogs. As soon as they pull out we'll be getting on ourselves."

Kit faced his brother in startled recollection. "Say!" he exclaimed. "I'm under arrest—a fugitive from the police. I'd darned near forgotten. They spotted me a couple of days ago—impersonating an officer—"

"Who did?" interrupted the sergeant.

"Devon and Cross." Kit grinned ruefully. "Murder too. They think I made away with you."

"Really?" Jerry was amused by the notion. "Good! You'll have to take good care of me if you want to clear yourself of the murder charge." He laughed calmly. "I guess it'll be all right. If Cross and Devon are like the usual run of the mounties they'll be a couple of four-square chaps whom we can tell the truth to and trust to keep their mouths shut afterwards."

The Yellow Knives were moving away. Kit heard the cracking whips and the shouts of the dog drivers. The tribesmen had started down the river to look for Oogly, to find out if the blood-debt were really paid.

As soon as the last of the creaking sledges had drawn off out of range Kit climbed the embankment again and walked out on the prairie. The Yellow Knives, with cynical unconcern, had left their white companion as he had fallen. It needed but a moment's investigation to establish the fact of death. Here at least was one who never again would trouble the crown's lawful forces.

At that moment Kit's stinging eyes saw as much as he cared to have them see. The broad, bearded face, with the missing front teeth—the man undeniably was Bruyas. Kit lingered only to unlace the upturned snowshoes, and he carried them under his arm back to Jerry.

"Jim Durand's square-webbed snowshoes!" he remarked. "We guessed right. It was Bruyas who killed him and dumped him out of the cabin window, who found use for the snowshoes, who helped himself to Dad's old service gun. Bruyas—who tracked me into the barrens, and shot Oogly—

"It's funny," he puzzled after an interval of silence. "Durand evidently timed his return to this country to coincide with Hell Bent's release from prison. His idea must have been the same as yours. He must have expected Bent to come back after the hidden gold sledge, just as you were sure that he would. Like you, I gather that he intended to ambush himself in the Great Owl woods so that he might catch Bent red-handed when he tried to recover his loot."

"It would seem so," agreed Jerry. "And this Durand would have even a blacker account to settle with Bent than you and I. We thought that Bent had something to do with Dad's disappearance. But Durand knew! He was an eye-witness. He'd seen his sister shot down. You can guess what he meant to do!"

"The woman." Kit's half-seeing eyes turned broodingly towards the south. "If she was Durand's sister and Diane his niece, then she either was Diane's aunt or her mother."

Jerry tilted his head sidewise to regard his brother searchingly. "You call her 'Diane' now, do you?"

Kitchener wasn't listening. He fumbled in his shirt pocket and brought out a fragment of paper that had been crumpled and then carefully smoothed afterwards. "Here's a note she wrote when she left me yesterday. I haven't been able to read it."

Without comment Jerry took the sheet and spread it open in his left palm. In a faintly mocking tone he read aloud:

DEAR COCKY-BIRD:

I don't know any other name for you, and I guess maybe it's better that I don't. I'm leaving you because I don't want to go north, and anyhow I'd be a hindrance to you. You and Oogly'll travel faster without me. You may believe me—I'll never hint to the police which direction you went.

You remember the bad thought I had, that gave birth to Shedim, the owl? And I couldn't tell you what it was. But now that we'll never see each other again I think I'd be not quite so unhappy in the years to come if I knew you knew.

From the very first I guessed that you were no policeman. I don't quite know how you fit into the horrible crimes at Great Owl Run, but I know that you do, somewhere, somehow. When I see you and talk with you it's something that is utterly impossible to believe. But I've had to force myself to believe it.

I ought to hate you, and I don't and can't. And my bad thought is simply this: that it is filled, days and nights, with nothing in the world but you. Good-by. I'm praying that I'll never see you again.

DIANE.

Jerry folded up the paper and bent a brotherly grin at Kitchener. "A demon with the girls!" he remarked. "How do you do it, Oakheart?"

Kit took the note back and tucked it into his pocket and buttoned the flap.

"I can see where she might mistake you for an old crow," remarked Jerry, "but an owl—"

"Shut up!" Kit broke in fiercely.

"It's turned out to be the craziest mess that anybody ever heard of," ruminated Jerry in a sobering voice. "Everybody ramming and bulling around at cross-purposes. We picked Durand out for Hell Bent. And you thought Diane was a crook, and she thinks you're one."

"Diane has gone back to Great Owl Run to wait for Durand," said Kit, and softly shook his head. "And he'll never come."

"It's odd," reflected Jerry, "the way everybody's scuttling all over the place waiting for this Bent bird to get out of prison. He's been out now for two or three months, and none of us has seen him or heard a thing of him yet." His forehead creased perplexedly. "What I'd like to know is where the deuce is Hell Bent?"

"How do I know—" Kit started to say, and then stopped with his mouth open.

"There was a man at the police post the other night!" he burst out. "A big, ugly-looking cuss with a scarred face. His excuse for being in the woods in mid-winter sounded phony to me. But I didn't give it much thought until this minute—

"He heard me say I'd moved the gold bags, and that Diane knows where I hid them." Kit's face looked ghastly in the dying sunlight. "Diane is alone at the Great Owl cabin, and this man is loose in the woods.

"Jerry!" It was a stricken cry. "He must be Bent. I know it! As sure as the devil it's Hell Bent!"

CHAPTER XXVIII
SNOW-BLIND

Kit was on his feet, grabbing for the shotgun with one hand and his mittens with the other. He was like a man demented. A dozen miles or more back to Great Owl Run, and night was at hand and he could barely see and Jerry was badly wounded and the dogs were dead. Diane would be waiting at the old cabin, at the mercy of the monster who had come back at last like an evil genius to hunt out the scene of his bloodiest crime.

Kit knew now that the stranger he had met at the police shack was Hell Bent. He knew it, not merely by surmising and guessing, but by an inward conviction, a clear and absolute prescience that left him without doubt and without hope. He knew it as positively as he had known all these weeks that he loved Diane. If anything happened to her before he could see her and pour out all the astonishing things that were in his heart, if he lost her now after she had vouchsafed him a glimpse of loveliness and incredible happiness that might have been....

He was nearly frantic with his visions of her, alone in the dismal night, needing him.

"Nothing else counts," he told Jerry. "We're leaving now."

"Righto!" Jerry was perfectly willing to undertake the killing march across the barrens, but when he stooped to tighten up his snowshoes he simply doubled in the middle like a grain bag and pitched headforemost into a drift of snow.

Kit was down beside him, pulling his face out of the snow, propping the sagging back against one of the sledges, peering beseechingly. "Jerry! What is it—what's wrong?"

The sergeant let his legs sprawl apart for added support, and managed something like a laugh. "Just went dizzy all at once. A minute ago—a big, hulking slob, and now— I thought I was going to faint—or something. Kit—you go on!"

Kitchener unloaded the topmost sledge and hauled it into the lee of the terrace. He got his hands in his brother's armpits and stumbled backwards, and bedded the slack, awkward body in a nest of blankets. There was no need to ask questions. Jerry's forearm had been smashed by one of the Yellow Knives' dum-dums. This after weeks of snow-travel that would have broken most men. The shock and the loss of blood and an accumulated fatigue fought off for days and nights: it was a miracle that he had not collapsed when he was hit. He stood up for a while on sheer nerve, and then the physical creature finally had demanded payment.

"I'll be all right here for a few days or a week," said Jerry, trying to make his voice sound as big as it ever had been. "I guess—I don't believe I'd better go with you."

Kit stripped up his brother's sleeve and bathed the swollen, darkened flesh, and removed the tourniquet that had begun to cut too deeply. He kneaded the shattered bones into place as truely as his inexperience could accomplish the job, while Jerry looked on with a set, awry grin. Splints and bandages were speedily improvised, and the arm was bound stiff against the body, like an unused pump handle.

This much, at least, Kit could take the time to do. And then he lingered for just another moment. "It's rotten to leave you like this, and yet, I don't see what else to do."

"What would I want with you?" returned Jerry scornfully. "I've got plenty of blankets and plenty to eat and an oil stove. And anyhow—you know—" His glance sought the reposing shape beside the second sledge. "It's better to have somebody to sit here and keep the wolverines away. And—I don't know—I'd like to be the one to keep the vigil. You can come back or send for us when you have a chance."

Kit drew his hood closer about his mouth and pulled on his mittens. "Can you still see the Indians?" he asked.

"Just barely. They're following the river and'll be out of sight in a few minutes. If I were you I'd cut more southeast than the river runs. You'll save several miles. The wind's southwest. Keep it on your right cheek."

"So-long, Jerry!" Kitchener shouldered the shotgun, and then he bent down and the brothers' left hands met and clasped.

"We'll be waiting for you," said Jerry lightly.

Kit started to speak, and then decided that he'd better not attempt it. He nodded and tried to swallow the choking feeling in his throat. Then he turned his right shoulder to the vanishing sun and started off across the barrens.

"If you're in doubt about the direction of the wind," yelled Jerry, "rub your face with snow." His reckless, graceless laughter was the last sound that Kit was to hear that night. "Give my love to Diane. And give Hell Bent hell."

There were only a few more minutes left of the chilling daylight and then the early, arctic gloaming began to spread down into the awful silence and lonesomeness of the barrens.

Kit struck off at a gliding trot, his raquettes crunching pleasantly over the icy surface of the snow. He felt fit enough for enormous undertakings. The clean frosty air filled his lungs and set his blood tingling. He could keep up this sort of a dog-jog all night if he must. Not more than twelve miles to go—if he held the straight line he ought to reach Great Owl Run long before dawn.

The day vanished quickly and the night grew as dark as it ever is around the dusky circle of the north. Kit hurried on with his eyes almost shut. There was no need of seeing the ground ahead. His feet could follow the gentle undulations of the unbroken prairie.

If there were only a moon he'd have fewer misgivings. The moonshine, shifting around his head, would have given him a constant check on the compass points. But there would only be stars to-night. He could look up and feel the shimmer of the stars in his face, but he could not see well enough to pick out individuals for guidance. Only the southwest wind was trustworthy, and he kept its breath on his right cheekbone.

He counted his steps, and allowed twenty-five hundred to the mile. This ought to be approximately correct. The multiple of twenty-five hundred by twelve was thirty thousand. The total was appalling. Yet he'd already counted past the five thousand mark. He must be at least two miles on his way.

Jerry was back there, probably with his little stove alight and coffee boiling and his eternal pipe smoldering, while he gazed into the night and sat in dreamy quiet beside the man he had loved.

Every stride was taking Kit farther from Jerry and nearer to Diane. His thoughts were like restless terriers, sometimes lagging behind, but more frequently racing ahead. His longing for Diane and his fears for her existed as tangibly in his mind as actual forerunners on the trail, frantically beckoning to him, calling him on. His legs were always trying to keep up with his anxieties, and his better judgment was constantly reminding him that if he ran too fast he would spend himself too soon.

Ten-thousand foot-paces and fifteen-thousand—it seemed to him that he had been traveling thus for hours, automatically counting the feet into miles. "Ninety-seven, ninety-eight, ninety-nine, fifteen thousand three hundred, one, two, three—" A deadly monotonous business this, saying numbers to himself, over and over and over again, exactly in the rhythm of his breathing and his stride. But he kept it up. If he lost track he would never know how far he had come or how far he yet must go.

As he switched the shotgun from one hand to the other it occurred to him that he did not know what loads it contained. He snapped open the breech without slacking his stride, and made sure that there were two shells chambered. They might carry buck-shot, or only a charge of "6s" for ducks and ptarmigan. He ought to have asked Jerry before he left. Well, it was too late to worry about that. Whatever the gun had in it he'd use it if he had to.

Two or three times during the next hour or so he had lost the feeling of the wind in his face. But before he was seriously alarmed the lightly fanning breeze sprang up again. He went along confidently for a while, and then all at once realized that he was moving in an apparent calm. Either there was a sudden lull, or else his skin was not as sensitive as it had been. He halted abruptly and tried Jerry's plan of rubbing the face with snow.

It seemed to work. The right cheek felt much colder than the left. Once more he trudged onward with the assurance that he must be going the right direction.

After this he paused every now and then to gather a handful of snow and dab it over his stinging face.

Time and distance—how long he had been slogging ahead, how far he had come, he hadn't a faintest notion. The numbers he had counted were beginning to jumble up meaninglessly in his head. He couldn't seem to recall whether he was in his twentieth or thirtieth thousand. He began to think of himself as a minute, selfless object moving eternally in endless, invisible space....

In the middle of his long, hurrying stride he halted as abruptly as though he had hit a wall. His head turned one direction and then another, and his breathing stopped. A puff of icy wind had struck the left side of his face.

Kit flung off his hood and stood aghast in the vast silence. There was a distinct breeze quartering his path from the sinister side. Either he had unwittingly changed his direction, or else the wind had veered.

He was careful to keep his feet planted exactly as they were when the alarming change pulled him up. He mustn't get excited. It wasn't any use being frightened. As deliberately as he had ever moved in his life he pulled out his flash-lamp, and laid his compass in the palm of his hand, and snapped on the electric beam.

It is a peculiarity of snow-blindness that the vision is more befogged and the eyes hurt worse at night than in the full daylight. The glare of the search-lamp made him blink. It was easy enough to differentiate between light and darkness, and he even caught the glint of the metallic disc in his hand. But that was all. He couldn't make out the compass card or the arrow. He couldn't tell which point was north and which was south.

Kit deliberated, with a stern effort to keep his head. He had to reach the Great Owl cabin to-night. Even now he might be too late.

The breeze seemed to be much stronger than it had been. Coming off from the left. Jerry must have been certain that it would not change its point during the night. But Jerry was not infallible. It might have shifted. Or in a moment of aberration Kit perhaps had swung off his course. How was he to know?

He put away his useless torch. His head pivoted blindly in a half-circle. There was no sound nor scent to guide him, nothing that he could touch with his hand. He stood in the midst of barrenness and desolation, completely at sea. And in his heart was the tantalizing, maddening conviction that Diane was in desperate straits somewhere near, needing him frightfully—and he did not know which way to go.

The compass was clenched in his hand. In a sudden fury with himself and his sightless eyes he started to fling it away. Then, just in time, he checked his arm. It occured to him that perhaps he might read his directions by the sense of touch. He stooped to one knee, laid the compass firmly on the other knee, and tapped the crystal with the hilt of his knife. The glass shattered into fragments. The sharpest point of the needle, he recalled, was the magnetized end. He slipped his hand out of his glove, and with a gingerly forefinger he tried to trace the line of the wabbling sliver of steel.

But he was overanxious, and his hand was not as quiet as it might have been. His blundering finger dislodged the needle from its jeweled post. He heard the needle slide across the card, and it was gone before he could save it.

He went after the tiny metal arrow with his bare hands. In a widening circle he groped and searched. He dug up handfuls of snow and explored minutely among the frozen crystals. And before very long his flesh was ice and all sense of feeling had left his fingers. He wouldn't have recognized the compass needle if he picked it up.

Now he needed his self-command. He was aware of the beginnings of that strange form of insanity that attacks lost men: the raging desire to do something, to be somewhere else, to walk off whichever way the feet are turned, to break from a walk into a run, to keep on running from the multiplying horrors that can run faster than a man.

This was the time for Kit to remember that he was one of a hardy line whose men do not lose their heads in the wilds. The old lessons of wilderness lore had been drummed into him from the days of his infancy. When in doubt, don't move. Sit down. Cover up. He put his freezing fingers in his mouth, and did not budge.

There was nothing to be done now. He'd have to wait for the sun. He pulled his hood over his head and sank down in the snow, despairing, and shivering with cold.

And from off in the darkness, a long while afterwards, he thought he heard a sound. He was crouched in a ball with his head on his knee. His body had grown so cold that he was almost in a torpor. It may be that he had dozed now and then. He didn't know. His faculties were nearly dormant.

But he did hear something. He raised his head. His breath had congealed under his hood. With his sleeve he wiped the frost rime from his face and eyes. Both arms were so stiff he half listened to hear them creak. What was it that had aroused him?

He remembered. There was a noise of some sort off across the tundra. He leaned forward on his hands and labored drowsily to stand up. There it was again—far off in front of him. A voice in the air—a ghostly whistle changing into faint chuckling laughter.

He was on his feet now, swaying a trifle, staring vacantly. For some reason he had picked up his shotgun. Listening until the pulse of his heart seemed to wait—

The cry! This time it was nearer—a grotesque, quavering note that reached his ears and trembled all the way down his backbone. He knew it now—the sound that had awakened him other nights in the sweat of an unearthly abhorrence—the horrid, hunting call of a great owl.

Kit stumbled forward. The creature was ahead of him. It would be time soon for it to be going home. The owls lived off there somewhere in the depths of the forest, on the other side of the creek. They circled over the barrens at night and went back at the first crack of dawn.

Whether it was night or morning, Kit didn't know. He couldn't even see the glimmer of the stars. His eyes had gone totally blind while he huddled in the cold. But he could hear the complaining of the owl. A low, gasping sound, with a hoarse croak at the end.

Why, it was Shedim—the bird that had caught cold in Hades! It was Diane's owl.

Kit's legs had refused to obey him for a minute or two. But he had staggered on somehow, and now he was beginning to feel his feet under him. His snowshoes were gripping the crusty snow. He was getting into his stride.

At moments there was utter quiet, and then he would hear the throaty wheeze in the air, at his right or at his left, or sometimes off in front of him, but always drifting farther ahead, leading him on.

He ran full tilt into a clump of bushes, and rejoiced in the frozen branches that cut his face. This was no longer the bleak tundra. He was getting somewhere at last.

The owl was still ranging ahead, and Kit charged on recklessly. There were other patches of brush in his path, and now and then a group of dwarfed trees. Usually his outgroping hands saved him.

The ground suddenly sloped down from his feet. He crashed through a tangled barrier of small growths, and then all at once he caught the clean, pungent smell of pine woods. Shedim was somewhere behind him. But he did not wait. He picked his way cautiously down the declivity, and was gladdened by the sound of running water.

Here was the creek. This must be Great Owl Run. He felt his way along the stream and found a place where the thick ice reached out from the bank. On his hands and knees he crept precariously across the slippery bridge to the opposite bank.

He no longer heard Shedim, but there was something else—not far away—rhythmic thuds of chopping, an ax blade ringing in wood. Through a border of willows and alders he thrust a path and emerged into an open space.

The chopping went on briskly, close at hand it seemed. He turned towards the sounds, started forward, and hit his knee on a stump. The axman must have seen him. The strokes stopped, and there was intense quiet. Kit had a feeling that he was being stared at.

And then something like a spurt of wind crashed past his face, a red flame leaped at him, a rifle explosion battered his ears.

He flung his shotgun to his shoulder and fired both barrels. The double shock, the dreadful hush that followed, and then a woman's cry throbbing wildly....

"Diane!"

Kit leaped forward, and tripped, and fell. The uproar in his head faded to leaden silence.

CHAPTER XXIX
COCKY-BIRD

The quiet and drowsy warmth; the languid pleasure of stretching out weary legs; shadows that soothed his heavy, aching eyes; the cheery crackling of a hearth-fire and wavering of ruddy firelight: Kitchener's reawakening senses went adrift in a spell of dreamy contentment.

He was under shelter somewhere, wrapped in a soft blanket, his head on a pillow. It seemed to him in those moments that he had never felt a keener consciousness of well-being. Something stirred gently beside him. He tried to see, and couldn't, quite, and so he closed his eyes again.

"Who is it?" he asked.

Somebody came closer, and a hand strayed to his face, and then ran its fingers through his hair.

His heart stopped, and then swelled in mighty beating. He reached for the hand, but it was gone.

"Diane! Where are you?"

"I'm here." The voice held him thrillingly awake.

He sat up and threw off the blanket.

"Diane! Are you all right? I was all night getting here. I was so frightened—I wanted to get to you so—and I couldn't see—"

"It's all right," she told him. "You got here in time—you got here just in time." There was something like awe in her muted voice. "I'll never understand what it was, but—deep in me, all the time I had the strangest feeling that you were coming—that you'd get here. And you did."

"What happened?" he asked. "I don't quite remember."

"You stumbled over a stump and fell and hit your head on the sill of the cabin. You've been lying here without knowing anything for nearly five hours."

Kit put up his hand to feel an enormous swelling above his right eyebrow. "I don't mean that," he said impatiently. "That's nothing. But before then?" He scowled in an effort to collect his faculties. "I remember the chopping, and then somebody fired at me, and I let him have it."

"He was chopping down the door of the cabin," Diane told him, and shivered. "He came here last night and demanded that I tell him where the—where those old bags were hidden, and I wouldn't, and he said he'd make me. I never heard anything as frightful as his talk. He went away, and some time later he came back with an ax and started chopping down the door, and I had no gun or anything, and I was just crouching in the corner, when—when I heard the rifle and then the shotgun. And I knew it was you."

"I guess I killed him," said Kit.

"No, you didn't. You must have had bird-shot in your gun. A few of the shot hit him in the forehead and temple, but they were too tiny, and only glanced. They only knocked him out for a few minutes."

Kit started to get up and grope for his boots. "My God!" he exclaimed. "Where is he? Where is he now?"

"No. Don't!" Diane's flexible arm was around his shoulders, holding him. "He's safe. As soon as I'd made sure that you hadn't been killed, I went to him and tied him up tight. And then two or three hours later the policemen came."

"Policemen?" he echoed.

Diane moved discreetly away before Kit had time to regain his breath. "Devon and Cross. They were searching the woods for you, and happened to pass here this morning. Cross is outside now, with a tent pitched and a handcuffed prisoner lying in it."

"Hell Bent?"

"It was the man we met at the police shack the other night—he called himself Pettijohn."

"Yes. I knew it. I figured that out when it was just almost too late. He's Hell Bent."

Kit sat straighter. "Listen!" he said. "I want to see Cross right away. I want him to go, or send, for a wounded man down in the barrens—"

"All right," interrupted Diane. "Devon started a couple of hours ago. When I dragged you in here you muttered something about rescuing a wounded man. So Devon went as soon as I told him. He's following your back trail. Poor Oogly. I hope he isn't badly hurt."

"It isn't Oogly," said Kit. "It's my brother Jerry."

"Who?" Kit was aware of the intensity of the girl's glance.

"My brother. Sergeant Buck Tearl, the man I was pretending to be. The one who put you in handcuffs that night, long ago. It was he who put me up to the masquerading business, and sent me on the trail of Jim Durand, mistaking him for Hell Bent."

"You—" Diane stopped in bewilderment. "What are you talking about?"

"About you and me and the muddle of everything in general." Kit spoke decisively. "We've got to straighten it out. You thought I was mixed up somehow in that old tragedy here at Great Owl Run, and I thought your uncle was. See? I was after him—after the wrong man, and you thought I was some kind of a beastly scoundrel, come here to smear my hands in those rotten bags."

"Oh, wait—wait a minute!" protested Diane. "You're going so fast."

"We can't clean this up fast enough for me. Jim Durand—your uncle—he was here in that fight twelve years ago, wasn't he—when the gold sledge was lost, and the woman—"

"My aunt," broke in Diane softly. "I was only just a little girl, but I remember, Uncle Jim—coming home without her. She was so beautiful—"

"Remember about the man who was with your uncle?" asked Kit. "Who fought side by side with him—who disappeared and was never seen again? Inspector William Tearl, R.C.M.P.—did you ever hear of him?"

"I heard—I knew there was a policeman. I may have been told the name. If they told me, I've forgotten."

"He was my father," said Kit.

Kit felt the girl move abruptly, and he did not need his own vision to feel the potency of her eyes looking at him in the shadows. "I didn't know," she whispered. "You say he was—then you—then you're not—"

"I'm not anything excepting just Kitchener Tearl, who came here to help Jerry and to find Bill Tearl."

"But why—why the imposture?" Diane demanded in a shaken voice. "Why did you impersonate somebody else? Explain please. I've got to know—I've got to know the truth."

"Bill Tearl was lost, and Jerry had to go hunt him, that's why," Kit told her. "And somebody had to stay around here and watch for that devil—for Hell Bent. We thought it would be better if I was in uniform. So I traded clothes with Jerry, and he went north and I stayed here. That's all there was to that."

"Oh, God!" Diane was beside the bunk on a box. Her face had suddenly buried itself in her hands and she was sobbing. "Then you—oh, how could I have thought for a minute that anything was wrong! Of course not! I might have known!"

"I might have known too," said Kit. "Taking Jerry's word, like a darned fool. Well, I've learned something. I've learned only to believe what I see with my eyes and feel in my heart."

Diane had straightened on her box, and somehow seemed to have regained her self-control.

"What a frightful thing it all has been," she gasped. "I can remember when Uncle Jim came home, so long ago. He'd been traveling all over, from city to city, crazed with grief and horror, after he'd seen his sister's death."

"Did he know what had become of Hell Bent?" Kitchener asked.

"He found out some way that one of the men—the worst of the lot—had gone to prison. And so Uncle Jim waited. He knew that the man would come back here to the woods as soon as he was freed, and so he waited—with one idea, with one fixed purpose."

"I don't blame him," said Kit.

"Oh, I know. Of course not. But it was so terrible. Uncle Jim, the sweetest man that ever lived, but a stubborn and dangerous one, brooding over one thing, living his life for just one end. He kept away from the police. He didn't want anybody to interfere. He wanted to do it with his own hands—here in the woods.

"He was so restless," Diane went on in a musing voice. "He spent most of his time wandering over the world, just—just marking time until the day. Sometimes he took me with him. I am the only thing on earth he cares for. But he would never talk to me about what had happened here—just kept his mouth shut, with that terrifying look of his.

"And one day," she said, "he left me in Ottawa and told me to wait there for him. After he was gone I guessed—intuition told me. I found out that he had started for the north—and I came after him. I thought—I hoped—if I could catch him in time I might be able to prevent a second tragedy. That was why I followed.

"But I never found him." Diane sighed heavily. "Uncle Jim! I don't know what ever happened to him."

Kit's teeth closed in his lips. He didn't want to tell her now of the body that Jerry had found in the river. "I wonder," he said, "if it wasn't your uncle who sent the radio to Jerry about the white man who was living on the north sea, who—it has turned out—was Dad?"

"I don't know," she said. "But it is possible. He probably did."

"But it was signed, 'Diane.' Why would he use your name?"

"I suppose he didn't want to use his own. So he just signed anything—the first one that came into his mind. And the first name Uncle Jim would think of, always, would be 'Diane.'"

"Me too!" said Kit.

"What?" He heard the box scrape on the floor.

"Diane! Come here!"

"No." And then, after a briefest pause. "What for?"

"I want you."

"Why?"

"Because I love you."

There was a lingering silence after that, until a log on the fireplace suddenly broke in two and a shower of sparks sizzled in the chimney. Kit put one foot on the floor and strove with hungering eyes to see the shadowy figure that stood so quiet in the dusk. He could hear Diane's breathing, but nobody moved and nobody spoke.

"Do you remember Shedim?" Kit asked at length, with a little, husky laugh.

Still Diane said nothing.

"Last night when I was out there on the barrens—snow-blind—knowing I had to come to you, and not knowing which way to turn—Shedim flew over me, and I heard him, and he led me here. I wouldn't have got here if it hadn't been for the owl. Your bad thought that you couldn't kill—"

"And didn't want to!" she declared defiantly. "And never would have—never!"

His forehead was screwed up in a straining effort to visualize the shadowy face that always seemed to elude him. And suddenly he heard faint laughter, and something reached to him and gently poked his left eyebrow.

"Hello, Cocky-bird!"

"Diane! Please!" Kit's arms reached forward vacantly. "I can't see you. I can't find you!"

"Need you see?"

And Diane was in his arms then, and her young, warm body was clinging to him, and her lips were feeling their way to his. "You don't need to find me—not while I can find you."

THE END